Praise for *In the Cards*

"Infused with . . . fresh detail. Between the sweetness of the relationship and the summery beach setting, romance fans will find this a warming winter read."

—*Publishers Weekly*

"Fans will love the frank honesty of her characters. [Beck's] scenery is richly detailed and the story engaging."

—*RT Book Reviews*

"[A] realistic and heartwarming story of redemption and love . . . Beck's understanding of interpersonal relationships and her flawless prose make for a believable romance and an entertaining read."

—*Booklist*

Praise for *Worth the Wait*

"[A] poignant and heartwarming story of young love and redemption [that] will literally make your heart ache . . . Jamie Beck has a real talent for making the reader feel the sorrow, regret, and yearning of this young character."

—*Fresh Fiction*

Praise for *Worth the Trouble*

"Beck takes readers on a journey of self-reinvention and risky investments, in love and in life . . . With strong family ties, loyalty, playful banter, and sexual tension, Beck has crafted a beautiful second-chances story."

—Starred review, *Publishers Weekly*

Praise for *Secretly Hers*

secretly hers

ALSO BY JAMIE BECK

In the Cards

The St. James Novels

Worth the Wait

Worth the Trouble

The Sterling Canyon Novels

Accidentally Hers

secretly *hers*

A Sterling Canyon Novel

Jamie Beck

Montlake
Romance

Published by Montlake Romance, Seattle

www.apub.com

Amazon, the Amazon logo, and Montlake Romance are trademarks of Amazon.com, Inc., or its affiliates.

ISBN-13: 9781503936225
ISBN-10: 1503936228

Cover design by Laura Klynstra

Cover photography by Regina Wamba of MaeIDesign.com

Printed in the United States of America

For Katherine. I'm sorry I can't bring Trip to life for you, but I can make his story yours.

Chapter One

Kelsey adjusted her plastic tiara and entered Sweet Cakes bakery, smiling. Her niece, Fiona, clutched the cheap satin skirt of Kelsey's Sleeping Beauty costume with one hand while the other waved a bejeweled princess wand through the air.

The child's blond curls bobbed as she bounced on her toes, her pale blue eyes—the same icy color as her own princess costume—twinkled as she studied the rows of cupcakes behind the glass display case.

Kelsey could practically hear the Ballard sisters raising their eyebrows as they snickered in the corner. It wasn't the first time Kelsey had been ridiculed in the tiny Rocky Mountain ski town of Sterling Canyon, and she doubted it would be the last. Not that she cared one whit about other people's opinions of her or of her tendency to go overboard for the people she loved.

And there were few people she loved as much as she loved Fee. So if Fee wanted them to dress up as princesses on her fifth birthday, then Kelsey would happily grant her wish.

"Priiiiin-cess Fee-yoh-na," she announced, "which do you prefer: chocolate, vanilla, or red velvet?"

"All of them!" Fee pressed her little nose against the glass before glancing upward, shamelessly batting her lashes. "Please, Aunt Kelsey."

Kelsey grinned even though she could hear her older sister, Maura's, exasperated voice echoing in her mind. *If she hadn't come from my body, I'd swear Fee was your daughter.* The thought prompted both a surge of pride and a pang of jealousy. She and Fee did look and act like mother and child, but they were not.

Kelsey ached to be a mother, but today she'd content herself with being the best darn aunt this side of the Mississippi. Tomorrow she'd heed her panicky biological clock and resume her search for a happily-ever-after with someone worthy, whoever he turned out to be.

"All three?" Kelsey pretended to carefully consider the idea. "Sprinkles, too, I suppose?"

"Oh, yes!" Fee jumped twice.

"Okay, pumpkin." Kelsey fingered Fee's curls. "But don't tell your mom I gave you three cupcakes, or this will be our last princess birthday."

Kelsey could imagine Maura lecturing her about healthy habits, but spoiling Fee was an advantage of being an aunt.

Kelsey paid for the small box of cupcakes then considered her surroundings. She didn't regret coming to town midweek, dressed like a buffoon, but she didn't need to prolong the spectacle, either. After all, she had current and future clients to consider. Her real estate business was taking off, and she intended to keep it that way. Contrary to most people's opinions, being blond, buxom, and big-hearted didn't make her stupid. Kelsey understood that faux-crystal-embroidered costumes did *not* scream "professional."

"Shall we take these home to eat?" She affected a British accent. "We can dine on the balcony and preside over our royal subjects."

"And watch for Prince Charming!" Fee twirled on one foot, her wand once more slicing through the air.

"Oh, honey, I think Prince Charming and all his brothers have fled the land." She grinned at Fee's pout. "But never fear! We princesses will take control of our own destinies."

Fee's forehead creased in confusion as they departed the store. *I know. Prince Charming does have his benefits.*

Kelsey lifted the hem of her gown, focusing on her stiletto-clad feet while descending the two steps leading to the sidewalk of the old silver mining town, with its one-hundred-thirty-year-old Victorian buildings nestled in the shadows of the San Juan mountain range. Her gaze remained fixed on the rhinestone ankle clasps of her awesome new shoes until she collided with Trip Lexington and stumbled backward.

"Gotcha." Trip's hands gently squeezed her waist until she wriggled free. To her irritation, her pulse sped up when his cool green eyes sparkled with amusement and testosterone.

At least he'd caught her before she landed on her butt.

The box of cupcakes? Not so lucky. "Sorry." She tipped up her chin and, once more, straightened her loosened tiara.

She expected Fee to wail over the smashed goodies, but her niece's gaze seemed riveted on Trip, who was a stranger to Fee.

Oh, dear. She really is just like me. Kelsey shook her head, knowing the wear-your-heart-on-your-sleeve romantic mentality would probably hurt Fee one day, just as it had stung Kelsey over and over again.

Fee's eyes widened; her little cheeks pinked up, too. Nearly breathless, she said, "Look, Aunt Kelsey! Prince Charming!"

Trip shot Kelsey another curious look before facing Fee. "At your service, little lady."

Of course, Trip did look like Prince Charming and Adonis rolled into one, with a hefty dash of feral vitality thrown into the mix.

At six-foot-three, he towered above her. Glossy, dark hair contrasted with his sea green eyes, complementing his chiseled cheekbones and nose. Trip's clean-shaven face—a rarity among the mountain men in town—allowed admirers to appreciate his strong, masculine jaw and sensual lips, which seemed to be set in a permanent smirk. And if physical perfection weren't enough, years of skiing steep and deep in the backcountry had given him an athlete's swagger.

Yes, when Trip Lexington passed any woman between the ages of eighteen and eighty, her ovaries sang with more worship than the Mormon Tabernacle Choir. The problem with that was the fact that he knew it. Worse, he used it to his advantage.

He'd been in town for only eight months and, if rumors were true, had already slept with most of its single women. But not with Kelsey. Although they had been thrown together socially because his business partner, Grey, was dating Kelsey's best friend, Avery, until now their interaction had consisted of a mixture of lighthearted antagonism and false flirtation.

Just as well, she supposed. She was hunting husband material—a man who wanted a wife and children. Trip was *not* that man, and even *she* wasn't so stupidly romantic as to believe she could change him. Besides, she'd already wasted too much time chasing after Grey before he'd fallen for Avery. The last thing she needed to do was get mixed up with Trip, even if he did have more raw sex appeal than any man she'd ever met.

His gaze roamed Kelsey from head to toe, quickly but appreciatively. He inclined nearer, murmuring, "Funny, but I've always seen you as more of a Jessica Rabbit type than a Sleeping Beauty."

His hot breath brushed against her ear, sending tingles tumbling down her neck like fairy dust. Kelsey gripped her hips to silence the chorus coming from her own set of traitorous ovaries. Before she could manage an answer, Fee chimed in, flashing a giddy smile and spinning on her toes. "We're princesses!"

Trip smoothly turned to Fee, removed his cowboy hat, and produced an exaggerated bow. "It's an honor, your highness. What brings you to town when you look dressed for a ball?"

"My birthday." Fee stretched her arms wide apart, wiggling her wand.

"Ahh." He grinned. "And how old are you?"

Kelsey bent over to retrieve the fallen box of cupcakes, pretending not to watch the scene unfolding on the sidewalk. Always flip with women, Trip's apparent ease with children took Kelsey by surprise.

"Five." Fee began swinging her body from side to side, one hand delicately holding up part of her skirt. *Little flirt.*

"Might I inquire as to your name, which I'm certain will be as lovely as you." Trip smiled, and Kelsey had to hide a grin at the effort he made to speak in a princely manner.

"Fiona," squeaked the rapt voice.

"Princess Fiona, my name is Gunner Lexington the third, but everyone calls me Trip."

Fee giggled. "Do you fall a lot?"

"Never!" Trip knelt on one knee, palm splayed against his chest, facial expression exaggeratedly horrified. "Not even from the tallest mountains." Then he flashed a genuine smile. The kind of smile that could coax Kelsey into believing there was more to him than he let people see. In other words, a lethal smile. "Yet I may have just fallen for you."

Fee swooned. Yes, *swooned* before asking, "Will you marry me?"

Kelsey grinned at Fee's bold question until Trip's smirking face spun toward her as he said, "My, you're training her early." He then returned his attention to Fee. "I wish I could. But by the time you grow up, I'm sure you'll think me an old toad."

"How old are you?" Fee tilted her head, eyes narrowed.

"Too old, I'm afraid." He stood up again and grinned.

"Then marry Aunt Kelsey." Fee's delighted expression proved she believed she'd just solved a crisis. "She's old, too!"

"*Fee!*" Kelsey sputtered.

Trip burst into laughter. "Positively ancient, I agree."

Fee stared at him with one of her darling puzzled expressions until he controlled himself.

"In lieu of a wedding ring, may I buy you a birthday cupcake or cookie?" he finally asked.

"Three!" Fee clapped.

Trip's brows rose as he glanced at Kelsey. "Three?"

"Does Prince Charming *object* to indulging his beloved princess?" Kelsey tilted her head, tsk-tsking. "Stingy princes always get banished, no matter how charming."

Trip looked as if he had a snarky retort beating against his teeth, but he must've bitten it back for Fee's sake.

"Quite right. Three cupcakes it is." He held out his elbow, but had to crouch so Fee could grab hold of him. "Lead the way, Princess Fee."

Kelsey followed them inside, fighting against her heart's pitter-pattering as she watched Trip delight her niece. Five minutes later, they exited Sweet Cakes again, this time without any clumsiness.

Trip bent down, raised Fee's hand to his lips, and kissed it. "I hope I see you again."

Fee looked at Kelsey. "When you and him get married, can I be the flower girl and wear this dress?"

Convinced her cheeks must look like overly ripened tomatoes, Kelsey brazened on. "When *we* get married, pigs will fly and you can wear whatever you want. You can even ride a unicorn right down the aisle. Now, we'd better get going soon, or we won't have time for tea before I have to take you home." Collecting herself, she glanced at Trip and pretended no part of her felt wistful about their illusory nuptials . . . or wedding night. "See you around."

"Princess Kelsey, I'll be counting the minutes." He bowed before sauntering away, whistling as he went.

Kelsey dragged her gaze from his butt and grasped Fee's hand. "By the way, thirty's not old, Fee. It's mature!"

Perfectly mature, she thought, despite the fact that she was strolling through the dusty streets of town wearing a pink costume.

♦ ♦ ♦

Three blocks away, Trip meandered toward home wearing a smile on his face. Kelsey's typical wardrobe revealed a lot more flesh than that ridiculous costume, yet watching her play dress-up with her niece held a unique, if baffling, appeal. And little Fiona! She promised to be more of a terror to men than her aunt, whom he and his soon-to-be partner, Grey, had nicknamed Boomerang due to the stalker tendencies she'd exhibited when she first met Grey.

Admittedly, Kelsey's rockin' body had *always* intrigued Trip. A few rounds in bed with her might be worth the clinginess. Stacked, with a curvy ass and shapely legs, she was all woman. The way a woman should be built. Whiskey-colored eyes, a turned-up nose, and pouty lower lip enhanced her sex appeal. Her thick blond hair hung in loose curls down past her chest. The kind of hair you could wrap around your wrist and . . .

Trip shook his head, clearing his throat. Grey had warned him to steer clear of Kelsey, convinced Trip would hurt her, which he probably would. That kind of tension could stir up trouble between Grey and his girlfriend, Avery. So Trip had agreed.

At the time it hadn't seemed like a big sacrifice—plenty of fish in the sea. Sometimes, though, he'd see Kelsey in town and find himself daydreaming about stripping her out of whatever tight dress—or loose-fitted costume—she was wearing . . .

He stopped and shook his head again. Clearly he needed ski season to begin, which always brought a fresh influx of single women on vacation looking for a little short-term fun. Until then, he should probably steer clear of Kelsey. Shouldn't be too difficult, considering the important business issues he and Grey had to address.

He strode into Backtrax—the backcountry ski and mountain climbing expedition business in which he would soon be a partner—passing through the reception area and down the hall to the private office. "Grey, you back here?"

"Yeah," Grey called.

Trip entered the windowless room to find his friend parked behind the computer with a lollipop sticking out of his mouth. Typical Grey.

Grey tossed a manila folder toward Trip. "These are the new partnership papers we need to sign once you get the money to buy into the company. How's that coming?"

"Just got back from the bank. Still no deposit." Trip sat in his chair and tipped his hat back, feigning confidence he didn't quite feel. "Don't worry, partner. I'll get the money."

"You asked me not to ask too many questions about your situation, but, if there's a problem, you need to tell me *before* I settle with Andy's insurer." Grey kept his gaze locked on Trip.

Trip knew Grey wanted to settle his legal claims against Avery's brother Andy—who'd driven while drunk and injured Grey last winter—quickly and for as little money as possible. In order to do so, Grey was relying, in part, on Trip's promise. Failure to secure the funding wouldn't just be a major disappointment to Trip and put Backtrax on shakier ground, it could wreak havoc on Grey's personal life, too. "I'll have the money, Grey. Soon."

"Okay. Dealing with Wade Kessler's hotel project was only one part of saving this business. Your investment is still key." Grey glanced at his watch. "I'm going to pick up the van from the shop. Catch you later."

"Sure." Trip watched Grey leave and then he stared at the manila folder in his hands. He drummed his fingers on the arm of his chair. Anxiety threaded through his chest, tightening it along with the muscles in his shoulders.

Dammit. He picked up the phone and dialed his father. "Hey, Dad."

"Gunner, I've been waiting for your call."

As always, love, resentment, and disappointment knotted in Trip's stomach at the sound of his dad's voice.

"Then you know why I'm calling." Trip kept his own voice polite, if detached.

"Yes. I got the request to release funds from your trust last week. Needless to say, it surprised me, considering you've never touched that money. In any case, we need to discuss it first."

"What's to discuss? I thought it was my money."

"It is." His father sighed. "But until you're thirty-five, I'm still the sole trustee, which means I can't allow funds to be misused or wasted."

Trip scowled at the implication. "You think I'm going to blow the money on something stupid?"

"Can't honestly say I know you well enough these days to answer that question, but that's beside the point." His dad paused. "As trustee, I'm bound by a fiduciary duty, and I'm never derelict in my duties."

Except your marital ones. His dad had been derelict in his duty to his wife by catting around with Trip's mom, which was how Trip came into existence and why Trip's mom had named him after *her* father.

Now, however, wasn't the time to point out his father's selective memory, or dwell on how that sophomoric affair had shaped Trip's outlook on love and life.

"So what do you need from me to move this along?" Trip hesitated. "There's a bit of urgency on my end."

"I figured there must be or you wouldn't have asked for the funds. Describe this investment, and be specific. The email you sent my assistant was scant on details."

Trip set his hat, brim up, on the desk and rubbed his forehead. "In December, I decided to work for a good friend who'd recently bought a backcountry expedition business. It sounded fun, and he's a great guy, so I figured I had nothing to lose. We get along great, and I've been able to make a real contribution here. Now I'm ready to commit more time and energy to this town and buy a stake in the company. I'm getting a fifty percent ownership interest for the money." After a brief pause, he said, "You should be happy. I'm finally growing up."

"I am, son. And I respect your attempt to forge your own path. Reminds me of myself when I was younger." He chuckled as if enjoying a flashback of his younger years. Of course, whenever his dad made a comparison between himself and Trip, it always served as one reminder of why Trip chose to remain a bachelor. He *was* a lot like his dad, which meant he couldn't be counted on to commit to one woman for life. "Where exactly *are* you living these days? You haven't set foot in Denver in almost two years. At least not to see your family."

Trip had breezed through Denver during that time period, but he didn't consider his stepmonster, Deborah, or older half brother, Mason, family. They'd made it their mission to interfere with the father-son relationship he and his dad might've been able to build. Made it real easy—enjoyable, even—for Trip to play out the role of the Cutler family's bastard black sheep.

Despite his dad's efforts to balance everyone's needs, Deb and Mason's behavior destroyed any chance they'd had at being a functional blended family. Trip's dad still hoped they could all reconcile, but Mason and Deb's hatred had merely cooled to indifference and neglect over time. Not exactly the stuff of happy family reunions.

"We're in Sterling Canyon." Trip cleared his throat, as if doing so might clear away the ugly memories crowding around him.

"You don't say! We've just submitted a bid to W. Kessler Group regarding a construction contract for a sizable resort and condo development there," his father said, pleasant surprise in his voice. "What do you know about it?"

Trip grimaced. *Of all the bad luck.* "I know Wade. Had to negotiate an easement over that development so we could retain access to our section of U.S. Forest property. He's a decent guy, from my limited experience, anyway. But he's destroying pristine land for oversize condos and a big hotel."

He heard his dad chuckle, which didn't surprise him considering his father had amassed a nationally known empire with Cutler Construction. "Still on that soapbox, I see. You do realize little towns like yours depend on amenities to draw tourists, right? Your business needs those very same tourists, so count your blessings."

"I've made Sterling Canyon my home because of its natural beauty and ample outdoor adventure. I'm not looking to get rich here. Just want to make enough money to ski, climb, drink a good beer, and eat a good burger."

"Easy to say when you're already very wealthy."

Reluctant acknowledgement tempered the hot streak of indignity that flashed through Trip. He closed his eyes, wishing he hadn't needed that trust fund money for this deal. "This is the first time I've ever tapped my trust, and I'm barely touching it."

"I don't want to argue, I was just making a point." His dad paused. "Maybe Mason and I should jump on the jet and come see you. You could give us a personal introduction to Wade before he chooses a contractor."

Trip scrubbed the back of his neck. The office suddenly seemed muggy and hot. He did not want his dad—or worse, his pompous half brother—snooping around town. Of course, Mason would probably be all too happy to come cast judgment on Trip's lifestyle.

"Silence isn't exactly the warm response a father wants from his son." His father's voice jerked him out of his daze. Just like that, guilt seized Trip's shoulders, tugging them back.

"Sure, Dad. I'll introduce you."

A defeated sigh came through the other end of the phone. "One of these days we need to have a heart-to-heart, Gunner. I realize our family isn't picture-perfect, but I've been there for you since your mom died."

For the first decade of Trip's life, his mother and *her* father—his beloved Poppy—had raised him. But when his mom was diagnosed with pancreatic cancer, she'd introduced Trip and his father to each other. Trip's dad spent the ensuing months convincing his mom and her father that he could better provide for Trip's future than Poppy could. But when Trip had finally been taken from Poppy's home just two weeks after his mom died, Deb's resentment had made it impossible to openly grieve his losses.

As a man, Trip understood why Deb had disliked having a constant reminder of her husband's infidelity staring her in the face each day. But as a boy, it had been brutal. At first, Trip had been eager to meet his older brother. Unfortunately, Mason turned out to be an entitled, self-centered brat who despised sharing his father. Trip suffered through almost five years of torment before Mason went off to college.

His father continued, "Don't you think it's time everyone made peace with our situation?"

Trip pinched the bridge of his nose and inhaled slowly. "No one's fighting, Dad. I just don't live in Denver or work for the family business. I'm pretty sure Deb and Mason are happier without me in the picture, too."

He imagined his dad waving his hand dismissively, scowling.

"Dammit, son. You and Mason are brothers. It's time you two talked, man to man. Don't think I haven't spoken to Mason about all this, too. Meanwhile, I'm not getting any younger. And Mason's been having a tough time since Jen filed for divorce. He could use a brother."

Trip pounded a fist against his breastbone, trying to break up the ball of acid burning through his esophagus. "Mason may be my *half* brother, but I doubt he wants to confide in me. He'd probably take out his best Remington and shoot you if he knew you just shared that tidbit about Jen. So can we not argue about him right now? Let's focus on why I called, and deal with the rest some other time. I really need you to release the funds before I lose this opportunity."

While Trip had no sympathy for Mason, he didn't feel very proud of disappointing his father. Every fiber of his being resisted being hog-tied by guilt, but those ropes were chafing him anyhow. Dammit, he knew there'd be a steep price to pay for tapping into his trust fund.

"Send me the financials so I can give them a look and make sure you're not getting ripped off. If everything is in order, I'll wire the funds by the end of the week."

"Thanks." Relief trickled through Trip, easing the muscles in his back. "I'll email the most recent statements. Call me if you have other questions . . . ," he paused, "or if you decide to come to town."

"Gunner, think about what I've said. If you and your brother can't solve your own problems, you're going to force me to find a way."

"I hear you." Trip hung up and tossed the phone on the desk. He blew out a deep breath, clasped his hands behind his head, and closed his eyes.

Their dad had tried and failed to negotiate peace in the past, and Trip remained certain they were all better off apart. If only he could squash that tiny voice inside that whispered about owing his dad more attention and respect.

Grey walked back through the door and went straight to his center desk drawer. "Got all the way there before I realized I forgot my wallet." He then looked at Trip, eyes narrowed. "You look like you're about to barf. What happened?"

"Went a few rounds with my old man." Trip folded his arms across his chest. "But I should have the funds by the end of the week."

On his way back out of the office, Grey slapped Trip on the shoulder. "Sorry this has caused you trouble with your family. But our partnership is worth it. You'll see."

It had better be, Trip thought, because he might've just opened the door to a whole lot of misery by using that money.

Chapter Two

Kelsey walked with Fee the six blocks across town from her condo to her sister's house. As they approached the yellow clapboard home, she admired her sister's small garden, manicured lawn, and picket fence—a private outdoor haven compared with the shallow balcony of Kelsey's second-floor unit.

They passed through the front gate and started up the walkway.

"I see you've changed out of your costume." Maura smiled at Kelsey from the front porch.

Fee scampered up the front steps and flung herself into Maura's arms. "Mommy!"

Maura hugged her while kissing the top of her head. "Did you have fun with Aunt Kelsey?"

Fee nodded. Maura then looked at Fee's costume, her eyebrows rising as she noticed the streaks of chocolate and vanilla icing smeared across its skirt. "Looks like you got a treat . . . or two."

"Three!" Fee exclaimed, apparently forgetting Kelsey's earlier warning as she thrust three extended fingers in Maura's face. Maura raised one eyebrow at Kelsey, who shrugged and flashed a guilty smile. "And we met Prince Charming, too, but he says he's too old to marry me." Fee flashed a wide-eyed smile. "So I told him to marry Aunt Kelsey."

"Aren't you thoughtful?" Maura chuckled before patting Fee's bum and sending her inside to change. Then she turned toward Kelsey. "Well, your day sounds interesting. Park your butt on the porch swing and give me the scoop."

While following Maura to the far end of the porch, Kelsey noticed her sister hadn't quite lost all her baby weight since giving birth to Tyler ten months ago. Of course, even on their best days, neither she nor Maura would ever be considered skinny. They looked like sisters, although Kelsey's hair was a shade or two lighter, and six inches longer, than Maura's. At five-foot eight, Kelsey also stood about two inches taller, and her cup size was at least two sizes bigger, too—as Maura often lamented.

"Where's Ty?" Kelsey asked as she settled onto the swing, which creaked as they began to rock.

"Napping." Maura held up a baby monitor before setting it back on the windowsill. Her eyes radiated girlish mischief. "Now, who exactly is Prince Charming?"

"Trip Lexington."

"Oh, no!" Maura giggled. "Were you mortified? Did he catch you in that ridiculous getup you were wearing?"

"Yes, literally. I collided with him on our way out of Sweet Cakes." Kelsey shrugged. "But I'm not *mortified*. It's not like I'm interested in him."

"Really?" Maura tilted her head, using her sisterly intuition to sniff out Kelsey's self-deception. "I've never met the man. Only seen him in town. But Fee's right, he does look like Prince Charming."

A flush of heat prickled throughout Kelsey's body. "I have eyes, so I can appreciate his 'most gorgeousness.' But these eyes also see how *he* appreciates himself. I like a confident guy, but Trip's cocky. He's probably a great one-night stand, but definitely not boyfriend material."

"Until someone comes along and rocks his world." Maura wiggled her brows suggestively, prodding Kelsey with an elbow to the ribs. "Someone like a strong, sassy Callihan girl to bring him to his knees."

That's how Maura had always referred to them—the Callihan girls—and she said it like a boast, like they knew life secrets no one else had figured out yet.

On the surface, Kelsey and Maura didn't have much in common. Maura, sixteen months older, had been a tomboy and rarely wore makeup. "Doing her hair" meant taking it out of its ponytail and running a brush through it. And fashion? Well, Kelsey sometimes thought her sister's ratty cutoff shorts might one day get up and walk away on their own.

Yet deep down, the sisters shared values and a romantic outlook on life. They talked big, dreamed bigger, and loved biggest of all. So Maura's not-so-subtle encouragement regarding Trip didn't shock Kelsey. Romantic fancies were practically a reflex for the Callihan girls.

"I'll pass."

"Come on. You're single; he's single. Don't tell me you've never even fantasized about him."

"The fantasy of that guy is probably better than the real thing. And if Trip's better in real life than in my fantasy, well, that might be the worst thing that could happen." When Maura failed to appear convinced, Kelsey poked her leg. "I told you, I'm done with guys my age. They're too immature, just like every guy I've ever dated since middle school. They look at me and see sex—period. I've learned good sex won't make someone love me. Now I've got to go about it a different way, or we'll have no shot at raising our kids together like we always planned.

"In the meantime, I'm putting energy into my career, which has been taking off. The commission on Wade's deal alone is six figures. And, confidentially, I told him the Copeland family is thinking of selling their tract of land just outside the northwest corner of town. He might be interested in another commercial development here. At this point, I'm the only broker in the deal. That could translate to about five hundred grand in commission. If that happens, I can start to invest in small apartment buildings in town, which would be debt-free by the time I retire."

"Wow! I'm proud of you, sis, although I wonder how the community will react to another major Kessler development." Maura waved away her concern, threw one arm around Kelsey and squeezed her. "But weren't you interested in a more personal payoff with Wade?"

Kelsey wrinkled her nose. "Yes, but I don't think I'm getting anywhere with that negotiation. He's friendly. We've had a few meals together while looking at the property. But he hasn't made a single move." She sighed. "Maybe I should be more like Avery, you know? For years she's tried to get me to see the 'he's not that into you' signs. Wade's signs aren't exactly flashing 'I want you' in neon."

"Maybe he thinks someone as young and pretty as you wouldn't be interested in him?" Maura's sincere expression made Kelsey want to laugh out loud, but she shook her head instead.

"What rich, forty-year-old man thinks any unmarried, thirtysomething girl wouldn't be interested?" Of course, maybe Kelsey should take one last shot before giving up on Wade.

"Good point." Maura slapped Kelsey's thigh. "So maybe Wade's not 'the one.' There are other guys. And anyway, you're lucky to have independence, the ability to be spontaneous, a solid career, and disposable income. Your life could go in any direction at any time, and that's pretty exciting. Me? My boobs will look like deflated balloons by the time I'm done breastfeeding Ty. I spend my days cleaning up baby food and poop, and folding loads of laundry. If I read *Goodnight Moon* one more time, I might actually go crazy. And Bill, while a great husband, can be like having a third child at times. Married life with young kids is not very romantic."

Easy for Maura to say, when she already had the life Kelsey wanted. Kelsey never understood why so many married women liked to groan about being a wife and mom. The truth was none of those women would trade places with Kelsey.

After all, Maura got to fall asleep with Bill, a man who'd vowed to stick it out through thick and thin. She got to come home at the end of a disappointing day at work and talk to someone who actually cared, someone who maybe even offered a backrub. She got to snuggle up and read a book to Fee and Ty, whose hugs and kisses could wipe away the worst kinds of trouble.

Those thoughts zipped through Kelsey's head, but she knew her sister meant well. And to be fair, Kelsey really could consider alternative futures now that her career had begun to take off. Futures that included exotic trips, new hobbies, and challenging business deals. So, rather than debate the finer points of marriage, she chose to nod and make light of her singleton status. "Thanks. You've just squashed any lingering interest I might've had in seducing Wade or Trip into wedded bliss."

If only using the words *seduce* and *Trip* in the same sentence didn't heat her blood.

"Anytime, sis." Maura smiled. "Anytime."

The sun had just peeked above the horizon when Kelsey pulled her car up to the Weenuche Inn to pick up her friend, Emma, for their six thirty yoga class. She scanned the windows, looking for signs of life, while wondering how Emma didn't feel stifled working and living there with her mother year after year.

Kelsey checked her watch, then exited the car to hurry Emma along. She had just turned around when she spied Trip making a hasty exit through the inn's front door. That man loved female tourists—fresh meat that didn't hang around town long enough to expect a second date, let alone a commitment.

When he spotted Kelsey at the end of the walkway, his surprised expression quickly morphed from chagrin to something sly as his pace slackened. He called out, "Good morning, princess."

If he thought he could embarrass her by bringing up last week's costume incident, he was about to be taught a lesson.

"Don't slow down on my account." Kelsey leaned against her car, arms folded in front of her chest, verbal assault at the ready. "And while it probably will blow your mind, just consider this: the woman you're so keen to sneak away from might not be all that interested in chasing you down."

"In my experience, satisfied women always want more." Undaunted, he came within a foot of Kelsey, his strapping frame casting hers in shadow. He leaned near, his eyes briefly dipping to her cleavage, which was scrunched together by the sports bra she'd worn for class. "And trust me, she's more than satisfied."

"Oh yeah?" She eyed his cowboy hat, half tempted to knock it off his head. Egos like his were the reason women like her were still single. "Well, in *my* experience, most men tend to overestimate their ability in the bedroom."

"Lucky for me, I'm not like most men." Trip's lips curled upward in that sexy, arrogant way he'd perfected. When she rolled her eyes, he said, "If you need proof, just say the word."

For just a second—a millisecond—she wanted to, badly. Attitude aside, he was hotter than a branding iron, even when mussed up and wearing last night's wrinkled clothes. And it had been, *ahem*, a while since she'd been wrapped up in a man's arms and legs.

Her slight hesitation ignited a spark of energy between them, which appeared to shoot an extra twinkle straight into his eyes. Her body flushed in response.

"No, thanks," she finally managed. "I wouldn't want to demolish your delusions of grandeur."

He chuckled, his throaty laughter making her smile despite her best efforts. When her lips quirked, he raised one brow. Planting one hand on the roof of the car, he leaned forward and murmured, "If you ever change your mind, you let me know."

It took a lot—a real lot—of resolve to hide the way her insides quivered as his voice skimmed across her ear. Thankfully, Kelsey saw the flash of Emma's red hair emerge from the inn before Trip could break her down any further. He pushed off the car and faced Emma.

"'Morning." Trip tipped his hat, smiling. "If you ladies will excuse me, I've got a busy day ahead."

"Fancy seeing you here early in the morning . . . again," Emma quipped. She narrowed her green eyes. "I might have to ban you from the property so people don't start getting the wrong idea about this inn."

"If you were smart, you'd use me to attract repeat business." When Emma snorted, Trip winked and raised both hands in surrender. "Okay, okay. I'll stop. Don't want to keep you two from your exercise class. Lord knows how much we men appreciate the results."

Before Emma or Kelsey could form a retort, he winked and jogged away. Emma watched him for a moment, shaking her head. When she turned to get into the car, she looked over the roof and said, "I know things didn't work out for you with Grey, but thank God it was him you liked instead of his partner. What a disaster a crush on Trip would've been!"

An understatement, yet Kelsey couldn't deny that some demented part of her brain and heart and other body parts might've been willing to risk the fallout.

Trip stepped out of the shower and rubbed the steam off the mirror with his towel. He rested his hands on either side of the sink and stared at himself. The hot water hadn't eased the tension in his shoulders or around his mouth. An hour from now he'd see his dad for the first time in nearly two years. He guessed the only thing that might loosen him up at this point was amber in color, came in a bottle, and went down the hatch with a bite.

He shaved the scruff from his face, trying to ignore the memories pounding against his skull.

Trip's father sat on the edge of Trip's bed, waiting for him to stop crying. His mother had been gone only a month, but it had felt like a year. He missed her. He missed his old room, his old neighborhood and school, his old friends, too.

"Now, son. I know this is hard. Losing your mom so young will leave a hole in your heart for the rest of your life. But now you've got a dad. And I've got a chance to help you become a man. And part of becoming a man is learning how to face a setback."

But Trip didn't want to be a man. He didn't want to listen to lectures from this virtual stranger, however well-intentioned. "When's Poppy coming to take me for a sleepover?" The remaining bright spot in his life involved his visits with the man who'd been the real father figure in his life, his namesake, and the man he had always admired.

"He'll be here soon." Trip's dad sighed, then laid a hand on Trip's leg. "Since you brought him up, I wanted to ask you something. Now that I've adopted you, I was wondering if you might like to change your last name to mine. What do you think?"

Trip's body curled away from his father's touch. "No!" When he noticed his father's defeated expression, he softly added, "Sorry."

Even now Trip winced at the recollection. That exchange had kicked off a pattern of his dad reaching out and Trip pulling back, never quite able to accept the love and attention as genuine. The circumstances surrounding his adoption, and Mason and Deb's nasty barbs, had always left Trip feeling like an outsider, a runner-up, a mistake his dad had to "be a man" and handle.

Maybe he'd never given his dad a fair shot. Maybe the time had finally come to try to accept the fact that they shared DNA, among other things. Maybe this visit would be the one to change the tide of their relationship.

Trip sat in the lobby of the hotel where Wade was staying, his stomach growling. A few weeks ago he'd sat here with Grey and Wade, hammering out a deal for access over part of Wade's planned development. Now he was sitting here with his dad and Wade, which kind of blew his mind.

He studied his father, tuning out his dad and Wade's conversation for the third time in thirty minutes. The gray hairs at his father's temples had spread throughout his dark hair, giving him that distinguished "salt-and-pepper" look. At sixty-five, Ross Cutler looked younger than his years. Perhaps Trip would age well, too. They shared some features, like olive-colored skin, dark hair, a square jaw. But Trip's green eyes came from his mother's family, as did his height.

He knew his dad and Mason had always hated being five inches shorter than him, although for different reasons. Trip suspected his dad disliked the height difference because it came from Poppy, serving as a reminder of the whole gulf between Trip and his dad.

As for Mason, Trip's size and athleticism has only further divided him from his more bookish brother, especially because their dad had openly admired Trip's physical prowess. The nail in the coffin had come when Trip had been only thirteen and happened upon Mason, then a high school junior, being bullied. Thinking he might salvage some relationship with Mason, he'd jumped into the fray and taken down the two bullies within minutes. Mason, however, only grew more hateful after that incident. Whether that was from jealousy or humiliation, Trip was never sure.

He was chewing on that thought when his dad's deep chuckle snapped him back to the present.

"Thanks for coming here to discuss the project in person, Ross. I'll be making a final decision very soon." Wade smiled. "If things don't work out, perhaps we'll get another opportunity in the near future with another tract of local land I've got my eye on. Apparently the owner recently died and his heirs might be interested in selling, so my timing is perfect."

Trip jerked his gaze toward Wade. "What land?"

"Eight acres at the northwest corner of town."

"For what purpose?" Trip heard the bitter edge in his voice, but Wade appeared indifferent.

"Upscale retail and office space."

Disgust gripped every muscle in Trip's body, but he shook it off when his father shot him a stern look. Now wasn't the time to raise objections, but Trip would not stand idly aside and let Wade Kessler or anyone else destroy Sterling Canyon's charm. First he'd get informed, then he'd form a plan—mobilize others who were sure to see things his way and try to convince the heirs not to sell.

"I hope we don't have to wait for another shot," his dad interjected. "I've got a good feeling about this development and know we can deliver what you want, on time and on budget, and better than any of our competitors. I pride myself on my reputation." Ross nodded. "Now if you two will excuse me for a minute, I need to make a quick call. Son, I'll meet you back here in a few. Wade, you have a good day."

Ross shook Wade's hand and meandered about fifteen feet away, phone at his ear.

Trip heard the click of Kelsey's heels tapping against the marble lobby floor before he saw her crossing to the concierge desk. He had to bite his tongue to keep from whistling.

Snug blue dress, cut high and low in all the right places. Cute shoes that showed off the red polish on her toenails. Dangling earrings calling attention to that nice spot along her neck. His only quibble with her appearance this afternoon would be the fact that she'd tied up all that awesome hair in some kind of knot. He much preferred when her mass of golden curls hung loose, like they had when he'd bumped into her this morning.

"Looks like my next appointment has arrived a few minutes early," Wade said, standing to greet her.

Trip stood, too, and noticed Kelsey flashing Wade a gigantic smile and flirty wave. If she was surprised to find him with Trip, she hid it well. However, her smile faded a bit when she acknowledged Trip's presence with a slight nod.

"Wade," she began, laying a hand on Wade's forearm, "I'm so excited to show you two of these properties today."

"You've got *another* project in mind?" Trip asked Wade, his gut burning once more.

"I'm thinking about buying a vacation home." Wade grinned congenially at both Trip and Kelsey while rocking back on his heels.

"Why not take up in one of the luxury condos you're building?" Trip asked, hoping his sarcasm hadn't quite registered with Wade. Seriously, how much shit did one guy need to own?

"I think it's best to put some distance between myself and the future condo association. Plus, Kelsey here has piqued my interest in looking for a unique vacation home."

"Not just a unique one," Kelsey said, using her eyes to enhance the come-hither smile on her lips. "The *perfect* one. Something in a prime location. Something cozy. Something special. And I think I've got just the place."

"Well, Kelsey, I can't wait to see what you've got." Wade winked, but based on his brotherly demeanor, Trip felt sure he didn't intend the double meaning that immediately popped into Trip's head.

Meanwhile, Kelsey was putting on quite a display for Wade throughout the conversation. She stood a tad too close to him, touched her hair and her collarbone flirtatiously, and licked her lips once, too. If Wade didn't have a hard-on yet, he was gay or impotent.

What did Kelsey see in Wade, Trip wondered? The guy was at least a decade older than her and not very charismatic. He wasn't bad looking, but he wasn't exactly handsome. Average height, average build, dark blond hair, nothing distinguishing about his face except perhaps a strong-looking nose.

Sure, the guy seemed friendly, but that didn't seem like enough to capture the interest of a woman like Kelsey. Normally he might suspect Wade's "bucks deluxe" of being the big fascination, but Kelsey had never struck him as a gold digger. He'd seen his fair share of those in Denver, including his brother's wife. Yet another reason he never spoke of or pulled from his trust fund. At least he knew the women he'd been with had been interested in him, not his wallet.

Wade's phone rang, so he excused himself for a minute and stepped a few feet away. Trip noted Kelsey's gaze following Wade.

"You're trying too hard," Trip whispered to Kelsey, while crossing his arms over his chest.

Kelsey stuffed the real estate listings back into her portfolio. "I don't know what you're talking about."

"Oh, yeah, you do." Trip chuckled. "You're coming on too strong. Trust me, it's only going to send him running in the opposite direction."

She scowled. "Well, you *would* know about running."

"I know about men. And men like to hunt, not be hunted." When she tilted her head in response, a little curl of hair fell out of that knot. Instead of twisting it around his finger like he wanted, Trip kept his hands locked beneath his armpits. "You want Wade's attention? Quit being so obvious about the fact you like him. Make him come to you."

"Why do men like games?" She shook her head.

"It's not about games. The chase is half the damn fun. If you take it away, you lose the anticipation and all that other good stuff."

Kelsey rolled her eyes. "You may think I'm desperate, but I'm not so desperate as to take love life advice from *you*, for God's sake."

"Fair enough." Trip raised his hands, his words dripping with sarcasm. "Do it your way, since it's worked so well for you so far."

Her cheeks turned pink, and he almost apologized, but Wade returned. "Ready to head out?"

Trip had to hand it to Boomerang—she recovered quickly.

Kelsey smiled at Wade, although less radiantly, Trip noted with a smug sense of satisfaction. "Absolutely. Let's go find you a new house."

"See you later, Trip." Wade escorted Kelsey through the lobby.

Trip smiled when Kelsey put a little more distance between her body and Wade's. Of course, he didn't want to think about why that made him happy.

His gaze followed them out the door, or, more honestly, he watched Kelsey's hips sway until they disappeared.

Before he realized it, his father had sneaked up beside him.

"She's a real looker." His dad's alert gaze remained fixed on the entrance. "Was that Wade's girlfriend?"

Trip's dad seemed almost as enthralled as him. Yes, something else he'd apparently inherited from his old man—an "appreciation" of beautiful women. And an ego big enough to go after them. Precisely why Trip wouldn't make the same mistake his dad did and commit to just one.

"Not yet." Trip glanced at his dad.

"That's good." Ross's blue eyes lit up.

Trip stuck his thumbs through his belt loops, irked by his dad's interest in Kelsey. "Last I checked, you were still married to Deb. Didn't you learn your lesson, yet?"

As soon as the words left his mouth, he wished he could swallow them. His father's head drooped as he sighed. "I wasn't talking about me, Gunner. I meant good for you."

"For me?" Trip grimaced. "What the hell do I care if Kelsey dates Wade or not?"

His dad slapped his shoulder. "Oh, you care. I'm old, but I'm not blind."

What did that mean? The parts of his body that enjoyed watching Kelsey walk out the door weren't anywhere near his heart, for God's sake.

"She's pretty, sure. But Boomerang's not on my to-do list. Trust me."

"Boomerang?" His dad rubbed his chin.

Trip closed his eyes, sighing. "Long story."

"I've got time. Take me to lunch before I catch the jet back to Denver. You can fill me in then."

Chapter Three

Kelsey woke up late on her birthday and stared at the ceiling. *Thirty-one*. Normally she loved any extra attention on her birthday, but not this year.

Thirty-one years old!

On her thirtieth, she'd painted the town red with a group of friends and acquaintances. This year she'd threatened everyone—no big parties or hoopla. All she wanted was a quiet day with the people she loved. Lunch with her besties followed by an evening with her family.

Of course, even though she'd made modest plans, she still wanted—needed—to look fabulous. An hour later, makeup done and hair smoothed, she left her home wearing a smart-looking caramel-colored wrap dress and platform beige suede heels.

She met Emma and Avery at Smuggler's Notch. Late-July sunlight streamed through the plate-glass windows of the recently renovated tavern. Reclaimed hardwood floors were all that remained of the old building. The stone-and-steel interior finishes were what Kelsey called "cowboy chic," where the Old West meets Manhattan. While she enjoyed Sterling Canyon's historic appeal, Kelsey liked modernization, too, and appreciated when local businesses upgraded and remodeled to keep up with the times.

"Happy birthday to you, happy birthday to you—" Avery and Emma sang, standing and greeting Kelsey with hugs and kisses.

Kelsey curtsied in jest and then they all sat down. In front of Kelsey's seat was a gift-wrapped box.

"Thanks, guys." Kelsey toyed with a bow on the package. "You didn't need to buy me anything."

"Oh, shut up and open the gift." Avery said, the flecks of gold in her blue eyes sparkling. "You knew we wouldn't listen."

Kelsey raised her wineglass in the air. "Cheers to that!" After practically chugging its contents, she started to untie the ribbons.

Em chuckled. "I have to admit, I'm happy to see you so upbeat today. I know you've been trying your best to ignore this birthday."

"I'm not exactly thrilled about it, but it is what it is." Kelsey stopped unwrapping the gift to look at Emma before swigging more wine. "Might as well embrace it."

"Love the attitude." Avery raised her glass. "So what's your birthday wish this year?"

"My old standby—falling desperately in love with the guy who will love me back just as much."

"I've always teased you about that, but now I have to confess, it is a worthy goal." Avery's cheeks flushed. A notorious *un*romantic, that admission had to have killed her. Never mind the bitter irony of Avery finding love before Kelsey, despite the fact *Kelsey* had been the one actively pursuing it for the past decade. Kelsey wasn't proud that a pinch of envy clouded her happiness for her friend, but she wouldn't lie to herself either.

"If you'd have asked me five years ago where I'd be at thirty-one, I've have said married with kids." Kelsey grimaced, rolling her eyes in a self-deprecating manner. "Epic fail. Not only am I not married or pregnant,

I'm not even dating. Haven't even had sex in . . . well, no need to get *totally* depressed. Too long, that's the only important point."

"Not as long as me." Emma wrinkled her nose. She and Kelsey giggled while Avery's cheeks darkened from pink to red.

"At least my career is going great." Kelsey sipped more pinot grigio, hoping the wine would help her better accept her loveless status. "In fact, I just got my commission from Wade's hotel deal, which brings me to another wish. I want to plan that girls' weekend I mentioned at the jazz festival."

"I'm in. Just need to check my schedule." Avery took out her phone. "When and where were you thinking?"

"You'd mentioned Santa Fe." Emma leaned forward. "Is that still the plan?"

Kelsey shook her head. "No. I'm thinking bigger . . . better. How about Cabo in mid-September?"

Emma and Avery's shocked expressions drew the first hearty laugh of Kelsey's day.

"Sounds fabulous, Kels, but I don't have that kind of money." Emma sat back.

Kelsey patted her hand. "I told you, this is my treat. I'll buy plane tickets and rent us a nice suite. You just need spending money."

"That's so extravagant." Avery swung her silky, chocolate-brown hair behind her shoulder. "Are you sure?"

"Yes! Please let me share my good fortune with the people I love most. We'll have a blast." When her friends looked skeptical, Kelsey added, "You have to say yes. It's my backup birthday wish."

Avery smiled. "If you're really sure."

"I am." Kelsey squeezed Emma's hand.

"Okay, then," Emma replied. "Who am I to say no to a fairy godmother?"

"Oh, please. No fairy tale jokes. I'm still living down the whole princess birthday thing I did with Fee the other week." Kelsey relaxed into her chair. "Turns out one of my clients saw me from a distance and was a bit perplexed."

Avery's lips twitched. "Grey mentioned something Trip had said, too." Then her eyes widened. "Well, speak of the devil."

Trip had been headed toward the bar until he noticed them and changed course. He tipped his hat just before he pulled a free chair from a nearby table, turned it backward and set it between Kelsey and Emma, then plopped his cute butt down. He surveyed the wineglasses and partially unwrapped gift. "Ladies, looks like quite a celebration."

"It's Kelsey's birthday lunch," Emma said, her voice cracking. Trip's over-the-top flirtations had a way of making shy women like Emma nervous. Kelsey, on the other hand, took them as a challenge.

"Happy birthday, princess." He grinned, leaned closer to Kelsey, and practically purred in her ear. "Does the birthday girl want a kiss?"

Yes. Her insides sprang to life like Mexican jumping beans, but she remained outwardly calm. "No, thanks. No telling where those lips have been in the past twenty-four hours."

She smiled sweetly even as Emma and Avery choked on wine.

"Don't be jealous." He winked and glanced at the table again. "No cake. No candles. Too bad. I would've liked to have seen you pucker up and blow."

"Would you have?" She knew her next move would be risky, but his cockiness drove her to distraction. She leaned in, placed her lips close enough to his jaw that she could almost taste his skin, and gently blew into his ear. His jaw clenched and she thought he might've even shivered, which made her limbs all tingly. "How's that?"

He drew a deep breath and pinned her with those gorgeous green eyes. "If I were a smoker, I'd be lighting up a cigarette now."

Kelsey shook her head, pretending to be annoyed. But deep in her chest, her heart clenched even harder than his jaw had. It didn't help that he kept staring at her like she was some kind of whipped cream dessert he was dying to lick.

Avery cleared her throat.

"Well," Trip said, looking a little dazed while rising from his chair. "I'll let you ladies return to your lunch." Then he leaned nearer to Kelsey. "Maybe tomorrow after you're done helping me with Backtrax's website stuff, we can revisit your birthday wish."

Emma started to giggle and Avery rolled her eyes.

"If there's one thing I know for sure," Kelsey began, "it's that you, Trip Lexington, will never, ever make *my* birthday wish come true."

Emma and Avery both broke into peals of laughter, but Trip kept his focus on Kelsey. "You don't know me well enough to make that statement. Who knows? I might surprise you one day."

If only. The second that thought crossed her mind, her face scrunched up in horrified anger. What the heck was she doing fantasizing about this womanizer? "Bye, Trip."

"Are you sure it's a good idea to spend more time with that man?" Emma asked after Trip walked away.

Kelsey held up a hand. "I'm sure it's a terrible idea. No doubt he'll spend the whole time pushing my buttons. Don't worry, though. Grey will be there to keep things clean. And anyway, those two yahoos need some help with their social media. But let's drop guy talk. No Grey, Trip, Wade . . . none of it."

She really did not want to think about Wade and his continued disinterest, or why Grey had rejected her for Avery, or Trip's ability to whip up a flurry of hormones she had to beat back to avoid doing something stupid.

"Let's get back to our Mexican extravaganza. I might be able to plan a five-star trip if my newest project with Wade comes through." Kelsey fiddled with her fork.

"What new project?" Avery asked.

"He's considering another lucrative land deal. If I can help him pull it off, I'll have a bundle of money, most of which I'll use to invest in small apartment buildings. Step one to building up my balance sheet and future income stream."

"How exciting!" Emma beamed. "Look out, Sterling Canyon. I think Kelsey Callihan is going to end up being a big mogul . . . and not the kind on the slopes."

"I'm so glad to see you focusing on your future this way." Avery said no more, but Kelsey knew Avery had always worried about the emphasis Kelsey placed on romance and men. No reason to spoil Avery's delusion that her true heart's desire had changed.

"Cheers to that, too." Kelsey raised her glass, and they toasted to future success.

◆ ◆ ◆

Later that evening, she rang the doorbell at Maura's house. She'd been looking forward to a home-cooked dinner, maybe a game of Apples to Apples, followed by a little cheesy reality TV while nestled on the comfy corduroy sofas in Maura's living room. A perfect ending to her day.

Fee answered the door, dressed in a frilly summer dress, her curls pushed back behind a sparkly headband.

"Surprise!" she squealed, jumping up and down.

Kelsey's brows had just begun to knit together when she heard groans and laughter coming from inside the house. Apparently Fee had just ruined some kind of surprise. Kelsey stepped inside to find not only her family in attendance, but also Emma, Avery, Grey, Andy, and Trip.

Her cheeks burned as she surmised her perpetually matchmaking sister had used this birthday as an excuse to throw Trip and Kelsey together. Poor Avery probably had no idea she'd been so easily manipulated as part of Maura's schemes.

And poor Andy looked almost as uncomfortable as Kelsey felt. He was currently serving probation for his "post-happy-hour" vehicular assault charge, and had been keeping a low profile around town. Andy and Grey were polite to each other for Avery's sake, but not exactly close.

She quickly took in the pink streamers and balloons, which looked like leftover decorations from Fee's recent birthday party. Oh dear Lord. Any hope of a relaxing evening disintegrated within seconds of seeing Trip winking at her from across the room.

"Surprise!" the group shouted, despite the fact that Fee had spoiled their plans.

"Wow, you got me." Kelsey grabbed Fee up onto her hip. "No costumes for my birthday?"

Fee shook her head. "But Prince Charming came."

Kelsey rolled her eyes and tried to ignore Trip's smug smile.

"Prince Charming?" Avery asked.

"Yep. Him!" Fee pointed at Trip. "He's going to marry Aunt Kelsey when pigs fly, and I get to be the flower girl on a unicorn."

Stifled laughter and stunned faces made Fee scowl in confusion. Trip's self-satisfied smile briefly faltered as Grey and Andy mocked him, but then he played along with a princely bow. "Fee's wish is my command."

Kelsey set Fee down when Maura approached with a glass of champagne, mumbling, "You probably need this right now."

"Yes, very much." Kelsey shot her sister a stern "we're going to talk about this later" look before glancing at everyone and raising her glass toward the group. "Thanks for coming. Bottoms up!"

"Hear, hear." Trip's velvety voice rose above the crowd. She immediately regretted making eye contact with him. His cocked brow clearly proved he'd intended to draw attention to the double meaning of her last words. As if she hadn't caught it, or felt it flutter low in her stomach.

Not that she'd let him know it. As she drew near him, she muttered, "In your dreams."

She brushed past him, the brief contact sparking like static electricity. To distract herself, she hugged her parents and observed the feast of home-cooked favorites Maura and her mom had prepared. The dining room table displayed quite the buffet: barbequed chicken and vegetables, corn on the cob, loaded baked potato salad, Caesar salad, homemade buttermilk biscuits, and pitchers of extra-sweet lemonade.

She scanned the comfort foods dripping in butter and oil, sighing. No wonder she and her sister always had a bit of meat on their bones. Of course, Kelsey also opted to keep drinking the champagne, which probably added to her waistline.

Inadvertently, she smoothed her hand over her stomach. *Oh, screw it.* She grabbed a corn muffin and slathered it in honey butter.

"You've got a real nice family, princess," Trip said over her shoulder. "I see where you get your big ideas about love and happiness."

She turned in surprise. "Thanks, I think." Somehow his compliment sounded a bit backhanded. "Your tone suggests that your family life was less than perfect."

A mix of uncertain emotions raced across his face within the span of two seconds. "My early childhood was great, but then things took a surprising turn." His brows gathered together and his gaze grew distant.

Curiosity urged her to pry into this story, but intuition warned her not to press for details. She laid her hand on his forearm. "I'm sorry, Trip."

He patted her hand, his cool green eyes warming. "No need to turn your birthday into a pity party. I love my life now."

"Hey!" Fee appeared from nowhere and clasped his long leg like a koala in a eucalyptus tree. "You said you'd play with Lolly and me."

In a swift move, he hoisted her up onto his hip and tweaked her nose. "I did, and I never break my promises. Where's Lolly?"

Fee pointed to the living room sofa, where her baby doll lay near a toy cradle. Trip smiled at Kelsey before wandering away. "Excuse us for a bit."

Kelsey watched Trip sprawl out on the floor with Fee, who taught him how to change, swaddle, and bottle-feed Lolly. Fee then crawled onto his lap with an *Olivia* book, which he proceeded to read to her while she snuggled Lolly and sucked her thumb.

A ribbon of warmth traveled from Kelsey's heart through her limbs while she spied on them. This was the second time she'd observed Trip with Fee, the second time he'd displayed wonderful instincts with a child. Who could believe Trip had a heart? Did this also mean he might even be able to love someone other than himself? That he could be a good father some day?

Everything in Kelsey screamed to reject the idea, because she could *not* afford to think of him as anything other than a calculating man-whore. She twirled on her heel and dashed off to find the nearest glass of champagne before anyone caught her staring at Trip Lexington—most especially Trip Lexington.

By the end of the evening, Kelsey surveyed the damage: the ravaged buffet table, the half-eaten birthday cake, Maura and Bill struggling to settle their hyper kids. She wistfully acknowledged that these happy family gatherings sometimes made her yearn harder for her own home and husband and kids.

She and her sister had always assumed they'd be raising their children together. At the rate Kelsey was going, Fee could be in high school before Kelsey had a diamond ring on her left hand.

"What's that look about?" Maura asked as she approached Kelsey.

"Just appreciating the evening. This was really sweet of you." Kelsey deflected her grim thoughts by wrapping an arm around Maura's shoulder and directing her away from the group. "I may be pretty buzzed now, but don't think you fooled me tonight. You railroaded Avery to get Trip over here, didn't you?"

"I don't know what you're talking about." Maura did her best to appear innocent, but she didn't fool Kelsey. "I asked Avery to invite a few friends, that's all. But Trip did bring those gorgeous lilies, so he can't be all bad."

"He did?" Kelsey turned, tottering a bit on her heels, to look at the stargazer lilies in the center of the dining table, which she'd assumed her sister had added for decoration. "Are they for you or me?"

"I think he brought them as a hostess gift. I'd told Avery no birthday gifts because I thought you'd be uncomfortable otherwise." Maura glanced at the flowers. "But you can take them home with you."

"No, don't be ridiculous." Kelsey hiccupped and scrunched her nose before she said, a little too emphatically, "I don't want flowers from him, anyway. And I already got a gift from Emma and Avery."

"Did I hear my name?" Avery appeared out of nowhere. "Maura, the food was delicious. Thanks so much for including us. I think we're going to get out of your hair so you can put the kids to bed. Can I do anything else to help clean up before we go?"

"No, no!" Maura waved her hands. "Bill and I have got it covered."

"Okay. Well, our gang is heading out, then." Avery turned to Kelsey. "Do you want to walk back with us?"

"There might be live music at On The Rocks tonight," Trip chimed in from a few feet away. "Let's move the party there."

Kelsey hesitated, resisting the pull of his eyes. Already beyond buzzed, she knew drinking in a bar with Trip, of all people, would likely end badly. "You all go. I'm going to tuck my little lovies in and hang with my sister a while longer." Kelsey looked down at Fee, who was now clinging to her leg. "Thanks for coming, everyone."

She stood at the door and kissed everyone good-bye. When Trip passed through, he leaned close and whispered, "Sweet dreams, princess."

He jogged down the porch steps and disappeared into the dark with the others. Kelsey closed the door, leaning against it for a minute. She told herself the tingling sensations jetting down her arms came from all the champagne she'd consumed, not from *him*. Nodding to herself, she pushed off the door and grabbed Fee's hand to take her to bed.

♦ ♦ ♦

"Who wants to hit On The Rocks?" Spending a couple of hours in the loving bosom of the Callihan family had left Trip rather desperate to get back into his familiar habitat—a bar filled with anonymous faces.

"I'm out." Grey tucked his arm around Avery's shoulder. "But something tells me you're on a solo mission anyhow."

Avery rolled her eyes. "What's new?"

"Fine. You all go home at—" Trip glanced at his watch, "ten o'clock on a Saturday night. How pathetic."

"Different strokes," Emma's quiet voice offered.

"Damn straight." Trip stopped in front of the bar. "See you all later."

As soon as he stepped inside the rowdy space, he felt better. The memories of Maura and Bill's modest home, filled with comfortable furniture and lots of love, began to fade. Good thing, too, because watching the casual affection between Kelsey and her family had reminded Trip of the life he'd lost when his mother died.

A life that seemed more like a dream than reality after so many years. And the kind of loss he'd never suffer again so long as he didn't risk re-creating a happy family for himself. Free and easy, the only sane way to live.

He cut through the crowd without stopping until he got to the bartender. "Red Rocket." Trip threw his money down. While he waited for the cold bottle of beer, his thoughts ran backward again, first to the few hours he'd spent across town, and then to his mom.

In addition to old memories being dredged up by his dad's recent visit, tonight he'd been forced to watch Kelsey in her element. The prickly vibe she gave off around him had disappeared thanks to her comfort with the group and multiple glasses of champagne. She'd smiled and laughed and patiently attended to Fee and Ty, love oozing from every pore of her body.

She'd looked hot, too. Funky high-heeled shoes with a little bow at each ankle, pink shorts, sleeveless lace top. That hair hanging loose, swaying every time she moved or laughed.

His growing obsession with her was Grey's fault, dammit. Clearly the promise Trip had made not to touch her had only made him want her more, like the chocolate cake women craved when forced to diet. He just needed a bite to be satisfied, then he could get on with his life.

Hell, if he couldn't have Kelsey, maybe he could find a substitute for the night. Someone to distract him from all the memories now swarming his brain. Someone who wanted from him only what he wanted from her: a good-time girl who wasn't searching for a relationship.

He tipped back a swig of his beer and turned to scan the crowd. Ten minutes—and a second bottle of beer—later, he spotted a cute blonde near the front window.

She didn't look familiar, which surprised him. She must not have been from Sterling Canyon, because he'd have noticed her before. He pushed off the bar and sauntered over to her and her friend, adjusting his Stetson and pasting a smile on his face.

"Good evening, ladies." He stood beside the blonde.

She smiled at him, jutting one hip outward. "Hey, handsome."

Bingo.

"You having a good time tonight?" he asked, nodding politely at her friend before returning his attention to her.

"It's getting better." She pushed a section of hair behind her ear and held out her hand. "I'm Susie. This is Beth."

"Nice to meet you. I'm Trip." He took a swig of beer. "You mustn't be from around here, 'cause I'm sure I'd have noticed you if you were."

"Oh, no. I'm from here, I just haven't spent much time in bars." She sipped her drink.

"Don't like the crowds?"

Susie glanced at Beth and then laughed. "I love crowds, but I only turned twenty-one last month."

Twenty-one. Legal. But eleven years his junior. Was that too young? Jesus, even having that damn thought depressed him a little. Made him feel old standing there in the bar—alone. He shoved aside the unwelcome realization. "Ah. That explains it."

Through the window, he caught sight of another blonde tottering along the sidewalk under the streetlights—a very familiar blonde. *What the hell is she doing walking alone at night?*

"Excuse me a minute, I need to check on someone." He hurried away without thinking about it and dashed onto the sidewalk. "Kelsey? What are you doing?"

She turned, her eyebrows rising, appearing to wobble a bit on those shoes. "Oh, it's you."

"Why are you stumbling through town alone in the dark?" Trip felt himself frowning. "Not too smart."

"I'm fine." She waved her arms at him, all flopsy. "This is *my* town. I'm perfectly safe. I always walk to and from my sister's house."

"I can't believe she and Bill let you leave like this." Trip gestured up and down with his hand, concern warring with arousal.

"Let me?" Kelsey made a *phfft* sound. He hid a smile at her drunken behavior. Alcohol robbed her banter of its typical sarcasm, replacing it with bravado. "I wanted to walk home and so I did."

"Well, how about you let me see you the rest of the way home?" He realized he was still holding the beer in his hand, so he chugged it and tossed it in a nearby garbage can. "Come on. Just how many glasses of champagne did you drink?"

Kelsey shrugged. "It's my birthday. I celebrated!"

"For someone who's celebrating, you don't look too happy right now." He grabbed her by the elbow to prevent her from falling over. As soon as he touched her, he felt that connection everywhere. "Which way?"

She pointed to the right then yanked her arm away and ran a hand through her loopy curls. "Happy? Ha! Happy . . . I'm flippin' thirty-one.

Thirty-one! That's like . . . like *seventy* in guy years. Thirty-one, alone on a Saturday, and . . . and my feet are killing me."

He heard a little squeak of exasperation. Before he said anything, she briefly covered her face with her hands and shook her head. "Oh, God. I *must* be drunk or I'd never give you any ammo to use against me later. Just pretend I didn't say anything. You never saw me."

She took two steps, twisted her ankle, then bent over with a frustrated groan to unbuckle her shoes. Trip enjoyed the nice view of her ass in those shorts until she kicked off her shoes and stood up.

"You can't walk home in your bare feet, Kelsey. There's broken glass and rocks and stuff."

"Well, I can't walk in these new shoes anymore, either." She held them up, scowling. "They're not broken in yet."

"No amount of breaking those stilts in will make them good walking shoes." He crossed to where she was standing and leaned down closer to her face. "I can appreciate heels as much as the next guy, but why do women buy shoes *this* high?"

"They make my legs look thinner." She stared at him like he must be the dumbest man on the planet. He might've laughed if he weren't feeling so stirred up while she obviously felt nothing more than disdain.

"You've got great legs. You don't need shoes that make you practically as tall as me."

"You think I have great legs?" Her genuine skepticism surprised him. He'd pleased her, which felt oddly good.

Great legs, great ass, great rack, great face . . . and awesome hair. Of course, he didn't want to admit any more than necessary. Instead, he turned his back to her and squatted a bit. "Jump on. I'll carry you home."

"I'm too heavy." She sighed. "I'm fine to walk."

"I've carried backpacks up the mountain that weigh more than you. Just jump on so I don't have to throw you over my shoulder." Now he was getting annoyed by having to beg to help her.

But a whole lotta other sensations squeezed out his irritation the minute she wrapped her legs around his waist, rested her chin on his shoulder, and let some of her fragrant hair cascade around him. Holy hell, she felt good, like he knew she would. Made him wish he was carrying her face-to-face instead of piggyback style.

"Thanks." Her soft voice brushed across his neck. He was just tamping down a new set of tingles when she lifted his Stetson off his head and stuck it on her own. "Now I'm a cowgirl instead of a princess."

A cowgirl. He wondered if she intended him to note the sexual connotation of that phrase, which now had his jeans feeling too damn tight. He needed to dump her at home quickly and head back to the bar.

"One more block, that way." She pointed up ahead. Ten seconds later, she asked, "Trip?"

"Yeah?"

"Do you really think men like Wade would like me more if I were less nice?"

His grip tightened around her thighs as he frowned. It was rare—hell, never—that he had a girl wrapped around his body and all she could think about was other men. He set her down in front of her building.

He wouldn't have responded except she looked up at him with pleading, amber puppy-dog eyes. "It's not about being nice. You're just too eager. It's written all over your face, and most guys aren't ready for all that so soon."

"So my being open and thoughtful means I'm too easy?" Her brows drew together. "I'm not *that* easy. Jeez, it's been like . . . a *while* since . . . you know." Even in the dark, he could read embarrassment all over her face. Boy, tomorrow she was going to regret drinking all that champagne if she remembered everything she'd admitted tonight.

But right now she was suddenly looking at him in a way that set off his radar, because at that moment she was thinking about sex and him, not other men. He liked that idea way more than he should.

The conversation had veered into awkward territory, so he did what he did best. Flirt. "I'd be happy to remedy that particular problem for you. You shouldn't go too long without. Consider it a birthday present."

She tipped her chin up a bit, studying him. "You would, wouldn't you? Just sex and nothing else. And that's good enough for you? You don't get lonely?"

"I'm not lonely." He inched even closer, lowering his voice. "I get what I need. I don't hurt anyone. And I have a damn good time in the process." He peered down at her, insanely hoping she might surprise him and take the bait. "You should try it sometime."

The air seemed to crackle and he realized he'd been holding his breath. Would she actually accept his offer? One night in bed with her would mean he'd deal with the stalker otherwise known as Boomerang for weeks or months. But he already knew it would be worth it. At least, that's what his body was shouting.

He inclined nearer to her, finding it hard to breathe while she stared at his mouth for several seconds.

Then she shook her head as if waking from a strange dream, and straightened. "Guess it's something to think about. Thanks for the ride home, cowboy."

Kelsey turned, shoes in her hand, and scampered down the walkway to her building. She glanced back over her shoulder and gave a little wave. "Good night."

It wasn't until a block later that he realized she'd never given him back his hat—one of very few mementoes he had from Poppy. He stopped for a second, but then kept walking. If he'd turned back, he might've done or said something really stupid. He'd get Poppy's hat tomorrow when she came to work on the website.

Right now he needed a cold shower or a woman, but he couldn't be with some other woman if he was just going to be picturing Kelsey's pouty mouth. Man, he hated cold showers.

Chapter Four

Kelsey peeked out from beneath the pillow and popped one scratchy eyelid open to find a vintage brown Stetson beside her on the bed. The throbbing in her cotton-stuffed head intensified as she scowled and peered under the covers. *Whew!* Pajamas. Her nightgown and the empty, neatly made sheets to her left thankfully answered her prayer that she hadn't done anything too stupid with Trip.

She rolled onto her back and sighed. Self-restraint was a good thing. Of course, being naughty might've also been a good thing, at least in the moment. Glancing back at Trip's hat, she pictured him lying there wearing it . . . and nothing else.

Oh, bad idea. Very bad idea. The mere image sent a shiver down her spine.

Kelsey sat up, her back pressed against her pillows, and hugged her knees to her chest. She rubbed her sore feet, which summoned a memory of last night's piggyback ride.

Carrying her three and a half blocks to keep her from getting hurt after she'd kicked off her shoes in the middle of the street would've been kinda chivalrous, if one could believe he didn't have an ulterior motive. But his affinity for children aside, Trip always had a motive when it came to women. It started with an *s* and ended with an *x* and came with a side of "don't call me, I'll call you."

Sighing, she forced herself out of bed. Grey and Trip were expecting her at eleven for a little advice on updating their social media sites. Last time she'd gone to Backtrax to help, Grey had rejected her and pissed her off. She might not have agreed to try helping again had he and Avery not been dating. Now she'd have to face Trip so soon after all that champagne caused her to let her guard down.

Keeping her cool would be a challenge. Perhaps she could simply focus on the sizable challenge of bringing Grey and Trip's business into the twenty-first century. Or better yet, the challenge of studying a few more chapters of the real estate investment book Wade had recommended.

Given her itinerary, Sunday would not be a day of rest.

After downing a healthy portion of greasy eggs and bacon to deal with her hangover, she stood in front of her cheval mirror, appraising her Abercrombie navy-and-cranberry-print summer dress and red strappy sandals. Yes, her sore feet rebelled against yet another high-heel shoe, but they were the perfect ones for the dress. The fact Trip thought she had nice legs had nothing to do with her decision to wear that particular outfit or those particular shoes, no sirree. She'd be sitting for most of the morning, anyway.

Once more her gaze drifted to the Stetson, with its fraying hatband. How unlike Trip, a man who took pride in his appearance, to wear such a beat-up hat.

She lifted it off the mattress, her fingers brushing against the supple, well-worn brim. Grinning to herself, she piled her hair atop her head and then donned the Stetson, tipping it back a bit. Looked cute. Maybe she should add hats to her wardrobe in the future.

No doubt Trip expected her to return his today. Of course, he owned several, including a gorgeous black felt one and a summer straw one, too, so this old thing couldn't be too important. Maybe she'd keep it for a while . . . bribe him or make him earn it back or just generally torment him a bit by "forgetting" to return it.

Tormenting Trip sounded like fun.

She set his hat on the chair, grabbed her purse and Guy Kawasaki's *The Art of Social Media* book, and strolled out the door.

When she breezed through Backtrax's empty reception area, she called out, "Yoo-hoo! You guys back there?"

Trip appeared at the end of the dim hallway, wearing olive-green cargo shorts, a gray T-shirt, and leather flip-flops. His snug cotton tee hugged his broad shoulders and pecs, reminding her of how she'd clung to that same body just last night. She licked her suddenly dry lips, praying he didn't notice her reaction.

As always, he greeted her with a smile and a quick once-over. His gaze stopped at her feet. Shaking his head, he teased, "I see you didn't learn your lesson last night."

She walked up to him and patted his cheek. "Oh, I learned a lot last night."

"Me too. But what did *you* learn?" He looked down at her, brows raised. His face was so close she could see the little cleft in his chin and appreciate that clean-shaven jaw. Miraculously, she repressed the urge to run her fingers along his jawbone.

"Beneath this whole playboy persona is a bit of a gentleman. Just a bit, of course. But it's in there. Once upon a time, your mom must've taught you how to treat a lady." His momentarily haunted expression surprised her. Did he prefer people to believe him to be shallow and self-centered? "Don't worry. Your secret is safe with me." Kelsey peered inside the office and glanced at her watch, pretending not to notice the way Trip's gaze automatically fell to her cleavage. "Where's Grey?"

"First things first. Where's my hat?"

"You mean that old thing that belongs in a thrift shop?" She might've laughed at him if his shoulders hadn't stiffened and tight lines pulled around his mouth.

"I need it back, Kelsey." Although he stared at her without blinking, she thought she saw a hint of panic in those green eyes. His body gobbled up most of the space in the doorway, making hers prickle from the nearness.

"Settle down, cowboy. You'll get your hat back." She tilted her head. "But now you've got me curious. What's so special about that one? You have at least a dozen others."

Trip leaned back against the doorjamb. "It belonged to my grandfather."

She'd known him for eight months and yet, until last night, had never heard a single word about his background or family. Now several new questions sprang to mind, but she chose to tease him instead of pressing for answers he'd probably never give.

"Don't tell me you have a sentimental streak, too. That's too cute, Trip. Makes you almost . . . human." Seeing another hint of vulnerability worried her because it could actually make her start to fall for him, which would surely be a disaster.

"You've only got that partly right." He grinned, slipping back into his detached persona. "Haven't you heard? I'm *super*human."

Disaster averted.

"So where's Grey?" She sighed.

"Grey's put me in charge of this project." Trip set his hands on his hips. "Looks like it's just the two of us."

She hoped he didn't see her alarm at the prospect of being cooped up alone with him. "Well, then, let's get started."

Trip pulled an extra chair over to the desk and sat directly in front of the computer. Kelsey sat beside him, put her bag on the floor at her feet, and slapped the manual onto the desktop.

She pulled a hairclip out of her purse and twisted her hair atop her head so it wouldn't fall in her face while they worked. From the corner of her eye, she noticed Trip frown. Of course, he ignored her questioning glance.

Shrugging, she pulled the keyboard over to her side of the desk while asking, "May I?"

Trip chuckled, leaning close. "By all means."

The mere sound of his voice tightened her nipples. Kelsey thanked God she'd worn a loose dress so he couldn't see her body's response.

"Let's look at your site." She typed its URL. "Now tell me, what do you like about it?"

She watched his eyes scan the neatly aligned row of tabs and the column of links to forms and waivers. "It's easy to navigate and to find relevant information."

Kelsey laid her head on the desk, closed her eyes, faked a snore, then popped back up singing, "BOR-ING!"

"Functional." Trip crossed his arms, frowning.

She drew a deep breath and stuck out her chin. *Men.* "Websites and social media should give some sense of the product or service you're selling. What are you selling, Trip?"

"Guided backcountry ski and rock climbing trips."

"No." She rolled her eyes.

"No?" Trip tilted his head, frowning. "We're not selling those trips?"

"Nope." Kelsey shook her head. "You're selling 'adventure.' You're selling adrenaline and excitement. You should be appealing to guys who want to be like you, and women who want to be with you." As soon as she heard those last words, she realized her mistake.

"In other words, all women?" he interjected, wearing a smirk and twinkling eyes. When she rolled her eyes, he chuckled. "Sorry to interrupt."

"Does *anything* on this site promote a sense of adventure?" She thrust her index finger toward the screen while scrunching up her nose.

He scanned the green-and-beige page for a few minutes, with its Backtrax logo and stodgy fonts, before he admitted defeat. "No."

"You and Grey are *not* old Bill Batton. You two need to get your handsome faces on this site, and then load it with recent tour pictures. Make it fun and fresh."

"You think I'm handsome?" He leaned closer, his eyes scanning her face like a predator.

So flippin' handsome. Fortunately, she pressed her lips together before the words escaped. Suddenly she wanted to fan herself, but that would only encourage his flirtatious behavior. "Stay focused, please."

He took his time sitting back. "When I'm stomping big air, I'm not pulling out my iPhone to snap photos."

"Surely you shot some footage with a GoPro. Grab some frames, maybe even upload a video or two."

"That might look cool." He sat forward, his expression thoughtful. "But how will it bring people to visit the site?"

"For starters, join Facebook groups or communities that involve climbing and skiing." She hit a few keystrokes and brought up several rock climbing groups on Facebook. "You need to interact on these sites often, but not to directly 'sell' your services. Submit stories of your own and suggestions. Answer people's questions about places you've been, techniques, gear, and other stuff like that. Gradually people will get interested in your expertise and start looking you up. That's when they'll find your new and improved website."

Trip's expression grew pensive as he considered her advice. She tapped the keys again and *Powder* magazine's online site appeared. "Submit articles or guest blog posts here. Getting your name out a couple of times a year will build a following among your main client base."

"I'm impressed, Kelsey. Beauty *and* brains." Trip studied Kelsey with a wide smile, as if for the first time he noticed she was more than perky body parts. Not that she minded his appreciation of her appearance, but she liked being seen as something more, especially by a guy like Trip, who probably never thought of women as anything more than sex dolls. "It all sounds great, but how do I design a site or set up all those other things?"

Kelsey patted the manual to her right. "Between this book, YouTube videos, and other free information, you can get this all done with very little cost if you're willing to put in the time."

"I thought you were going to help me do it." Trip murmured in the smooth tone she recognized as one of a man trying to woo a woman into doing his bidding. Like a full-bodied red wine with a lingering finish, his seductive voice could lull her into all kinds of trouble.

Kelsey didn't want trouble. Or rather, she couldn't afford to waste time on trouble, not at her age.

"More like you hoped I was going to do it *for* you. Well, I'm not. I'll help a bit, but I've got my own business to deal with, plus the homework Wade gave me."

Trip sat back, arms crossed, head shaking. "Homework from Wade? What harebrained scheme are you using now to get his attention?"

Kelsey kicked Trip's calf.

"Hey, those shoes hurt!" He rubbed his shinbone.

"Sissy." Kelsey shot him an arch look. "It's no scheme. I'm expanding my business and getting into real estate investing, too."

"Don't tell me you're in favor of what he's doing to this town?" Trip's playfulness fled.

"Of course I am. I'm making great money from Wade, plus his developments will bring in more tourists and create jobs, too."

"Temporary construction jobs and low-paying retail jobs." Trip's peeved tone stunned her. "This town already gets plenty of tourists—people who come for its antique charm and natural beauty. If guys like Wade keep destroying the land to put up new buildings, tourists will start going elsewhere to 'get away' from it all."

She hadn't considered that before, but she wouldn't concede anything to Trip. "Fancy hotels and luxury shops won't drive tourists away. Look at Aspen."

"Yeah, look at Aspen—a once great, funky ski town that has slowly been transformed into a 'see and be seen' place for posers. In my opinion, it's lost all its personality."

She resisted the urge to frown. He wasn't totally wrong. Aspen had kinda lost *some* of its magic. Still, Sterling Canyon needed a boost. This old mining town wouldn't be destroyed by one high-end retail development. And maybe she couldn't control making her dreams of family come true, but she sure as heck would take control of her career.

"We'll just have to agree to disagree, Trip," Kelsey said. "I'm all for more options in this little town. And I'm counting on the commission from this deal to set me up to invest in some rental properties of my own."

"I wouldn't rely on that if I were you." His tone and posture issued a warning, but what did Trip know about investing?

"Leave Wade and real estate to me, cowboy. Stick to what you know best—the slopes and women."

He shook his head before he cocked it. Studying her thoughtfully, his eyes never drifting below her chin. Perhaps she'd gained a little of his respect? Then his facial muscles relaxed and he ruined the moment by wiggling his brows suggestively. "Tell the truth, your real interest in Wade's got nothing to do with these deals, does it?"

"Why is your mind always in the gutter?"

"It's fun in there." He lazily leaned back in his chair, which he'd turned to face her, stretching one leg forward until his foot nearly touched hers, like the snake in the Garden of Eden. "In fact, I think you should join me for a while before you wind up married and bored."

"Bored?" She cocked her head, annoyed. When he started fiddling with a pink eraser, she asked, "Why would I be bored?"

"Because everyone who gets married ends up bored. One person—forever?" He tossed aside the eraser he'd been tapping on the desk. "Good God, I'm bored even thinking about it."

"Naturally *you're* bored. You can't even be with the same woman for a whole weekend." His unrepentant shrug prompted her to lean forward. "You may be proud of that fact, but it tells me you only have a few moves and no imagination."

His cocky expression transformed to heated indignation and then something . . . else. He hooked his foot around the leg of her chair and yanked it toward his own. After planting his hands on the arms of her chair and caging her with his body, he murmured, "Honey, you can't throw down a challenge like that unless you're willing to let me prove you wrong."

Before she could respond, he unclipped her hair and ran his fingers through her curls. Every hair on her body vibrated in anticipation as his gaze dropped to her mouth.

Bewildered. Excited. Confused. A little terrified. The conflicting emotions coursed through her veins, making the one at the base of her neck throb so hard she thought it might burst.

"Tri—" she began, but he silenced her with a breathtaking kiss. Firm, a little rough, a whole lotta hot. She didn't want his kiss, or at least she hadn't been angling for one, and yet its carnal power swept her away.

He groaned, making her heart thunder. In a fluid movement, he lifted her as if she weighed no more than a Styrofoam cup, plunking her bottom onto the desk. Settling his hips between her legs, he dragged her to the edge of the desk, using his hands to coax her legs around his waist. He crushed her against his body while hungrily kissing her mouth, jaw, and neck.

Whatever happened in the future, she could no longer make wisecracks about his skill. Her entire body burned like she'd been thrown in front of a bonfire.

His hands were everywhere—seeking, touching, kneading—turning her on way more than she could handle. Granted, it had been a while since she'd been with a man, but the way he overpowered her, took what he wanted, and knew what to do with it, well, it unleashed yearning buried deep inside, which took hold like some kind of drug.

He broke the kiss to catch his breath, then immediately pressed his mouth to her neck. She gasped as he pulled her closer to his body. He practically growled when the hard ridge of his erection rubbed against her panties, making her wet and needy and panicked.

This could not happen. Not here and now.

Not with *Trip*, of all men.

That thought broke through her lusty haze so she shoved at his chest. "Wait."

"Why?" He barely got the word out as he continued his hot assault on her body, his thumbs now circling her nipples through the fabric of her dress. "Let's do this, Kelsey. We both want it." He kissed her again, and like the hungry fool she was, she kissed him back. "That's my girl."

His cocky tone coupled with the little smirk she felt against her cheek gave her the strength to push him away.

"Trip, please. Stop." She kicked him again, this time in the thigh.

"Hey, those damn heels are lethal, especially in this vicinity." He waved his hand in front of his crotch.

She jumped off the desk and backed away. "I don't know *what* that was about, but it never happened. You are never going to tell Grey or Avery or anyone else."

"First of all, barely anything happened." He scrubbed his hand over his face. "Secondly, why the hell does a kiss have to be a state secret?"

"Look, Trip. I've grown up being thought of as some kind of blond bombshell, making it impossible to get a man to see me any other way. I don't mean to hurt your feelings, but if I get associated with you, no decent man in this small town will ever take me seriously. And whether or not *you* think it would be boring to be 'stuck' with the same person, it's the one thing I want more than anything else. So I will *not* muck it up just for twenty minutes of pleasure."

"Oh, at least an hour, darlin'." He was hard and horny and stunned that she'd shot him down. She looked damn gorgeous standing there, fired up and flushed, chest heaving, hair wild and flowing.

Kelsey rolled her eyes. "Go ahead, joke. It's what you do best." She straightened her dress and then bent over to pick her purse off the floor. "Return my book when you're done with it, please."

"Wait a second." He held up his hands. That little taste of Kelsey had only whet his appetite, confirming what he'd suspected all along. She would be H-O-T. Now he needed to convince her to loosen up and have a little fun . . . with him. "Tell me why you're so desperate to get married. I mean, shouldn't you actually meet someone and fall in love first? Maybe the reason you keep failing is because you're going about it all backward."

Kelsey hugged her purse to her chest, frowning. "Is this the part where you try to give me relationship advice again?"

"Now there's an idea." He smiled as he took a small step toward her.

"I don't want your advice." She stepped back. "I don't trust you."

"Ouch." He grabbed his chest, mocking the insult. "Between the shoes and that sharp tongue, I'm losing a lot of blood this morning."

"Look, I've got to go." She turned to leave.

"Go study for Wade?" The thought of her and Wade curdled in his stomach like sour milk. Wade wasn't a strong enough personality for Kelsey. She'd be bored within a month, no matter what she thought right now. Kelsey needed someone bigger, stronger, and more fun than Wade to keep her interested for a lifetime. Someone more like Trip—not that he was vying for the honors.

"No, not for Wade!" She whirled around, eyes blazing, and stepped toward him. "For myself, Trip. Expand my horizons. Fulfill my potential. Any of these concepts mean anything to you?" She shrugged one shoulder. "Of course, if it makes me more appealing to Wade and other men, then all the better. Eventually I'll find my happily-ever-after with someone who wants a family. Someone who won't be *bored* by the idea of a woman who adores him and supports him and loves him above all others."

"Settle down, princess." This time he inched closer. "I'm here to help."

"Yeah, right." Her nose wrinkled, skepticism written all over her face. "Help how?"

"When you find your next target—" She scowled at his word choice, so he stopped and rephrased. "When you meet the next guy you want to date, I'll help you reel him in."

"Oh, really?" She tipped up her chin, narrowing her gaze, apparently unaware that he'd taken another step closer. "How, exactly, will you perform that magic act?"

"By keeping you from making the mistakes you made with Grey and Wade, and whomever else, that pushed those guys away. I'll be your gatekeeper." Now he was close enough to touch her again, but he didn't dare just yet.

"And why would you take on that role?"

"I love a good challenge." He chuckled at her outraged expression and held up his hands to fend off the whack she aimed at his chest. "Seriously, Kelsey, I think you're a sweet girl and I know I can help you. But while you're looking around for Mr. Right, there's no reason you can't have a no-strings fling with me. Memories to keep you warm on those cold days in the future when you're *bored*." He winked.

"You don't know when to quit, do you?"

"Nah, that's no fun. Besides, last night you admitted it'd been too long since you had a 'good time' with anyone. We get along. If the past few minutes prove anything, it's that we'd be combustible. Let's enjoy each other's company without all the BS that screws up serious relationships. In the end, we both wind up happy, satisfied friends."

"You'd get what you want, but I won't. I just told you, a fling with you will make me undesirable to most of the men around here."

"We'll keep it a secret, then." Worked better for Trip anyway, considering Grey's request. "Hell, that'll even make it hotter. And Kelsey, don't pretend that kiss didn't make you hot."

At least she didn't argue that point. He noticed her cheeks turn pink even as she tried to feign indifference. "This is still not a good deal for me."

"Deal? It's not a transaction, princess. Just two single people having fun." He stepped closer still, sensing some interest on her part. "But if the broker in you is more comfortable treating it like a deal, negotiate your terms."

"Well, you get everything you want right up front, but you can't guarantee I'll ever get what I want most." Her voice wobbled a little as she registered his body crowding hers.

"I sure can. You're a beautiful woman. You're successful. You're kind, or at least you are to everyone else. And you're savvy. There are plenty of men out there who'd want you if you didn't scare them all away by coming on too strong." Her disbelieving expression spurred him on. "In fact, I'm so sure I'm right, I'd even be willing to make a bet."

"A bet?" She tapped her fingers against her bicep.

"Yep."

"I get to name the prize?" One corner of her mouth lifted.

"Wait a sec, you've got to promise you'll follow my instructions to the letter. I can't have you purposely screw up just to win the prize."

"I want a husband and kids more than anything you could give me, Trip." She tilted her head, assessing him. Her grin suggested something between suspicion and daring. "Since you're so confident, then I'm thinking your grandfather's Stetson should be sufficient motivation."

"You must have lost your mind when I kissed you."

"Hey, this was your proposition." She poked her index finger at his chest. "You're the one who seems so interested in a secret sexual relationship. You're the one who claims to have all the answers. You're the one who came up with the bet." Her grin transformed to some smug flirty expression. "If you want to call it quits, that's fine with me. I've got other things to do today, anyway."

She tossed her hair over her shoulder, releasing the perfumed scent of her shampoo into the six inches of space separating their bodies. Whether the aroma infected his brain, or those pouty lips of hers made him stupid, he wasn't sure. Either way, he heard himself saying, "Hang on. How about a thousand bucks instead of the hat? That should make you comfortable I won't renege on my promise."

"You're serious?" Her mouth fell open. "You'd *actually* pay me a grand if you fail?"

"I'm not going to fail." He refrained from touching her while he waited for her answer. His heart dropped a bit when she started shaking her head.

"Why are you suddenly so interested in my love life?"

"I'm not interested in your love life. I'm interested in your sex life, but I'm happy to help you with your love life, as a friend—one with benefits."

"You're going to an awful lot of effort just to sleep with me, Trip. Have I just stumbled onto the real reason why so many women fall into bed with you—do they all get this same deal? Or is there some other reason you're so intent on taking me to bed?"

"You want me to admit to fantasizing about what it'd be like to strip you down and heat you up? Fine. Busted. I want you. Now that I know you've got no interest in a relationship with me, that makes you the perfect woman." Trip linked his fingers with hers and tugged her against his body. He could feel her heart beating faster, which totally turned him on. Instinct urged him to grab her and kiss her into submission, but he refrained. "So are you down with this?"

Her eyes searched his as if she were trying to solve a puzzle. "Okay, cowboy. But forget the money—that makes me feel tacky. It's the hat or nothing."

Hell no.

"The hat is off the table." His mouth set in a grim line.

"Guess you're not so sure you can help me, then, which means everything else is off the table, too." She patted his shoulder, taunting him. "See you 'round."

She got about three steps away before he found himself chasing after her. He reached out and yanked her back so her heart-shaped ass smacked against his pelvis. "You win." Snaking one arm around her waist, he set his mouth right beside her ear while gently wrapping her hair around his other wrist to expose her neck, just the way he'd been yearning to do for months. "Or maybe I've won."

When she shivered, he kissed her neck to remind her of their explosive chemistry and ensure she didn't back out. Her body softened but then she braced against him, a little breathless. She cast a haughty gaze over her shoulder. "Know this: you're not winning anything I wasn't willing to give before I suckered you into that bet."

"Oh, really?" He chuckled and released her, slowly unraveling his wrist from her hair. "Go on and study. But get some rest, 'cause I'll be dropping by later tonight."

As she headed out of the office, she stopped briefly at the door. "You've talked a lot of smack since we've met, so I've just got one piece of advice. You'd better bring your A game, Trip Lexington."

And then she was gone, leaving him alone with a painful hard-on.

Trip read several pages of the social media book, but his mind kept getting distracted by visceral memories of the way Kelsey smelled, the texture of her hair and skin, the warmth of her mouth. By the mounting anticipation of seeing her again tonight—all of her.

Potent stuff. Intoxicating.

Enough so that she *had* gotten the upper hand and convinced him to risk losing his most treasured Stetson just to be with her. Dammit, he hadn't won anything. Somewhere in the middle of his attempted seduction, he'd lost control of the situation.

He scowled, wondering what other witchy spells she would cast on him before their little tryst ended.

Chapter Five

"Can you keep a secret?" Kelsey asked Maura the minute Bill took Fee outside on a nature walk.

"You know I can." Maura closed the dishwasher door and tossed her dishtowel on the spigot. "Guess now I know why you've been so fidgety for the past thirty minutes. Spill it."

Kelsey extended her pinky finger, waiting for her sister's pinky to latch on. "I mean it, Maura. I've just made a deal with the devil and I need to tell someone, but no one else—and I mean no one—can ever know. Not even Bill."

Maura pinky-shook and stepped back. "With that intro, I'll admit, I'm a little worried. Are you in some kind of trouble with the law?"

"What?" Kelsey set one fist on her hip. "Why would you ask something that ridiculous?"

"You're the one making this such a big deal. What am I supposed to think?"

"Certainly not that I'm some kind of criminal." Kelsey sipped her Diet Coke. "However, you might want to sit down."

Maura sighed, pulled out a kitchen chair, sat beside the round oak table, and cut herself another slice of banana bread. "This reminds me of when you lost Mom's pearl necklace and wanted to blame it on cousin Sarah."

"If anything goes wrong with this plan, I'll take all the blame." An attack of nerves caused Kelsey to rapidly tap the toe of her red shoe against the linoleum flooring.

"Okay." Maura placed her palms on the table. "Lay it on me."

Kelsey went still and drew a deep breath before spilling her guts.

"I've agreed to engage in a purely sexual fling with Trip Lexington." As soon as she said the words aloud, she covered her mouth with her hand, half stunned, half giggling.

Maura's eyes widened as she dropped the final bite of bread onto her napkin. "Why in the world would you agree to something so . . . so risqué?"

Kelsey twisted her hair in her hand before letting it fall around her shoulders. She then began ticking off her fingers as she spoke. "A, he's hot. Hotter than hot. Trip Lexington may be the hottest guy I've ever seen in my entire life, including celebrities."

Maura shook her head in disbelief, which made Kelsey eager to persuade her she'd made a good decision. "B, I haven't had sex in almost a year. Given a choice between sex with Trip or a battery-operated toy, there really is no choice."

"TMI!" Maura sank her head into her hands for a moment. When she looked up, she pressed her palms to her flushed cheeks. "Okay, recovered. Continue."

Kelsey rolled her eyes before she resumed her argument. "C, it's actually kinda freeing. Think about it. I've carried so many expectations into all my other sexual experiences. This will be completely different. I have *no* expectations or hopes. It's purely for fun, so I can live out some kinky fantasies without worrying about any repercussions."

"Again, TMI!" Maura's fingers drummed the tabletop. "I mean, *really*, Kelsey. You're not going all fifty shades on me, are you?"

"No." Kelsey's hand found her hip again, her brow lowering. "But stop being such a prude." Then she waved off the remark. "I'm serious, though. This will probably be the only time in my life that I can enjoy myself in bed without worrying about how it might affect the relationship . . ."

Maura's eyes grew as wide and round as golf balls. "Are you actually listening to the words coming out of your mouth, or do you think you're making sense just because you're talking fast?"

Kelsey waved her hand in the air. "I haven't even told you the best part yet. Trip's going to help me reel in the next guy I'm interested in dating."

"Stop." Maura raised one hand. "He's going to help get you together with some other guy? Honestly, that's not the best part. It's the *dumbest* point on your list."

Kelsey sank onto a kitchen chair. "Is not."

Maura nodded. "Yes, it is. You're telling me you're going to be having hot sex with Trip while simultaneously trying to woo some other guy? How does that even work?"

"We haven't discussed all the details." Kelsey frowned, realizing it could get tricky. "I wouldn't continue being with Trip once I started up with someone else, but who knows *when* I'll meet someone I really like. In the meantime, why can't I have fun sexy-times with a really gorgeous guy?"

"Because I know you. You're not going to be able to keep your heart out of the equation past your first orgasm. Then what? It's one thing to go out with him if you think there's a chance for something real. But if you agree to go through with this crazy deal, you're going to get hurt."

She knew her sister meant well, but Maura's delivery sounded more like a reprimand than concern. Kelsey wasn't a child.

"Not this time." Kelsey shook her head. "Trust me. I know what Trip is and isn't capable of, and I know what he does and doesn't want. This is a *mutual* decision—purely physical."

Maura leaned forward, brow furrowed with concern. "Kelsey, you don't do purely physical. I'd bet everything this was his big idea, not yours. He's seducing you with promises he can't possibly keep, and you're letting yourself get in way over your head."

Maura's lemon-face temporarily set Kelsey back on her heels.

"You know what I need from my sister right now? Support, not judgment." Kelsey cast a hard glare at Maura, then stood and tossed her empty can in the recycling bin. "I'm sure you, with your doting husband, picket fence, and two kids, can't imagine what it feels like to be thirty-one and alone and going crazy thanks to the ticking biological clock you can't escape or slow down. It's been a long, cold winter, spring, and summer. If I can find a little heat with a charming, if superficial, man, why would you try to ruin it for me?"

Maura stood and approached Kelsey, grabbing her into a hug. "I'm sorry. I'm not judging you. I'm worried about you. I *know* you, Kels. I know you're going to start to care for him, and from everything you've admitted, he's never going to give you what you deserve. What you really want and need."

Kelsey bit the inside of her cheek to keep from getting choked up by her own fears and doubts. "I know he's not what I need, but for the short term, he's a good substitute."

Kelsey stood before her mirror, her body humming in anticipation even as she tried to calm her nerves with a large glass of full-bodied Italian red wine. She glanced at the clock: 8:56.

Turning to one side, she examined herself. Four-inch BCBG black strappy heels—check. Sheer black negligee with lace trim—check. Spritz of Jo Malone Peony & Blush Suede cologne behind ears, on her cleavage, and behind the knees—check. Dimmed lighting, soft music, opened bottle of red wine. Blindfold, silk robe sash, edible body paint.

All set.

Well, almost. She picked up Trip's cowboy hat and stuck it on her head. Now she was ready.

Maura had been wrong. Kelsey knew exactly what she was doing. The blindfold would protect her heart by creating distance. The sash, well, that was just something she'd always wanted to try and, despite Trip's playboy persona, she knew he'd never hurt her. For one thing, Grey would kill him. For another, her intuition sensed an odd code of honor about him.

And by setting the stage tonight with her props and plans, she'd make it clear to Trip that she not only understood the terms of their deal, but was taking full advantage of them for her own reasons. Reasons that had less to do with him than with her own sexual curiosity. In an hour or so, after they'd both gotten what they'd wanted from this part of their bargain, she'd politely send him home without any regrets.

Inhaling slowly, she took another long, slow drag of wine from her glass to drown out any lingering misgivings. A short while later, she started when her door buzzer rang. Her heart raced. When she stood to answer the door, a dull roar rushed to her ears.

Here we go.

She pressed the intercom button. "Who is it?"

"Prince Charming," answered the smooth baritone.

"Come on up. Door's unlocked." She released the intercom and then sat—or rather posed, with her ankles crossed and her chest held high—on the arm of her sofa.

Trip knocked gently before opening the door to her unit. He stepped inside, his cocky grin fixed in place until he actually looked at her. Stopping midstride, jaw unhinged, he stood there blinking.

Score one for me.

In his right hand he held a single white rose, which made her lips part in surprise. Fortunately, she remembered the reality of their situation before her heart skipped ahead of her brain.

Trip collected himself quickly, handing her the flower. "Thought we should start off on a high note."

"Thank you." She lifted off the sofa and forced a calm voice even as six thousand butterflies took flight in her belly. Did he bring other girls flowers, or was this something just for her? "Pour yourself a glass of wine while I put this in water."

Before she turned away, she noted him swallowing hard as his gaze traveled over her body, which boosted her confidence. "You do not disappoint, princess."

"Did you think I might?" she said over her shoulder on her way to the small kitchen to fill a bud vase with water.

"No." He filled his glass but downed it like a cold beer rather than a pricey Amarone. "Did you finish studying?"

"In fact, I did." She slid the stem into the vase and set it on the counter. "Would you like to know what I learned?"

"Nope. I don't want to argue about Wade or his development right now. I'm just making sure I have your full focus for the rest of the night."

Oh, he had her attention. But she needed to remind both of them of their bargain. "First, share a dating tip to prove your good intentions about helping me."

Trip set his empty glass on the coffee table, pulled a folded sheet of paper from his jacket, and waved it in the air while walking toward her. "You'll learn I'm a man of my word."

He flattened the paper on the counter and pushed it toward her. She lifted the handwritten sheet, entitled "Trip's Tips," and raised one brow.

He snatched the paper back. "This can wait." His expression turned wolfish. "I can't."

This was it; she'd committed to this odd arrangement, for better or worse. It would be fine as long as she retained control of herself and the situation. But at that moment, with his strong body brushing up against hers and his green eyes shining with desire, she didn't know how in the world she'd manage to keep herself in check.

His fingers toyed with the ends of her hair. "You are a most beautiful woman, Kelsey Callihan." Then he removed the Stetson from her head, grinning. "If you don't mind, I'd rather not think about my grandfather right now."

As soon as he set the hat down, he cradled her head with both hands and kissed her long and deep. She opened her eyes to find his closed tight, almost painfully so. God, she needed the protection of the sexy fantasy she'd constructed before she started to actually feel something for this man.

"Trip," she whispered. "I want you to do something."

"What," he murmured against her neck just before planting another kiss behind her ear, one she felt all the way down to her toes.

"Come with me." She eased away, leading him by the hand toward her bedroom.

When they approached the edge of the bed, where she'd laid out the props she'd assembled, Trip's eyes widened before filling with electrified lust. "If I die tonight from pleasure, bury me with my hat."

She smiled and then kissed him, enjoying the way her body trembled under his touch. Her fingers fiddled with the buttons of his shirt, but he quickly took over and unfastened them himself, tossing his shirt to the floor and pulling her tight to his chest.

The hard muscles of his shoulders and chest flexed as her fingers explored the carved lines of his body—his big, athletic body. Way, waaay better than a vibrator.

She tugged at his belt, and within another minute, he'd stripped out of his jeans. Everything about his appearance was as perfect as his face: broad shoulders, narrow hips, and a tightly sculpted butt. If he were famous, he'd be at the top of *People* magazine's annual "most beautiful" list. No wonder he was so damn cocky.

She reached for the hem of her negligee, but he grasped her wrist.

"Keep this on," he ordered between kisses. "And the shoes, too."

He lifted her before laying her on the bed, pushing her arms over her head, and kissing her mouth, chin, neck, and chest. His hands followed, caressing her breasts and waist, the fabric of her nightie abrading her skin. Then he reached across the mattress and snagged the blindfold.

Trip sat back on his knees as he placed the blindfold over her eyes. For a minute, she regretted the mask because now she could no longer admire his physique. Lying in the darkness, her heart kicked up a few notches as she began to anticipate what he would do next. Her senses awakened with each passing second.

"Look at you," he murmured. The light brush of his fingertips traced parts of her body, creating a trail of goose bumps along her collarbone, the underside of her breast, the centerline of her abdomen, the inside of her thigh. His heavy breathing excited her, feeding her own gasps whenever she sucked in a breath under his touch. The wet heat of his mouth, and the weight of him as he shifted from his knees to his side to lying partly on top of her, overwhelmed her senses, as did the smell of his skin and spicy-scented deodorant. His kisses tasted like the wine he'd drunk not long ago.

Suddenly, she liked being blindfolded. Liked the way her heightened senses made her entire body purr from his attention. Liked the kind of sensual control she seemed to exert over him, too. In fact, she couldn't have been happier about agreeing to this whole plan.

His mouth trailed down her neck as his fingers went to the juncture between her legs. She licked her lips and lifted the small of her back off the mattress, like a serpent at the mercy of a snake charmer.

Aphrodite. Somehow she'd managed to control and yet submit to him at the same time. Impossible. Surprising. Sexy as hell. And maybe more than he'd bargained for tonight.

Trip opened his eyes to watch her respond to his kiss and touch. Her lips parted. Her muscles twitched. Her body quivered and arched, seeking him out.

He ached to bury himself inside her already, but wouldn't rush this pleasure. When she hooked her leg over his hip, he smiled. "That's my girl."

He rubbed his body along the length of hers while kissing her hard, harder, invading her mouth the way he planned to invade her body. She tasted like chocolate and wine. Her hair tangled up all around his hands. Her dusky pink nipples were tight and hard beneath the negligee.

"I like that," she moaned, her nails scratching along his shoulders and back with just enough pressure to feel good.

"I can tell." He then reached over for the lengthy robe sash and hooked it through one of the bedposts before gently binding her wrists. "Does my naughty girl like this, too?"

"She does." She writhed within the binding in order to get closer to him.

His heart raced even more than when standing at the top of any snowy cornice before hucking off the edge and into the deep powder.

As he finished the knot, he gazed at her—blindfolded and bound for him. For his pleasure. A rush of hot lust crashed over him, making him groan and descend upon her with a blitz of kisses. He sucked at her nipples through the see-through nightie, loving the way her body writhed for him. Adrenaline spurred him to get a little rougher with his mouth and hands.

"I want you, cowboy." She bucked her hips.

He parted her with his fingers, and teased her, caressing her hot center until she begged for release. "More," she pleaded, so he used his mouth and his hand to push her closer to the edge. "Oh, yes. Now!"

"Patience, princess."

Her heels dug into the mattress; her hands strained against the sash. He watched her body tighten with the pleasure he held just out of her reach. He didn't want to hurt her, but he wanted to control her. Make her moan and groan and beg. He wanted her to feel him, and feel the lingering evidence of him tomorrow.

"Trip, please."

She smelled and tasted like sweet, sweet sex, which worked him up into a lather. He continued his onslaught until he couldn't wait another second, and then, after tearing open a condom package with his teeth, he thrust himself inside her, making her call out in surprise.

"Oh, God, yes!" she exclaimed.

"Not God. Just me." He chuckled before kissing her.

She clenched around him, hot, wet, and so, so tight. He kissed her again, overwhelmed by desire and power and, oddly, a surge of tenderness. He slowly withdrew and then thrust inside her again, slowly, purposefully, opening his eyes and watching her flushed cheeks, her swollen lips, her heaving chest.

A thing of beauty, his princess.

Suddenly he was carried away on another wave of sexual frenzy. Swamped with a need to possess and consume her, he pulled out, flipped her over and yanked her hips into the air. Her arms were still restrained by the lengthy, twisted sash as he entered her from behind.

"You like this, too?" He grasped her breast with one hand while the other slipped between her legs, as he began beating out a faster rhythm.

"I do."

Then, moving one hand to grip her hip, he wrapped the length of her hair around his other wrist like a set of reins and yanked her more upright as he slammed into her body, practically growling with desire. "And this?"

"More," she moaned. "Harder."

He heard his own voice shout something as he pounded into her, more excited than he could remember feeling in years. Her groans and grunts escalated until he felt her shudder, her insides in a spasm, tugging at him. And then, before he was ready to let go, he careened over the edge, his body erupting into a series of uncontrolled tremors until he collapsed on top of her.

For a few seconds, he struggled to control his breathing. His body, drenched in sweat, lay wrapped around her gorgeous curves.

Holy fucking hell. Everything he'd hoped for times ten.

"Trip?"

"You gotta give me a few minutes to recover." He brushed her hair away from her neck and kissed her.

"Untie me, please."

"Whatever you want." He untied her hands, only vaguely aware of her oddly detached voice.

Once her hands were free, he rolled her onto her back to kiss her, but she blocked him by removing the blindfold. She smiled—a satisfied smile.

"I needed that more than I realized. I'll sleep well tonight, thanks." Then she gently exerted pressure on his chest until he rolled off her body. She finger combed her hair and glanced at him. "So, take a few minutes to get dressed or whatever. I'm going to get some water. Would you like a glass before you go?" She stood at the edge of the bed, looking even sexier than she had when he'd first arrived.

"When I go?" He sat up, confused and . . . irked.

"I'll be right back." She flashed a pleasant, if not exactly personal, smile. Nothing like the smiles she gave Wade. No, this smile was more like that of a damn flight attendant.

He flopped back on the bed and closed his eyes, playing with the sash while recalling the highlights from their first encounter. What the hell was up with her attitude?

Irritated, he yanked off the condom, and discovered it had torn. Had it torn during sex or just now when he'd removed the damn thing? He frowned, his brief concern supplanted by jumbled thoughts about

Kelsey's dismissiveness. He wrapped the condom in tissue before tossing it into the garbage can beside the nightstand.

"Here you go." Kelsey reappeared and handed him a glass of water, then sat in a chair three feet away from the bed.

The heart-stopping impact of seeing her in those heels and nightie made him hot all over again. He wasn't used to being told to get dressed and leave, and he didn't like it. Especially not when she sat there taunting him with her fuck-me heels, see-through nightie, and sexy hair, dampened from their lovemaking. He had no idea why she was kicking him to the curb, but wasn't ready for his time with Kelsey to end.

"You're not getting shy on me now, are you?" He gulped down the water while maintaining eye contact.

"No. Why would you ask that?" She leaned back and crossed her legs, one foot bouncing up and down.

"Because you're sitting way over there instead of crawling into bed." He set his glass on her nightstand, edged to the bottom of the bed, and reached one arm toward her. "Come on back."

Kelsey shook her head. "Let's not pretend this is anything more than what it is, okay? We had sex. Really great sex, just like we discussed. And now you'll go home or out or whatever it is you do at night, and I'll go to sleep so I can be productive tomorrow. I'll let you know when I need your help to make good on that other promise you made, but for now, I think we're all set, right?"

"All set?" Trip chuckled, but when he met Kelsey's blank gaze, he scowled. "I'm not all set. I'm just getting started."

"Are you trying to prove something to me—make me eat those words I said earlier about your moves and imagination? No need. I take them back." She stood up, giving him another gorgeous view of her body cloaked in sheer fabric.

His lower half stirred, demanding he seduce her back into bed. "Kelsey, you don't really want me to go so soon, do you?"

"I'm not saying this can't ever happen again, just not tonight." She wrapped a silk robe around her body and sighed. "I'd think you'd be high-fiving me right now. Not only did you get what you wanted, but also you don't have to cuddle or figure out how to sneak out of bed before the sun rises."

"Wow. You're just full of surprises tonight, princess." The snarky bite in his voice caused her to wince. He stood, watching her gaze rake over his naked body, so he took his time getting dressed while he brooded about the unceremonious way she was kicking him to the curb. "Guess I'll get out of your hair, then."

She followed him through the living room and to her front door. Before he opened it, she reached up to his shoulder, her indifferent mask slipping away for a moment. "Thanks for the rose, Trip. That was sweet."

Sweet? He wasn't sweet. And he wasn't about to leave her apartment being the only one who wanted more. He swooped down on her faster than a hawk on a mouse and kissed her, grabbing her ass with both hands.

Her resistance ebbed almost immediately and she kissed him back, digging her hands into his hair and moaning softly from her throat. He caressed her hips, and ran one hand along her upper thigh and in between her legs until he felt her knees buckle. Only then did he release her, leaving her panting and needy, just like him. Now they were even. "See you 'round, princess."

Chapter Six

Trip's Tips:

1. Don't return a new guy's interest right away. Force his hand. Get him to invest first.

2. Whenever a guy calls for the first time, end the call first because you've got to "run." Leave him wondering where you're going and who you're meeting. Jealousy is a powerful motivator.

3. Don't talk about the guy to anyone for the first few weeks (not with friends or Facebook or anyone else). Let it develop privately.

4. Don't text him all the time, or ask where things stand, or talk about your desire for marriage and family, for at least two months.

5. Under NO circumstances do you go to bed with him for at least five real dates. Make him work for it.

Kelsey refolded the paper she'd read at least a dozen times in the past ten days and tucked it back in her desk drawer. His obnoxious "advice" directly conflicted with her natural instincts, which made her want to reject it as stupid. But at thirty-one and hopelessly single, she had to consider perhaps her instincts sucked. Trip didn't understand women at all, but maybe he understood men better than she did.

Of course, thinking of him immediately launched her into yet another lusty daydream. She knew she should stop, but the memories were more addictive—and entertaining—than *Scandal.*

The alarm on her phone buzzed, pulling her from her thoughts. *Shoot!* She had just ten minutes to get her butt over to the groundbreaking ceremony. Grabbing her keys and purse, she dashed out the door.

She swerved her car into the dusty parking area of Wade's new project at 10:58 a.m., kicking up pebbles and dust. After checking her hair and lipstick in her rearview mirror, she exited the car and crossed the rocky ground toward where the crowd had gathered. She and the floral-print Miu Miu shoes she'd picked up online at a discount navigated the gravel and divot obstacle course without a major stumble.

As she approached the hub of activity, she smoothed her cream-colored tulip skirt and straightened her shoulders. Scanning the throng, she noticed Mayor Burns, Jimmy, the editor of the local paper, with his photographer, and Sandra, the local branch manager of the bank financing Wade's project. Wade and a few others were standing along a roped-off section of dirt, each wearing a hardhat and holding a shovel.

When she glanced past the assembly, off to the distant corners of the fifty-acre project, a swell of pride filled her lungs. This deal had not only earned her a bundle, but also had been a huge step in expanding her little company into a residential *and* commercial real estate broker-age. And if she succeeded in convincing the Copelands to sell, she knew exactly which small apartment complex she wanted to buy with that commission. Broker *and* landlord; maybe then people in town would start taking her more seriously.

Her gaze drifted back to Wade. At their first meeting months ago, she'd hoped to interest him in more than her listings, but looking at him now she felt less enthused. His friendly face and warm smile were still appealing, as were his sandy-colored hair and pressed clothing. His business acumen remained as impressive, his personality as affable. And yet he failed to make her heart race and her knees weaken. Truth be told, perhaps he never really had. Had she only set her sights on him because he'd been mature, which she'd assumed meant he'd be looking to settle down?

A mental image of Trip's muscled torso surfaced, causing her insides to quake like the San Andreas Fault. Flashbacks like that had been driving her crazy since he'd left her apartment. Thank God she'd avoided running into him in town since that night. She needed to get over their sexual encounter before facing him again.

At the outset, Kelsey had convinced herself she could protect her heart from that man. Then her stupid subconscious started leaking through the cracks of her defense shield. Cracks that wouldn't mend as long as she kept that now dry-pressed white rose beside her bed, or purposely summoned memories of the heavy, hot sensation of Trip's body. *Shoot.*

She forced herself to focus on Wade again, to listen to his pleasant voice as he spoke about the Sterling Canyon community, job creation, and the unique features of his planned five-star resort. People all around her watched him with admiration while he delivered the public speech with relaxed confidence. A copse of aspens swayed in the breeze of a beautiful summer day, providing a gorgeous backdrop to the scene. *Feel something, Kelsey.*

Nada.

Wade and his crew each lifted a shovel for the cameras and then took a first stab at the land that would soon be excavated. She clapped along with the crowd and then, when Wade caught sight of her and waved her over, walked around the cordoned land to join him.

"Kelsey, thanks for coming." Wade shook her hand and kissed her cheek in the same friendly business manner in which he'd always treated her. Still no sparks. "Can you join our little project team for lunch?"

"Not today, but thanks. I've got a client appointment at noon. How about a rain check? I'd love to discuss the Copeland property development more."

"Same. Shoot me a text with some dates and times and we'll get together again, ideally with one of the Copelands." He briefly diverted his attention to nod at someone in the distance. "I'm headed to Seattle for a week or so, and after that I'll be in and out of town as this project gets underway."

"I'll speak with Nick Copeland and get back to you. I'm sure we can put this together." She hoped she sounded more confident than she felt because, if Trip's opinions were shared by the majority, it wouldn't be a slam dunk deal. Fortunately, most folks like Trip only talked big and loud in the bars. "In the meantime, congratulations on all of this," she said, gesturing toward the acreage. "I hope everything proceeds without a hitch."

"Well, that'll be largely up to that guy right there." Wade pointed at an attractive man who was staring at Kelsey with apparent interest. "Hey, Mason, come on over and let me introduce you to this lovely young woman."

Except for a quick glance to acknowledge Wade, Mason kept his polite gaze fixed on Kelsey. He carried himself with self-assurance, which she always found appealing. She also appreciated his taste in clothes: dark denim jeans, cowboy boots, a tailored shirt, and linen-blend blazer.

When he removed the hardhat he'd donned for the ceremony, she noticed his closely cropped hair contained a few hints of distinguished-looking gray. The outer edges of his deep-set, coffee-colored eyes crinkled when he smiled, a pleasant smile that softened his dark features.

"Mason Cutler," Wade began, "meet Kelsey Callihan, Sterling Canyon's finest real estate broker."

"It's nice to meet you, Mason." She extended her hand, which he gently grasped with both of his. She felt something not unpleasant, although his open scrutiny suggested a certain familiarity she knew they lacked.

"Pleasure's all mine." Although Kelsey exceeded his height in her heels, Mason's smooth, deep voice belied his smaller stature. His expression turned a bit coy. "I've heard a lot about you."

Heard about her? She took a slight step back, glanced briefly at Wade, then returned her attention to Mason. "Cutler, as in Cutler Construction, I suppose?"

"Yes." He clasped his hands behind his back and cocked his head to the left. "We're very excited Wade chose us for this particular project."

"I'm looking forward to a productive working relationship, too," Wade said. "Now, if you two will excuse me, I need to speak with the mayor. Kelsey, I'll look for a text from you about getting together when I return to town. Mason, I'll see you at lunch."

Mason waited until Wade had walked away before resuming the conversation.

"You're not joining us for lunch?" His hands remained hidden behind his back. "That's disappointing."

Something about his shy, introverted grin intrigued Kelsey. Was he flirting? Another image of Trip raced through her mind, swamping her in guilt. Stupid guilt. Trip was a boy toy, not a boyfriend.

"Unfortunately, I've got a conflict today." She gripped her purse strap near her shoulder. Mason hadn't done or said anything unusual, yet she had a hunch he was a man with an agenda. "I'm meeting a client shortly."

"Speaking of which, may I have your business card?" He tucked his thumbs in his front pockets. "I'm going home for a couple of weeks, but when I return to oversee the construction, I'll need a decent rental. Perhaps you can help me find a good lease."

Ah, that was it. He'd heard about her from Wade and needed an agent.

A week ago, she'd have been grossly disappointed that he wasn't flirting. Today she could barely muster regret.

It was official. Trip had screwed her up.

"The long-term rental market isn't huge here, but I'll dig around a bit." Kelsey riffled through her purse to retrieve a card. "Here you go. Email me your wish list and then I'll see you when you return."

"Great, thanks. Am I embarrassing you if I say my outlook on living here just got a whole lot brighter?" Once again Mason's generous smile seemed flirtatious. It didn't exactly reduce her to jelly, but a little something bloomed in her chest. A little something was better than nothing.

Still, Trip's tip about not responding to perceived initial interest flared, causing her to project a professional, polite smile. "You're very kind, Mason. I look forward to working with you. Have a great lunch, and please tell Wade I said good-bye."

She walked away, glancing back over her shoulder in curiosity. Mason, who was still watching her, waved. Flustered, she waved back and then hustled to her car.

Perhaps Wade's project could result in a romantic payoff after all. Of course, the tiny blip of interest she felt about Mason paled in comparison to the whole-body sensations Trip aroused. But Trip wasn't available for anything more than a roll or two—or five—in the hay. She would not prove Maura right by allowing the shallow, physical, lusty *thing* between Trip and her to steer her off course.

Trip returned from leading three climbers up a cliff face, bothered by some of the chatter he'd overheard about Wade's latest plans. Rather than change out of his rock climbing clothes, he immediately settled behind the desk and made a list of elected officials and relevant board members to contact. Maybe there were wetlands on the property, or maybe he could persuade the Open Space Council to convince the town to buy and preserve the land. Anything to hold up the deal or make it less attractive to Wade.

Setting aside his list, he decided to load another GoPro clip from last March onto the Backtrax Facebook page. A death-defying reel taken when he'd shot over and cleared a fifteen-foot-high cliff face before making a perfect landing into twenty inches of fresh powder and then ripping through it to the bottom of the run. The footage looked almost as awesome as he'd felt flying through the air and snow.

"Hey, Avery and I are grabbing dinner." Grey stood in the doorway of the back office. "Want to come?"

"Nah, you two go ahead. I'm just getting into this stuff now." Trip nodded at the wad of cash on the desk. "When I'm done, I'll log those fees and tips into the system and then stick them in the safe."

"Keep your tips." Grey strolled over to stand behind him and view the footage. "Man, I missed out after the accident. Can't wait to get back out there."

"Me too!" Trip glanced up. "Hey, I want to talk to you later about Wade Kessler."

"What about?" Grey's hands rested on his hips.

"He wants to build some kind of mall and office park at the northwest corner of town if he can coax the owners into selling."

"Oh, hell no." Grey ran one hand through his overgrown hair.

"Exactly. We need to jump ahead of him somehow, but I need to keep my name out of it because of my dad's involvement with Wade. Somehow we've got to convince the owners not to sell, or make it too much of a headache for Wade to pursue."

"I'd imagine the local retailers will band together to keep national chains out of town." Grey snatched a lollipop from the cup on the desk. "Why don't you join Avery and me and we can talk about it more?"

"No. Don't say anything to Avery. I really want to keep a low profile, at least until I have more info. You go have a nice night. I've still got a ton of work to do on these website updates."

"Okay. See you later."

Trip returned his attention to the computer, jumping around to other ski enthusiast pages to leave comments and interact, just like Kelsey had suggested. The minute he'd thought of her—which had been happening all too frequently lately—he glanced at his phone.

He'd refrained from calling her or surprising her with a visit, although the thought had occurred to him more than once. And where the hell was Boomerang, anyway?

After meeting Grey last January and sharing one stupid public kiss, she'd dogged *him* for months with texts and drop-ins. Considering the mind-blowing sex she and Trip had enjoyed, he thought he should've heard from Kelsey by now. The fact she hadn't made any attempt to seek him out pissed him off. Hell, he wasn't ashamed to admit to himself it hurt his feelings a little, too. What the heck was so special about Grey?

A surprise after-hours visitor ringing the bell at the front desk interrupted Trip's unpleasant musing. Kelsey?

"Coming!" he called while shoving back from the desk and trotting down the hallway. He rounded the corner into the reception area, a flirtatious grin plastered on his face, but then skidded to an abrupt halt. "Mason?"

His anticipatory euphoria vanished, making room for shock and a little bit of dread.

Mason stood, hands in his front pockets, glancing around the dated room, clearly unimpressed. "Gunner."

In the far recess of Trip's mind, his dad's recent plea rattled. He awkwardly stuck his hand out to his brother, and Mason reluctantly shook it.

"This is a surprise." Trip crossed his arms and leaned against the counter. Mason was only three and a half years older than him, but his graying hair and thicker build made him look closer to forty. "What are you doing here?"

"Can't you guess?" Mason raised one brow.

Trip shook his head. "Honestly? No. I really can't."

"Dad sent me." Mason's face grimaced like he'd been force-fed a shot of cheap whiskey. "Put me in charge of Kessler's hotel project with the misguided idea it'll force you and me to deal with each other. Seems he's still holding out hope for some kind of family reunion. I told him you and I were fine with the status quo, but he's determined that we become one big happy family. Not sure why. You haven't seemed all that interested in being part of it for years."

Trip couldn't defend himself against that particular accusation. He had distanced himself from them since college with infrequent, brief phones calls and occasional holiday visits. Of course, Trip could lay some blame on Mason and Deb for their role in the family dynamic, but it didn't matter. If Trip were a better man or son, he'd have made more effort. "I suppose I can't argue with you there. I haven't been a model son."

Mason's brows rose, apparently surprised by Trip's confession. Someone else might be softened by such an admission, seeing it as a sign of maturity and remorse.

Not Mason.

"So this place is what Dad's been boasting about since he saw you the other week?" He smirked, gesturing around the drab room, with its creaky wooden flooring and fluorescent lighting. Mason eyed Trip from head to toe. "At least you don't have to wear a tie to the office."

In the space of a heartbeat, Trip was right back to being a young teenage boy, defending himself against another insult. One might think, by nearly thirty-six, Mason would've finally outgrown his need to best his little brother. Then again, at thirty-two, Trip hadn't matured much either, as he was about to prove.

"No tie, no nine-to-five. Just clean air, cliffs, and adrenaline. As for this place, it's not much to look at, but it's mine." Trip pushed away from the counter, standing to his full height, and thus physically, if not otherwise, proving who was the bigger man. "The fact I never rode his coattails is probably why Dad's impressed. Guess you wouldn't understand, now, would you?"

"Or maybe he's just impressed because he never expected much from you, considering . . ." Mason left the rest unsaid.

But Trip knew how that sentence ended. He'd overheard it from Deb many times, always muttered out of earshot of his father. *What can you expect from him, considering he's the son of a whore?*

It had always astounded Trip that she and Mason liked to blame the entire affair on his mother, who'd been an unmarried girl of twenty-four, instead of on the married man who'd actually betrayed them.

"Well, Dad's little plan is off to a great start." Trip forced a grin. "How long are you in town?"

"Leaving today."

"Guess you don't have time for a beer and round of pool, then?" Trip's sarcasm colored his words. He rested his hands on his hips. "Don't worry, though. I'll make sure Dad knows you came to see me. And, hey, we didn't break any windows this time, so that's progress."

Trip noticed Mason's uncomfortable reaction to the recollection of the fight they'd had. Mason had walked in on his then-fiancée, Jen, alone with Trip in their dad's study. It had been an innocent scenario, one in which Jen merely had been trying to learn a little about Trip because they'd never met. But Mason had immediately concluded that Trip had been out to sabotage his relationship.

He'd ordered Jen out of the room before barraging Trip with a slew of heated accusations. Naturally Trip's glib sarcasm had only enraged Mason, prompting him to toss a thick marble ashtray across the room. The projectile smashed through the palladium window, costing Mason a thousand bucks, not to mention his pride.

"I should've followed my instincts that day and called off the wedding. Could've saved myself a lot of aggravation and money." Mason's words were full of bravado, but Trip noticed a flicker of real pain in his eyes.

From what their dad had told him at lunch the other week, Jen might've been unfaithful. The parallel with how the Cutler family had been significantly altered by their dad's infidelity had probably rekindled all of Mason's antipathy toward Trip. For one second, he felt a trace of compassion for the insecure bully who'd tormented him for decades. Trip also knew Mason's girls would now suffer because of the family split—a kind of loss Trip could relate to.

"All our shit aside, Mason, I'm sorry your girls have to go through a divorce." Trip relaxed his posture in an effort to dispel the tension in the room.

"Concerned 'Uncle Gunner' now?" Mason sighed. He rubbed the back of his neck as he glanced out the window. In a quiet tone, he muttered, "Like you'd even recognize either of my girls if you saw them."

Trip raised his hands in the air. "I give up. Honestly, I've never been able to win with you. Not at ten, not at twenty, and not now. I wish I knew what the hell *I* ever did to make you hate me so much."

Mason's incredulous expression stunned Trip. He stared at his brother, trying to read his thoughts.

Eventually Mason shook his head, and when he spoke, his voice was oddly wistful. "My parents were happy until you arrived and ruined everything. For God's sake, my poor mom had to deal with Dad's garbage while having to help raise you. Imagine how she felt." Trip refrained from commenting that he didn't have to imagine, because Deb had never kept it a secret from anyone but her husband. When Mason spoke again, his tone had sharpened with disgust. "And Dad fell all over himself to make you feel part of our family. He just loved that you were so much more like him than I was, and *you* loved taking him away from us."

"No, Mason. That part was all in your head." Trip held up his hand to stop Mason's oncoming retort. "Trust me, I never wanted your life, and I didn't enjoy living in a house where the resentment was thicker than mud." Trip glanced at his feet and then back at Mason. "You know, when my mom introduced me to Dad, I was terrified. She was dying, my grandfather was sad all the time. I didn't know, or care about, this strange new man in my life. Everything sucked except for one thought—suddenly I had a big brother. The way Dad talked about you made me *excited* to meet you. But you never even gave me a chance to be a friend, let alone a brother. Given your feelings about me, I'd assume my staying away would've made it easier on you. Instead, you slam me for being neglectful. At this point I give up. Let's just go on avoiding each other like always."

"Fine with me," Mason said, resting his hands on his hips. "Unfortunately, I'll be back in two weeks and then stuck here for a year or so overseeing the construction, so we're bound to bump into each other in this small town."

Dammit. Memories of the many ways Mason had made life uncomfortable for Trip resurfaced, causing Trip's stomach to tighten.

Mason could easily come to town, try to damage Trip's reputation, and then walk away. Trip, however, had just committed a bunch of money and time to making this his home. He'd be stuck living in the aftermath of whatever Mason threw his way, which meant he was going to have to live wary for twelve months or more. And if Mason got a whiff of Trip's plan to stop Wade's next deal, he'd probably try to undermine him there, too.

Trip tamped down a wave of panic, determined not to let Mason see his worry. "For Dad's sake, let's call a temporary truce while you're in town. If we see each other, I'm just fine with us pretending to be polite acquaintances and going about our own business."

"Ditto." Mason glanced at his watch. "Suppose I'll catch my jet. Always a pleasure, brother."

Mason shoved open the door and disappeared around the corner, leaving Trip to stew. His father's timing sucked. Why would he push Mason into Trip's life now, when Trip had finally decided to settle down? When he'd decided to give his dad more respect and attention?

This was what happened when you let people into your heart. Things got messy, and then they usually fell apart. Trip didn't like messy, and he didn't like pain. Now both were staring him down, testing him.

Adrenaline pumped through his veins as he recalled Mason's smug remarks. What he needed was a release of the energy coiling in his gut. Without a destination in mind, he stormed out of the building and started walking.

Chapter Seven

Kelsey dragged herself to her sister's for dinner at six o'clock to hear some "big announcement." Based on Maura's tendency to exaggerate the significance of minor events, Kelsey suspected the announcement could relate to anything from buying new drapes to whatever participation award Fee might have won at summer camp that week.

She arrived just in time to help get the food to the table. While her parents and Bill were seating the kids in the dining room, Kelsey followed Maura into the kitchen.

"Don't think I didn't notice how you've been avoiding me these past ten days," Maura scolded as she tossed the salad. "And don't think you can escape questions about how it's going with you-know-who."

"It *went* fine. Better than fine." Kelsey transferred rice and beans from the pot to a serving bowl. She kept her heated face hidden from her sister. "In fact, it was awesome."

"In what way?" Maura set down the salad tongs. "I mean, is there more between you two than the purely physical nonsense you tried to sell me?"

"No." Kelsey snapped her head toward Maura. "I told you, I'm in control of the situation. It was just one much-needed, extremely exciting interlude that I'll remember for a long, long time. I don't know if it will happen again, and I don't care." *Liar, liar.*

Kelsey speared the rice bowl with a serving spoon before lifting it from the counter. "Now let's go eat so I can hear this big announcement."

"You know I just want you to be happy, Kelsey." Maura looked somewhat pained. "I want you to find someone to love so we can raise our families together."

"So do I. Trust me, Maura. My fling with Trip won't interfere with my life or my happiness. Now wipe that worried look off your face before everyone else starts asking questions."

The sisters entered the dining room and took their seats in time to say grace with the family.

"Okay, you two. Don't keep us in the dark any longer. What's the news?" Kelsey's dad asked just before he shoveled a heaping spoonful of rice into his mouth.

Her mom looked across the table at Maura with a knowing smile, which told Kelsey she either knew or guessed the secret. Bill grasped Maura's hand and kissed it, and then he turned to the table. "We're pregnant."

Kelsey tightened her grip on her fork, stunned. She hadn't expected this news. News that normally would make her crow with excitement. A rush of self-loathing blew through her for the envy eating away at her heart.

"A new baby!" Fee's joyous shout snapped Kelsey out of her daze. Forcing a smile, she kept her gaze on Fee while she collected her spinning thoughts. Fee frowned at fat little Ty, who'd smashed peas in his hair and all over his high chair. "Mommy, I want a sister."

"We'll see, honey." Maura looked at Fee, her expression glowing.

"Another baby?" Kelsey's dad shook his head, smiling. "Bill, you're keeping busy."

Maura slapped her dad's shoulder. "Dad, the kids!"

Kelsey finally offered heartfelt congratulations and managed to maintain a bright smile, but her insides were wrung tight. Maura was having her third child, her home becoming richer with family, while Kelsey's life stagnated. Big paychecks, real estate investments, and fancy trips to Mexico wouldn't fill up the hole in her heart or make her more lovable, no matter how much she hoped they might.

Lively chatter about the pregnancy carried on around her while Kelsey picked at her food. At one point, she glanced across the table and saw a private moment between her sister and Bill, in which he placed his hand over Maura's belly. The intimacy and love Kelsey witnessed plunged her once more into the depths of her own thoughts, doubts, and fears of never being loved, never being needed, never being any man's "someone special."

Fee crawled onto her lap and hugged her. "Aunt Kelsey, when can I have a sleepover at your house?"

Kelsey snuggled with Fee, uncaring that sticky little fingers tugged at her hair. "Soon, peanut. I promise."

She loved Fee, and, moreover, she loved the way Fee loved her. If she never found her own true love, could this be enough? She clung to her niece and kissed her head. Their special bond filled Kelsey's heart with emotion she couldn't even put to words. And yet that void remained—one she believed would only be filled when she fell in love with someone who returned her feelings and, together, they created their own family.

For the next thirty minutes, Kelsey celebrated the happy news with her family, but deep down she wanted to escape.

That chance came after cake. Kelsey helped her mom load the dishwasher and dry the pots, making excuses about being exhausted from a long day. She gave Bill another congratulatory kiss, then grabbed Maura and hugged her. "I love you, sis. I can't wait to meet my next niece or nephew."

She meant every word, too, despite her self-absorption.

"Thanks, Kels." Maura's eyes glistened, and Kelsey knew right then that, despite her attempts to hide her private sorrow, she'd failed. "Call me tomorrow."

Kelsey grabbed her keys, jogged to her car, and drove home, letting her tears flow. If she'd moved from Sterling Canyon to a bigger city years ago, might she have increased her chances of finding someone? At the time, she couldn't have imagined ever wanting to leave her family and closest friends.

Yet tonight the ridges of the San Juan mountain range encircling town felt claustrophobic rather than majestic. Familiar town streets cluttered with antique buildings seemed stagnant instead of charming. Perhaps she needed to take more drastic steps toward happiness than just playing secret sex games with Trip Lexington.

Two minutes later, she parked her car in the alley behind her building. A quick glance in the mirror reflected self-pity. Scowling, she slapped her cheek to snap herself out of her funk. Maura's pregnancy *was* great news for their family. And it would give Kelsey another infant to love.

As she made her way between her building and her neighbors', focused on those positive thoughts, her phone rang. She dug into her bag and saw Trip's name on the display. She stopped. Bit her lower lip. The last thing she could handle at that moment was talking to Trip, who, despite his appeal, personified the opposite of the kind of man she really needed. Tossing the phone back into her purse, she rounded the bend toward the front door.

When a man appeared out of the shadows, her heart skittered and her limbs went numb. "Oh!"

"Ignoring my call?" Trip asked, clearly insulted, as he caught her by the elbow before she stumbled.

"Trip! You scared me." Despite her attempt to stifle her emotions, she sniffled.

"Sorry." He tipped her chin up toward the glow from the porch light and studied her face with concern. As his thumb brushed away her last tear, his tone shifted to something fierce. "Okay, whose ass do I need to kick?"

"What?" Kelsey felt her forehead crease in confusion.

"You've been crying. Who upset you?" He loomed above her, chest puffed out. "I'll make him pay, just give me a name."

Utterly unexpected. Trip wanted to defend her. For some ridiculous reason, his concern made her happy. God, what a screwed-up pair they were.

"Not a *he*, and there are no asses that need to be kicked, so stand down." She raised one hand. "But I don't want to talk about it."

"I've never seen you cry, princess." He shocked her again by pulling her against his chest and murmuring, "Gotta say, I don't like it."

Her muscles relaxed in his embrace. She closed her eyes and enjoyed the warmth and strength he offered. The soothing sound of his strong heartbeat pounded against her ear, so she stayed there for a few extra seconds before easing away. "I'm fine. I'll be fine, really. But why are you here?"

Trip cocked his head, looking like he might continue to press the topic, but then he backed down. "Honestly? I didn't plan on coming. I bolted from the office to blow off steam and ended up here." The look on his face proved he was as surprised as she by that admission.

"To blow off steam?" She unlocked her door, already knowing she would let him come in. She didn't want to be alone just yet, and apparently neither did he.

"Among other things." Trip restored his playboy persona with the innuendo of his words and delivery. He followed her up the stairs and into her apartment and then proceeded to pace back and forth.

She tossed her purse to the floor, switched on a lamp and the gas fireplace, then grabbed a bottle of zinfandel and two glasses.

"Got any beer?" Trip asked while picking up various pictures and knickknacks to study them with a curious smile.

"Wine or water, sorry."

Trip motioned for the bottle with one hand then poured them each an extra-large glass. "Not sure who needs this more, you or me."

He clinked his glass with hers and proceeded to gulp it down like whiskey. When Kelsey slunk onto the sofa, Trip flopped beside her. He sank his head back against the sofa and closed his eyes, resting his hand on her knee.

Her body responded to his touch like a match to a striker. She watched the muscles in his face relax as his thumb massaged the outside of her knee. Despite her mood, his presence and signs of affection lightened her heart. But she couldn't let her heart misread Trip.

After a minute or two, he opened his eyes and faced her with a grin before sitting up.

"So what got you so riled up you had to take off?" She took another sip of her wine, but then he reached out for her glass.

He set it on the table and tugged her hand, drawing her closer to his body, his eyes clouded by trouble, his jaw clenched. "I don't want to talk about it. I just want to escape." He kissed her gently. "Want to take a ride with me?"

Before she could fire off a snarky reply, he kissed her again. Unlike their previous explosive encounters, this kiss simmered. His hold on her—the touch of his fingers along her jaw—was tender, like a kiss from a man who cared. He drew her lower lip into his mouth and gently bit down on it before kissing her again.

Like before, she opened her eyes, but his remained closed. He breathed deeply, his chest rising and falling as he pulled her across his lap and pressed her against his body. His desire fed hers and, if she wasn't careful, might trick her into believing he felt more than lust.

He caressed her back before his hand swept across her hip and up her waist to her breasts.

"You feel so good, princess." He opened his eyes and smiled, then kissed her again on the mouth before pressing kisses against her neck and down to her shoulder. He then stroked along the inside of her thigh. "I like this skirt, but I'd rather see you naked."

Part of Kelsey knew another go-round with Trip would seriously mess with her head, but the rest of her just didn't care. He tasted like heaven, and made her body resonate like no one else ever had. Maybe he couldn't love her, but he sure could *make* love like a champ, and that sounded pretty perfect at the moment.

She reached for the hem of his shirt and helped him tug it over his head. Then she kissed his shoulders, enjoying the way his breathing became uneven, the way the muscles in his chest twitched under her tongue.

Grunting, he kicked off his shoes and then began unbuttoning her blouse while kissing her. When she removed her shirt, he shoved her coffee table aside several feet and then laid her down on the carpet in front of the fireplace. Braced on his knees, he slowly removed her skirt and panties, his fingers skimming along her thighs. The flickering light caught in his eyes, which were glinting with their own heat.

Heat for her.

She slid her hands inside the elastic of his sweats and tugged them down until he yanked those off, too. She sat up and fondled the length of his erection before taking him in her mouth, making him gasp and grunt with pleasure.

He was a big man, so she couldn't accommodate all of him, but he didn't seem to mind. He dug his hands through her hair as he pumped into her mouth and uttered a breathless, "Kelsey."

She used her tongue and hands to excite him further, listening for and feeling what he liked and didn't by his body's response. Then he pulled away, laid her back and kissed her.

His entire body covered hers, the friction of the skin-to-skin contact heating her, making her purr.

"Should I go get the body paint?" she asked between kisses.

He brushed back some of her hair and looked at her. "Not tonight. No games. Just you. I just need you." Then he kissed her again, his finger traced her jaw before his hand went to her breast, followed by his mouth.

I just need you, he'd said. She arched her back and let him take whatever he needed, because she needed him just as much.

Everything about this woman turned him on. The feel of her soft skin under his calloused hands, the scent of the sweet perfume she'd spritzed on her body, the way she stretched and arched beneath his touch like a cat being petted, the ample proportions of all her curves.

He could stare at her and kiss her for hours. In fact, that was his plan. He'd lose himself in the exploration of her body, leaving no spot unattended.

As his mouth moved from her breasts to her abdomen and below, her little squeals and panting stoked the inferno blazing in his core. Each scratch of her nails or bite from her teeth spurred him to be more attentive, more impassioned.

He pulled away long enough to wrest the condom from his wallet and then buried himself deep inside her, kissing her, pinning her arms to the floor while pumping his hips.

She wrapped her legs around his waist, pulling him deeper inside. When he released her arms to cradle her head, she threaded her hands through his hair and then ran them along his back until she groped his ass.

They rode a wave of hunger until their sweaty bodies lay spent before the fire.

Kelsey Callihan was more erotic than any pinup girl of his boyhood fantasies, because in addition to her obvious sensuality, she oozed warmth. He'd done nothing to earn it, and yet she'd given it without reservation, thawing the chill of his sparring match with Mason.

She was way more than he'd bargained for, and he wasn't sure whether he should be glad or terrified.

Trip raised himself onto his elbows and brushed hair from her face, then kissed her before rolling onto his back and dragging her against his side. His fingers trailed back and forth along her waist while he stared at the ceiling.

When he'd stormed out of Backtrax, he hadn't intended to end up at Kelsey's. Yet here he was, sated and happy. She must be, too, because she wasn't crying anymore. Then the recollection of her tears nettled.

"Kels?" His fingers toyed with her hair, but he kept his eyes on the ceiling.

"Hmm."

"Tell me why you were upset earlier." He turned his head to look at her, but as soon as he spoke, she stiffened and looked away.

"It's personal."

"More personal than what we just did?" When he pinched her ass in jest, she swatted his hand.

"Yes, actually." She met his gaze. "What we just did had nothing to do with feelings. What upset me earlier is all about feelings, ones you'll make fun of, too. I'm not up to a verbal brawl."

Trip frowned, irrationally angered by her narrow view of him, despite knowing that was all he'd ever let her see. He rolled to his side and tugged one of her hands to his lips for a kiss. "I won't make fun of you, I promise. I'm a good friend, just ask Grey."

"Are we friends, then?" Her skeptical expression burned like a slap to the cheek.

"Of course we're friends, princess. Now, if you don't tell me why you were driving around town in tears, I'm going to have to go investigating on my own, starting with one Wade Kessler." Trip ignored the spark of displeasure that thought ignited.

Kelsey giggled, her smile lightening his heart. "He'd be mighty confused then, because it has nothing to do with him."

"Then what, or who, is the problem?"

"My sister." Kelsey blankly stared into space and bit her lip.

"Maura?" Trip curled his arm around Kelsey's waist. "But you two seem so close."

Kelsey nodded. "We are. I'm just being petty and stupid."

"How so?"

"She's pregnant, which is wonderful news, I know." Kelsey closed her eyes. "It's just that, instead of us being mothers together, her family keeps growing while here I am . . ."

She swallowed the rest of her sentence and flashed a rueful grin, but he could see the ache behind her eyes.

"Here you are wasting time with me, right?" He smiled so she knew he didn't blame her for the sentiment, although it did sting.

"That's not a slam against you, Trip. Honest. It's really about me, and whatever it is I do or don't do that makes me so undesirable." Little creases formed between her brows, which he promptly kissed.

"Listen up, princess. There is nothing—*nothing*—undesirable about you."

She shook her head. "I'm not talking about my body."

"Neither am I. You're bright, tough, ambitious, generous, and warmer than any woman I've met around here." He squeezed her waist. "If I ever wanted a wife, kids, and a picket fence, you'd be at the top of my list. So quit selling yourself short. You just haven't met the right guy yet, that's all."

About halfway through his pep talk, he noticed a change in her demeanor. Rather than thinking of her own issues, she'd shifted her focus to him. She rolled onto her side, so they were face to face. "Why are you so dead set against settling down?"

"Let's just say I didn't have the same kind of upbringing you seem to have enjoyed with your family." Mason's face zipped through his mind, stirring up the unpleasantness that had brought him here in the first place.

"Are your parents divorced?"

"No." His heartless chuckle caught her attention. "They were never married. My dad was already married when he had an affair with my mother. My mom raised me, until she died just before my eleventh birthday."

Kelsey reached out to touch his cheek. "I'm sorry you lost your mom so young."

"Thanks." That Kelsey had seized on that detail rather than the salacious elements of his response only proved what he'd said about her minutes earlier.

"What was she like?" Kelsey slipped her foot between his feet. He couldn't deny liking the way she kept physical contact with him while they talked.

"Awesome." He smiled at his memories. "She worked an admin job in a doctor's office. But at home she was super creative. Always decked the house out for the various holidays. Made a big deal out of birthdays. She wasn't a great cook, but hers are still the best chili-cheeseburgers I've ever had." He glanced at Kelsey and grinned at her rapt attention. "We lived in a normal house, a lot like your sister's. My grandfather lived a few blocks away, so he was around all the time. He and I remained close until he died."

"So that's why you don't want to part with that old cowboy hat." She looked up at the bookshelf, to where she kept his Stetson.

"Does that mean you'll give it back now?" Trip looked back at the hat. "And by the way, you should keep it upside-down when you aren't using it so the brim doesn't get misshapen."

"Okay. But no, I'm not giving it back yet. You haven't won the bet." She smiled, but he no longer had much enthusiasm for that damn bet. "He must have been like another dad, right?"

"Better, because he was more patient than most men. He never had a son, so he loved taking me fishing and hiking and camping. Got me involved in little league and pee-wee football. He thought I was the most amazing thing on the planet."

"That explains a lot about your ego." She bit his shoulder in jest, tempting him to bite her right back in more delightful places. "Tell me more."

"There isn't more." He reached over and caressed her hip, but couldn't shake the conversation from his mind. "I had a really happy early childhood, which made the loss more painful. Something I hope I never feel again."

Kelsey's eyebrow lifted, as if something had clicked into place in her mind. "What about your dad?"

"Like I said, I didn't know him until my mom got diagnosed with pancreatic cancer. She'd never told him about me because their brief affair had ended before she knew she was pregnant, and then she worried the news would destroy his family. But when she got sick, she reconsidered." Trip felt Kelsey's hand stroking his arm, the way one would caress a child to make him feel safe. Funny thing, it was working.

"Do you get along with your dad?"

"We don't fight, but we're not close."

"So you didn't see him much after your mom died?"

"Oh, I saw him. He adopted me." He avoided Kelsey's surprised gaze. "I'm sure he thought he was doing me a favor when he moved me into his palatial estate, as if a swimming pool or private school could compare with what I'd lost. Unfortunately, his wife and my half brother resented my existence and made my life pretty miserable whenever he wasn't around, which was often since he was busy building his empire."

"That's horrible. So you're not close to your brother, either?"

"Understatement of the year, princess." He quirked a self-mocking smile. "And here you were thinking *you're* the undesirable one."

"But if your dad went to the trouble to adopt you, surely he must love you."

"Not necessarily." Trip closed his eyes as if he could blot out the upsetting memory that had started playing.

Trip sneaked down the hall toward the kitchen for a late-night snack, starving because of the energy he'd expended taking his eighth grade football team to victory in the season championship game earlier that evening. As he drew near, he overheard Mason talking to his dad in the breakfast room.

"You love him more, just admit it. He's the kind of son you always wanted—popular, athletic. I can't wait to go to college and get away from having to watch you drool all over him."

"Of course I don't love him more, Mason. You're my firstborn son. You came into this world wanted by your mom and me more than anything. Trip wasn't born of love like you were, but he's my son, too. What kind of man would I be if I turned my back on my own flesh and blood, especially after his mother died? He's in our life now. You need to make peace with it. Show your brother some compassion."

Hunger fled as Trip's stomach clenched and his lungs burned. Despite his awkward, rocky start in this home, he'd begun to believe his dad actually loved him. But now he knew what he'd first suspected. He wasn't wanted and loved, not really.

"Let's just say I've never been convinced my dad loved me as much as he felt obligated toward me, that's all." Perspiration coated his skin, though whether it was due to the memories, the fireplace, or the nearness of Kelsey's naked body, he couldn't be sure.

"How could he not love you?" Kelsey tenderly ran her hand through Trip's hair and along his cheek. "You're his son."

"I'm sure you can't imagine it, but it doesn't mean you're right." Trip flopped onto his back and stared at the ceiling again. "That's actually what got me worked up today. My dad's pushing for a family reconciliation. I wouldn't mind being a better son to him, but I've no desire to mend fences with my brother or my stepmom. I tried for years, but they rejected every attempt. I'm done."

He braced for a lecture about forgiveness and the importance of family. Instead, Kelsey rested her head on his chest and nestled tighter against his body, pliant and warm. "I'm sorry you're still hurting. Maybe you can find some way to get closer to your dad without dealing with the others. In the meantime, you're not alone here."

"Because of Grey? He's around less often now because of Avery."

"Grey, and me." Kelsey propped her chin on his chest. "Whenever you need a soft place to fall, you call me and I'll listen."

"I'm sure I don't deserve that kindness." A surge of tenderness washed through him, prompting him to pull her in for a kiss.

"Probably not, but I'm notoriously foolish." She grinned. "Ask anyone."

He rolled over, cradling her. "And anytime someone hurts your feelings, you call me and I'll set them straight."

"Deal." Her fingers brushed through his hair again, shooting tingles down his neck.

"We strike good bargains, princess." He kissed her while twisting a lock of her hair around his finger.

"So far."

Somehow all this mushy talk had aroused him. He didn't want to think about why, especially when he had a more immediate problem. "I want you again, but since I didn't plan on coming here, I'm not prepared with extra condoms. Do you have any?"

"Why would a girl who normally doesn't have casual sex keep condoms?"

Why did the fact she hadn't had other lovers in a long time totally turn him on? He kissed her shoulder and then her breast. "Are you on the pill?"

"No. Maura told me her doctor made her go off the pill for three months before trying to get pregnant. I'm already thirty-one. Once I meet Mr. Right, I don't want to have to wait that long to get started."

He grimaced at being forced to think about babies when all he wanted to concentrate on was sex.

"So I guess I should stop kissing you, touching you." He kissed her again as he slid his fingers between her legs, which she parted willingly. His body throbbed in response to her hot, wet center. "Kelsey."

Her hips swiveled, her lips parted on a breathy sigh. "Are you clean?"

"As a whistle." He kissed her again, his body rigid with need. "I'll pull out."

She nodded before pulling him into a hungry kiss. Consumed by passion, Trip quickly pushed himself inside her body, disregarding all caution in deference to his fever to possess her. When she finally cried out his name, it took a Herculean effort to withdraw, but he hoped he'd managed just in the nick of time.

Chapter Eight

Kelsey's knees bounced so hard they banged against the desk just as she hung up the phone. She wiggled in her chair and drummed her hands on her desk, smiling. So close! Nick Copeland only had one sibling whom he'd not yet convinced of the benefits of selling their property. If she could pull this deal off for Wade, she'd be on her way to financial freedom.

After typing a quick update to Wade, she reviewed the email Mason had sent her outlining his rental unit preferences: two or three bedrooms, two baths, in or near town, updated interior, $3,500 per month rental rate. At that price point, she should be able to find something suitable, but why did he need the extra bedrooms?

That request had surprised her, mostly because she couldn't remember whether or not he'd worn a wedding ring. Normally she catalogued the status of a man's ring finger before asking his name. Last week, however, she'd been off her game.

Off her game from the moment she'd agreed to Trip's sexy proposition. And getting in deeper every day thanks to his nightly drop-ins this past week. Just picturing him caused her to absentmindedly stroke her neck, as if his fingers were toying with her hair.

She smacked her forehead to knock his image out of her brain, then bookmarked a few listings and scheduled appointments to go see two newer ones.

She glanced out the huge picture windows of her office at the cloudy skies hovering over town. Next month, she and her friends would be basking under the brilliant Mexican sun.

While sipping her latte, she studied the website of the Esperanza resort, where she'd booked a three-bedroom suite for four nights.

Sun-Baked Stone Massage and Cucumber Lime Facial sounded nice. Papaya-Mango Body Polish. Avocado Butter Mani-Pedi. Just as she got swept away by the menu of spa treatments, the devil breezed through her office door, throwing her emotions into chaos once more.

"Good morning, princess." Trip greeted her with a cheerful smile when he came to a stop on the other side of her desk. He glanced around the front room of her office, with its muted Tibetan carpet, cozy chairs, opaque glass lamp, and large mahogany desk—which she knew was a huge step above Backtrax's decades-old decor. "Wow. Nice digs."

"Thanks." From her desk chair, she craned her neck to meet his gaze. He looked as handsome as ever in faded jeans and an untucked blue-and-green plaid flannel shirt.

Her fingers itched to run through his shiny, dark hair. Her lips ached for his kiss. Her eyes raked over every inch of his six-foot-three-inch frame, coming to rest at the animal crate in his one hand and stuffed paper grocery bag in the other.

"Whatcha got in there?" She stood and walked around the desk, happy for an excuse to draw nearer to him, while trying to peer into the darkened interior of the crate.

"A surprise." Trip's radiant grin chased away the dreary skies and heated the room, even though she knew she shouldn't let herself get used to him brightening her days.

He set the bag on one of the two client chairs facing her desk, and then placed the crate on the table in between. Once he'd unlatched the door, he pulled out a tiny gray-and-white kitten. It wriggled in his large hands as he tickled beneath its chin. "Isn't he cute?"

Kelsey bit her lower lip to keep from chuckling. "I'd have pegged you as a dog person. How will Grey's dog handle this addition to that tiny apartment you two share?"

Trip furrowed his brow as he shook his head. "It's not for me. It's for you."

He thrust the kitten toward her, dropping it in her hands.

"For me?" Kelsey tentatively took hold of the living fur ball. Her mind raced, but her heart instantly warmed to the pint-size creature. Its teeny tongue grazed her fingers like a fine-grained nail file. She looked up at Trip, whose gentle smile softened an intense expression that caused her breath to catch. She cleared her throat and asked, "Why?"

Trip avoided her gaze while he stepped closer and stroked the kitten's back. "I know you've been a little blue. My buddy Jon's girlfriend's cat just had a litter of kittens. I thought you might like one." His cheeks had turned a bit red, and he cracked his knuckles in obvious discomfort. "It's cuddly. Girls like cuddly stuff, right?"

Her lips quirked at his awkward behavior. "Some of us do, yes."

Trip finally looked directly at her, his expression tentative. "If you don't want to keep him, I can take him back."

"Oh, just try and take him from me." She clutched the little kitten closer to her chest, still reeling from the fact that not only had Trip been genuinely bothered by her sorrow, but he'd also hoped to remedy it with this pet. "This is very sweet of you, Trip. What's his name?"

Trip shrugged. "Up to you, I guess." He scratched his neck, one side of his mouth curving upward. "I got kitty litter and some food and other stuff in that bag. Not sure what else you need, but this should get you through a couple of days."

Kelsey placed the kitten back into its crate and faced Trip, trying to square this considerate side of him with the womanizer she'd known for most of the past year. She stepped closer to him, cocking one brow, and lightheartedly poked his chest with her finger. "You know, this clinches it. Your carefree cowboy act is just that—an act. But don't worry, I won't tell anyone."

He narrowed his gaze and spoke with the playful cockiness he'd perfected. "I know you won't, princess, because that would mean you'd have to disclose our little fling, and I know that terrifies you."

"Touché." On impulse, she grabbed his hand and led him away from the prying eyes outside the street-level windows to the small storage room in the back of the office. "Now I want to show my appreciation. Tell me, what can I do for you?"

"Hmm." He tugged her ponytail free. "First, stop putting your hair in these contraptions. I like it better down."

"It gets in my way when I work." She shook it loose then wrapped her arms around his neck. "Besides, I didn't plan on seeing you today."

"That makes two of us." He brushed his hands along her sides, tugged at her hips, and then kissed her. "But I'm not sorry, are you?"

"No." Kelsey kissed him again, pressing herself against his body. His erection drove into her lower abdomen, making her chuckle. "You're always ready to go."

"Like Pavlov's dog whenever I see you. Hell, it happens anytime I think about you, actually." He lifted her and sat her on a file cabinet, then kissed her while running his hands up under her skirt along her thighs. "I want you right now."

His hands stroked her waist and breasts. The low rumble coming from his chest aroused her.

"I'm all yours." Kelsey spread her legs, locking her ankles behind his hips, wishing she could say those same words in a different context without scaring him away.

As she kissed his neck, he shoved her skirt up to her hips and unzipped his jeans.

Then they heard the front office door squeak open just before Avery's voice called out, "Kelsey? You back there?"

Trip froze. Kelsey slid off the file cabinet while yelling, "Just a sec, Ave. I'm coming."

"*Almost* coming, princess," Trip whispered in her ear, sending another wave of tremors through her core.

Kelsey pressed her fingers to Trip's lips to silence him and then straightened her skirt and smoothed her hair before grabbing a batch of paper and striding out of the storage room to greet her friend. "Sorry. What brings you by?"

"Emma and I wanted to take you to lunch to discuss Cabo. We're so excited, although Grey's a little crabby about it."

"He can do without you for four days." Kelsey dropped the paper on her desk. "But I can't meet for lunch today. I have a client appointment at twelve thirty. Maybe dinner?"

"Okay. I'll talk to Emma." Avery looked at the crate and grocery bag. "What's all this?"

"Oh." Kelsey had nearly forgotten about the kitten. She brought him back out of his crate. "A rescue kitten. Isn't he cute?"

"I didn't know you wanted a pet." Avery rubbed its leg.

"Neither did I, but he's just the perfect thing for me right now." Kelsey brushed her cheek against his soft fur.

"What's his name?"

Kelsey frowned for a second, and then smiled as it came to her in a flash. "Cowboy."

"Huh." Avery's perplexed expression made Kelsey smile. "Guess that's as good a name as any."

"It's the perfect name for this cat, trust me." Kelsey longed to share her private joke with her best friend, but she couldn't. The limitations of her and Trip's relationship—or whatever—tightened her chest, providing a stark reminder of one of many reasons why she should end their foolishness sooner rather than later. Yet her stomach pinched at the idea.

Besides, she saw no reason to call it quits with Trip until she met someone who wanted something more than casual sex. It wasn't like a bunch of men carrying little black velvet boxes were lined up at her doorstep.

"I'll take your word for it." Avery shrugged. "Anyhow, I looked into a little artisan community called Todos Santos, about an hour or less outside of Cabo. It might be a nice afternoon trip."

"Sure. I'm up for anything." Desperate to get Avery out of her office before her friend discovered Trip, she said, "Listen, I hate to rush you, but I've got to prepare for my appointment."

"Call me later about dinner."

Kelsey waved as Avery waltzed out the door and turned toward her physical therapy clinic. Once Avery was out of sight, Kelsey sagged against her desk and let loose a whooshing sigh. She placed Cowboy back in his crate and called to Trip, "Coast is clear. You can come out now."

When Trip emerged, he looked agitated and uncomfortable, stuffed back in his snug jeans. "Not a fan of being interrupted."

"Sorry." She reached out toward him, then remembered the street-level windows and dropped her hand.

"How about I come see you later tonight?" He stepped closer, but a quick glance at the street outside kept him from touching her. Still, the heat of his body pushed against her skin.

She should say no. She should stop pretending he might actually want more than a superficial fling. She should end this nonsense before she proved her sister right and lost her heart. *A couple of weeks more,* it whispered, despite common sense. "Sure."

A mix of satisfaction and relief flashed in his eyes before he turned to go, then he paused. "You never mentioned your trip to Cabo."

"Avery, Emma, and I are taking a little girls' trip."

Trip grinned, although his expression grew distant. "Three pretty girls in bikinis. I'm guessing you'll be surrounded by guys before long."

Was he jealous? Her stupid heart sped up at the idea. Why was she so prone to spinning fantasies instead of facing reality?

"No wonder Grey's been grumpy lately." Trip blew out a breath and then glanced at the animal crate and smiled. "Like the name, by the way. If you want, I'll watch Cowboy for you while you're away."

Aw, Cowboy was their cat—except "they" weren't really a couple, and no one could know that Trip had given her the kitten.

"That'd be hard to explain. Don't worry, though. Fee will love to be in charge of him for a few days."

Trip chuckled. "If she can break away from Lolly."

He remembered the doll's name. That had to mean something, didn't it? Or was she just grasping at anything—*anything*—to turn Trip into the man she wished he could be instead of the man he insisted he was? If only he'd always act like the cock of the walk instead of showing hints of a warm, caring man, she wouldn't have to fight so hard to keep perspective.

"True." Kelsey stepped away from Trip and toward her desk, needing space from him to get her head back together. "I don't mean to be rude, but I do have an appointment in a bit."

"With Wade?"

"Actually, yes."

"Is this about that property at the edge of town?" Trip's gaze narrowed while he placed his hands on his hips.

"Yes." She crossed her arms. "I know that makes you unhappy, but you'd better resign yourself to it. If it makes you feel better, I'm going to persuade Wade that the design of the project should be in keeping with the Victorian look of town."

"I'm hardly the only one in town not thrilled with the idea of another Kessler development. When you all hit a roadblock with the zoning board or whatnot, remember I warned you not to count on this one." The cool tone in his voice sent a shiver down her neck. But she wouldn't give in so easily.

"And I told you, I know what I'm doing. This transaction involves private parties, not public land. People may gripe, but there's nothing they can do to stop it, especially when a chunk of that land is zoned for light commercial use."

Trip opened his mouth and hesitated, as if he was considering saying something important. Ultimately he didn't. Instead, he lapsed into his playboy persona, winked and pushed open the door to the street. "I'll see you later."

Trip handed his carry-on bag to the attendant and then boarded his dad's Learjet 60XR late that afternoon, eager for takeoff. Things must be dire for Deb to have sent the jet to bring him home right away. Consumed by an abnormal bout of panic, he texted Kelsey to cancel their plans.

> Can't make it tonight. Flying to Denver. Dad had a heart attack and is having surgery. Not sure when I'll be back.

He put the phone in airplane mode and shoved it in his jacket pocket before buckling his seat belt and staring out the small window. Despite the wide beige leather seats, Trip had always felt cramped in the cabin. He glanced around at the burled wood and five empty seats.

It had been several years since he'd stepped foot on this plane. The last time had been six years ago, when he'd flown back from Mason's Caribbean wedding with his father and Deb. Trip had tried to keep out of Deb's way by reading and sleeping and listening to iTunes, but he couldn't avoid her entirely without appearing rude. So he'd suffered through her recitation of every *remarkable* thing about Mason's wedding: the ideal weather, the exotic floral arrangements, the phenomenal band, the delicious food, and the perfect bride.

Trip couldn't help but snicker at the thought that Deb probably didn't consider Jen to be the perfect bride any longer, then immediately derided himself for being petty at a time like this. He had to set aside his battle with Deb and Mason, at least while he was in Denver.

Trip didn't spend much time worrying about death, especially considering the risks he took on the mountain. But he'd faced losing a parent before. Although most memories of his mother's death were blurry and indistinct, a few sharp images tightened his throat: the one and only time he ever saw his grandfather cry, clutching his mother's hand as she drew her last breath, his new dad squeezing his shoulder while Trip walked out of his childhood home for the last time—crying—with his suitcases in hand.

Now, as the jet hurtled across the sky, his father was going under the knife for some kind of heart surgery. He could die before Trip had the chance to sit with him, man to man, to talk about why they never quite connected.

He pinched his nose to stop the tingling, then wiped the tear from the corner of his eye. Thirty minutes until landing, and then another forty-five or so before he could reach the hospital. Closing his eyes, he reclined his seat and prayed.

He entered his father's hospital room, where his old man lay in bed, hooked up to monitors, with his eyes closed. Mason and Deb sat together holding hands and talking quietly. Trip hadn't seen Deb in years but she hadn't aged much. Botox, most likely: that and auburn hair dye.

He'd never considered her brittle kind of beauty appealing. Today her uncharacteristically splotchy face and red-rimmed eyes shocked him.

How bad *was* his dad?

Mason looked up, as if hearing Trip's thoughts. His weary eyes barely flickered their normal resentment. "You made good time."

Trip nodded. "Thanks for sending the jet."

"Dad wanted you here." Mason glanced at Trip and then to the floor. "Sorry we couldn't get you here before the surgery. We were really caught off guard."

Trip stood across from Deb. "What have the doctors told you?"

Deb straightened up and donned the detached expression she'd always used with him. "It's better news than we'd anticipated. They inserted a stent in the collapsed artery. Fortunately, his heart muscle didn't sustain overwhelming damage from the heart attack and he didn't need a bypass. He'll go home tomorrow, but be on medication from now on, and will be in cardiac rehab therapy. The good news is that the recovery from this procedure is relatively quick. After a few days of taking it easy, he can slowly start to resume normal activities."

"Thank God." Trip briefly closed his eyes and blew out a deep breath. Now he had time to work things out with his dad. Not in the next few days, but in several weeks, once he'd recovered more fully. "Sounds like the best-case scenario under the circumstances."

His dad's eyelids fluttered open. "Gunner?"

Trip moved to the edge of the bed and touched his dad's arm. "Right here, Dad. Sorry I couldn't get here sooner."

"You're here now." His dad flashed a weak smile then winced when he tried to shift in the bed. "Help me raise the bed."

"Dad, can't you just lie still for a while?" Mason asked. "Consider it practice for slowing down and working less."

Before addressing Mason, Trip shook his head and winked at his dad. "Dad won't slow down until it's over. Nothing wrong with that, though."

"Nothing wrong with ignoring the concerns of his wife, children, and grandchildren who'd like him to stick around longer?" Mason rubbed his hands on the arms of the chair, muttering to himself. "Not that you'd miss him."

Deb placed her hand on Mason's thigh to silence him.

Trip bit his tongue even as his body flashed hot and cold. Mason had a way of twisting all of Trip's words around so they ended up sounding different than he'd intended. Still, he couldn't upset his father by engaging in an argument with his brother.

"Don't dig my grave just yet. The doctor assured me I'd be okay," their dad said to Mason. Then he turned to Trip. "How long will you stay in town?"

"Not sure. I got coverage for a client expedition tomorrow. Don't have anything on the books for the next day, but if things come up I can probably get more coverage. Figured I'd play it by ear and see how you were doing."

"Are you staying at the house?" His dad glanced at Deb, who quickly masked her displeasure, and then back at Trip.

Trip had planned to camp out in a hotel, but he lied to avoid being rustled into staying at the mausoleum the rest of his family called home.

"Actually, I thought you'd be in the hospital longer, so I made other arrangements with a friend. But I'll hang out all day and help Deb however I can while I'm here." His father's disappointed expression landed like a sucker punch to the gut. "Maybe I could change my plans, if that's what you prefer."

"Do that, son."

Trip caught Mason rolling his eyes behind his mother's back. *Great.*

They sat in strained silence for a few minutes while his dad raised the bed so he'd be a bit more upright, then Trip's phone vibrated. Welcoming a distraction, he removed it from his jacket and checked the screen. He looked at everyone apologetically. "Let me grab this in the hallway. Be right back."

Once he exited the room, he answered. "Kelsey."

"I'm sorry to call, but I got so worried when you didn't return my texts. How's your dad?"

Although he was loath to admit it, her concern burrowed inside his chest, opening it up and making it a little easier to breathe. "He's out of surgery and it sounds like everything will be okay. Not too much damage."

He heard her sigh of relief through the phone. "Oh, I'm so glad, Trip. I was sick thinking of how you would feel if you missed the chance to resolve things."

"Me too." He rubbed his hand over his face. He'd gotten lucky this time. Maybe he ought to stay a week or two and spend some quality time with his dad.

"What about your stepmom and brother?" Kelsey asked sympathetically. "Are they there with you?"

He liked the feminine quality of her voice through the phone, and the way her concerned tone relaxed him. "Of course."

"Are you okay? Do you need company? If I drive out first thing in the morning, I could be there by noon."

For the first time in hours, Trip smiled. Hell, yes, a big part of him would love to have Kelsey at his side for comfort, among other things. But the fact that his heart had swelled at the offer troubled him. He didn't want to care too much, or rely too heavily on her.

The anxiety he'd experienced during his flight had served as a harsh reminder of the kind of suffering Trip sought to avoid by keeping things light. She'd already begun to drift into his mind and beneath his skin too easily and often. He needed to maintain distance for his sake, and hers. "You're a sweetheart to offer, but I'm good, Kelsey. Stay put."

"Okay." A beat of silence passed between them before she spoke again. "I'm snuggled up here with Cowboy, anyway. He likes to cuddle up on my chest and purr."

"Already taking after his namesake, it seems." Trip smiled when she giggled, picturing her lounging on her sofa with the kitten under her chin—in that silky black nightie, of course. He squeezed his eyes closed, hoping to rein in his thoughts before he became overly excited here in the middle of the hospital.

"When will you be back?" she finally asked.

"Not sure." The connection growing between them beckoned like a highly addictive drug. Much as he genuinely liked her, he knew he couldn't give her what she most wanted. He had to keep things light, so he affected a glib tone. "But don't think about me. Plan your trip to Cabo. I'll be just fine."

"If something changes, please call me. Anytime, Trip. You're not alone, okay. Remember? We made a deal."

"I know all about our deals, princess." Trip frowned, thinking about the fact that, sooner or later, she'd meet some new guy and then call on Trip to hold up his end of their bargain. The fact that these thoughts thrust his heart into a deep freeze did not bode well.

Deb walked out of his dad's room and drank from a nearby water fountain. Trip didn't need her eavesdropping or sizing him up. Time to hang up with Kelsey. "Listen, I probably shouldn't stay on the phone long. We're not supposed to use them in the hospital."

"All right." She sighed, sounding dissatisfied. "Get some rest. And," she hesitated, "I think you're wrong about your dad. You're a kind man, Trip, and I've no doubt he sees that and loves you."

"Thanks, Kelsey." He swallowed through the tight knot in his throat. "I'll catch up with you later."

"Good night."

Trip returned the phone to his pocket just as Deb came back to where he stood. "Was that Kelly?"

"Kelly?" Trip's facial muscles contorted with confusion while the shock of Deb starting a conversation with him subsided.

"Your father told me about some woman he saw when he visited you . . . she had an unfortunate nickname." Deb raised one disapproving brow. "He thought you had a thing for her. I thought her real name was Kelly."

Panic gripped Trip's lungs. He didn't need Deb digging around in his business. "Close enough, Deb. Close enough."

"So was your dad right? She's someone important to you?"

No way in hell would he risk giving Deb any personal information. If she mentioned something to Mason, then he'd use it to screw with Trip back in Sterling Canyon.

The best way to throw Deb and Mason off his trail was to make believe Kelsey didn't mean squat to him. "Nope, not important. Just one of many pretty girls I know."

The lie singed his tongue, but he had no choice.

"As I suspected." She turned on her heel and went back into his dad's room.

Trip let a heavy sigh loose. Between his dad, Mason, Kelsey, and his intention to derail Wade's plans, Trip's life was quickly becoming a complicated web of half truths and secrets. He doubted he could keep juggling all the balls without dropping one. Whenever that happened, he hoped it wouldn't completely upend the life he'd been building this past year.

Chapter Nine

Kelsey stood in the kitchen of the fourth condo she'd shown Mason and watched him inspect the sleek, modern cabinetry. His streaks of gray hair glinted in the morning sunlight. She noted his intelligent, rich brown eyes analyzing every detail of the condo as he fingered the drawer pulls and inspected the storage space. It had been hard to focus on being professional when she kept mentally comparing the appeal of Mason's cultured refinement with that of Trip's masculinity and charisma.

"This is nice, especially with the dark granite." Mason ran his left hand—one without a ring, she confirmed—along a stretch of counter space. He stepped close to her again, like he'd been doing all morning. Unlike Trip, who smelled like soap and pine most of the time, Mason obviously wore light cologne—something citrusy. He wasn't witty or playful, but his sober, careful manner put her at ease—a not entirely unwelcome change of pace from the roller coaster she'd been riding with Trip.

Trip, who'd been in Denver for nearly two weeks and kept putting up a wall whenever she tried to get emotionally close. Although she had no right to be angry, his boundaries hurt. They reminded her of Maura's warning back in late July. They urged her to return her focus to her real goals instead of trying to spin gold from hay.

"It's masculine yet understated." She thought the apartment suited him. "Fits your Cary Grant vibe."

"Cary Grant?" Mason chuckled, then proceeded to shoot his cuffs. "I'll take that."

She smiled and gestured toward the open-concept floor plan, which was anchored by a massive stone fireplace. "This is probably the best we'll find. It's got both a spacious living area and nicely proportioned bedrooms."

"I agree." A slightly pained expression crossed his eyes. "I think my girls will like visiting me here."

"Oh? I didn't realize you had a family." Although highly curious, she maintained a friendly but professional tone.

"My girls, Lisa and Linda, are with their mom in Denver." He rubbed one hand over the back of his neck. "I'm in the midst of a divorce. Not sure how often they'll come, but I want to be prepared."

"I'm sorry, Mason. That must be hard." Kelsey refrained from probing for details about his wife and the reason for the divorce. "How old are they?"

"Three and five." His entire expression warmed. "The loves of my life."

Few things were more attractive than a man who adored his children. So what if Mason didn't strike her like lightning? Exciting men like Trip had always let her down. She had to wise up if she wanted a family of her own, and give other kinds of men a chance.

"My niece is five, so I'm up to speed on all the cool places around here for kids," Kelsey said. "I'll send you a list of things to do so you can show them a good time in our little town."

"That'd be great." Mason flashed a humble smile as he shoved his hands in his pockets, but his confident stare drew her in. "How about a list of grown-up things to do, too? In fact, perhaps you'd agree to be my escort?" Mason winced and his cheeks reddened. "Sorry, that came out wrong. I didn't mean *escort* . . . I just—"

Kelsey chuckled at his overreaction and discomfort. "Relax, Mason. I know what you meant."

"Good. So, would you consider going out with me sometime?"

"Maybe." Kelsey smoothed her hair to hide a flutter of nerves. Odds were Mason wouldn't end up being the great love of her life, but at least he wasn't proposing a superficial sexual tryst. At the very least, he'd be a great business contact. "In the meantime, let's go back to my office and complete the paperwork so you can move in as soon as possible."

"Perfect." He held the door open for her. "At least let me buy you lunch today, okay?"

"Oh, thanks, but I can't," she lied. Trip's list of tips raced through her mind, followed by an immediate heaviness in her chest. Her reckless heart wished he wanted more from her than sex, but her head knew better. So even though she wasn't sure she wanted to go out with Mason, she was determined to play hard to get. It felt a bit dishonest, but she'd been getting used to a certain level of dishonesty thanks to her relationship with Trip. "I've got another appointment."

"You keep busy." Mason sighed. "Or perhaps you just don't want to get mixed up with a divorcée with two kids?"

"Don't be silly. I love kids." Maybe his situation wasn't ideal, but at least he'd proven an interest in committing to someone. Unlike Trip, she thought to herself. Trip, who she hadn't seen in almost two weeks and, despite a couple of pretty interesting rounds of phone sex, was probably spending his nights in Denver with any number of women.

"Hmm. You look preoccupied. Is there someone else in the picture?" He tilted his head, narrowing his gaze.

Startled by his perception, Kelsey pressed her lips together and shrugged one shoulder. "Let's just say I'm better off focusing on my professional life than my personal life lately."

"Okay, Miss Callihan. I won't press you today." Mason followed her down the stairs and out to her car, where he opened the door for her. "So far, meeting you has been the best part of my relocation. I'm on my way out of town again this weekend, but don't be surprised when you hear from me soon."

Kelsey's heart thrummed a little at his compliment. She started the ignition and smiled. "Thanks, Mason. That's nice to hear."

◆ ◆ ◆

Cowboy was lapping up the milk Kelsey had set out when she heard her phone ping. Could it be Mason? He said she could expect to hear from him, but he probably didn't mean in just a few hours. She glanced at the screen and saw Trip's name.

I'm outside ur office. Where r u?

Apparently he'd finally returned from Denver. How like him, breezing back into town and expecting to see her as if she were just waiting around for him. Another reason she needed to move on from this secret fling and free—no, *force*—herself to go out with other men. Available men who wanted a real relationship.

This was it. She'd end things today, she vowed while typing: "Home early with Cowboy."

B there in 5.

Her stomach flipped. Setting the phone down, she steeled herself. In an attempt to create distance between her heart and Trip, she tried to conjure up Mason's face. Epic fail. Not even his kind eyes could shove away her excited anticipation of seeing Trip.

When he arrived, she buzzed him in and unlocked her door. Despite her private pep talk, her lungs ballooned the instant he strode through the door with his characteristic smile and swagger. Dark denim jeans clung to his powerful legs. Legs she yearned to grip again. Why couldn't he want more from her than a few laughs and good sex?

He crossed the room as if he owned it—cowboy boots clacking on the wood floors—and lifted her off her feet. "How can you look prettier every time I see you?"

Then he kissed her hard. Without thought she kissed him back, her body naturally molding to his, content in his embrace. When he cut the kiss short and set her back on her feet, she struggled to find her balance.

"How's your father?" she asked, ignoring her earlier vow to maintain emotional distance.

"Better." Trip squeezed her waist.

"Your brother and stepmom?" She kept her arms loosely thrown over his shoulders, her fingertips brushing the hair around the base of his neck, temporarily fooling herself into believing they were more than friends with benefits.

"We're all still standing. But let's not talk about them." He reached into his jacket pocket, his eyes twinkling, and retrieved a small box. "I brought you something. A thank-you for all the calls and sweet texts you sent me while I was away. I'm not used to anyone looking out for me. It was . . . nice."

"You didn't have to buy me anything, Trip. I cared about how you were doing. That's what friends do."

"Not all friends. Just like not all friends treat their friends to a Cabo trip." He gently touched her breastbone and winked. "That generous heart of yours is almost as sexy as the package it comes in. But I can be generous, too, with people who deserve it."

If he kept bringing her gifts and telling her how pretty she was, how would she ever end things? Was it possible he cared more than he was willing to admit? And if so, how could she confirm it?

Trip held out the small box. Not a ring box, but her pulse still raced.

"Aren't you curious?" he asked.

"You know I am." She took the tissue-wrapped package from his hand and unwrapped two bejeweled vintage hair combs. Holding them up to the light, she watched sparkles cast around the room. "These are gorgeous. Are they real antiques?"

"Of course. Victorian era, fit for a princess." His smile widened. He took them from her and gently tucked two small sections of her hair back with the combs, causing a light prickling sensation to race over her scalp and down her neck. "Now you can wear your hair down without it getting in your way while you're working."

She touched the combs, keeping her eyes on Trip's face. If only he would tell her he felt something more than friendship and lust, her heart would burst. She'd wrap him up in so much love, all the pain and loneliness he'd felt since his mom died would become a faint memory.

Although she'd never considered herself a coward, she knew she wasn't brave enough to have a frank discussion about their relationship. Perhaps a few subtle questions could uncover his true feelings. "Thank you. I have to say, you keep surprising me with thoughtful gestures. If you're not careful, I'm going to start thinking you're falling for me, cowboy."

His brief hesitation gave her false hope—until he opened his mouth and brushed off her statement with flirtatious joking.

"Princess, I fell for you the first time I laid eyes on you." He lowered his hands to her hips and tugged her against his body. "Now how 'bout we take this little reunion to the bedroom."

Before she could protest, he swooped her up in his arms and carted her off to her room.

"Trip—"

"Call me by my real name, not the nickname Grey gave me." Trip's deep voice grazed her cheek just before he nibbled on her ear.

He laid her on the bed. After withdrawing a two-pack of condoms from his pocket, he tossed them to land next to her. "I want to hear you say my name when we're alone like this."

Trip looked her in the eyes, cradled her jaw, and then kissed her, long and slow, before reaching for the hem of her skirt. A streak of goose bumps dashed up her thighs. She was putty in his hands, unable to resist the intimacy of his request. "Gunner."

He moaned in response, his hands quickly unzipping her skirt and removing her clothes and then his own. The sight of his bare chest and abs made her lick her lips as her hands caressed his well-defined muscles.

Before she could catch her breath, he rolled over and pulled her on top of him. "I want to see all of you. And when I'm buried so deep inside you that you fall apart, I want you to *scream* my name."

He matched the urgency of his command with the force of his kiss, then his hands cupped her breasts. Her nipples hardened at his touch, and every muscle in her body trembled.

"Kelsey, you always feel so damn good." His mouth covered her breast and one hand grabbed her butt.

"So you're not bored yet?" She ran her hands through his silky hair, holding him against her chest, recalling their first conversation about marriage.

"Not even close." The words resounded from deep inside just before he thrust himself inside her with a playful growl.

God, he'd missed her, and that scared him. He opened his eyes so he could watch her ride him. His heart beat hard against his ribs at the sight of her flushed skin and wild hair. Sitting upright, he forced her to wrap her legs around his waist so they could sit chest to chest.

He loved the way her hands felt on his back and in his hair. Loved the way her plush lips wet his neck and shoulder. Loved the way her supple body melded with his while her silky hair brushed against his skin. Best of all, he loved the way she somehow warmed him from the inside out.

With each mewl and whimper she uttered, he grew harder and hotter. And when she finally called out his real name again, he about lost his mind. Flipping her over, he pushed her hands above her head on the bed and drove into her over and over until they were both panting and breathless and completely spent.

Eventually, he fell to one side and pulled her up along his chest, hugging her close. "It's good to be home."

He thought he heard a small gasp, but then she teased him. "If I didn't know you better, I'd think you were lonely in Denver."

"I was lonely in Denver." He peered down at her, but she kept her face hidden, so all he could see was a tangle of golden hair fanned out on his body.

She lightheartedly pinched him. "Oh, stop acting like a man who just returned from a monastery. We both know that's not true."

Yet it was. He hadn't been with another woman since he started up his little affair with Kelsey, and that realization surprised him. He gripped her chin and tilted her face up to meet his gaze, considering confessing the truth, when her doorbell rang.

She snapped her head toward the bedroom door, eyes wide with anxiety. "Who the heck could that be?"

"Don't answer it." Trip kept his hold on her waist. He didn't want anything or anyone to intrude on their time together this afternoon.

The bell rang a second time.

"Stay here!" She pushed off the bed and grabbed her robe.

He waited, listening to her talk to someone through the intercom. A minute later, he heard her open the door, thank someone, and then say good-bye before closing the door.

Curiosity took over, so he grabbed his underwear and entered the living room. Kelsey had her back to him, so she didn't hear him coming.

She was concentrating on reading the card that had been delivered with a bouquet of pink roses.

Every muscle in his body stiffened. Who the hell was sending her flowers? What the hell had *she* been doing while he'd been dealing with his dad in Denver? She sure hadn't mentioned anyone else during any of their recent conversations.

He reached around her and snatched the card from her hand, which read: *Dinner next Friday? Say yes —Cary.*

"What kind of a girly name is Cary?" Blindsided, Trip flung the card onto the counter before corralling his jealousy.

"It's a private joke." She scowled and returned the card to its plastic holder. "I told him he reminded me of Cary Grant."

Trip laughed, feigning a nonchalance he didn't feel. "And he took it as a compliment?"

She slapped his shoulder. "It *was* a compliment."

Being an old-fashioned, highbrow pretender was a compliment? Is that the kind of guy she thought could make her happy?

"Who is this guy, and why is he sending you roses?" Trip affected a carefree tone, although his fingers itched to knock over the vase or throw it against the wall. "Do I know him?"

Kelsey stared at him for a moment, apparently weighing her options. "You know what? According to *your* tips, I shouldn't talk about this with *anyone*. I doubt you know him, anyway. He's a new client. I found him a condo this week."

"Those tips don't apply to me, Kelsey." He sighed when she winced at the bark in his voice.

"Oh yes, I think they do apply. Especially to you." Her fingers brushed the tips of the flowers and her brows knitted. "Maybe this is good timing, actually. When you texted, I'd planned to end the sexual part of our friendship, but then you surprised me with the gift and . . . well, I got carried away."

"I'd say you did." His lungs seemed to be struggling a bit to find air. How the hell did he get here? Before he could stop the words from coming, he cupped her jaw with his palm and said, "I thought we were having fun together. You've seemed happy enough."

"Happy with our secret booty calls?" She placed her hand over his and held it there before slowly lowering his hand from her face. Her next words were barely louder than a whisper. "Come on, Trip. You know me well enough to know our arrangement isn't what I want."

He couldn't say which bugged him most: the resigned tone in her voice, the fact that she was being pursued by some other guy, or the realization that somewhere along the way he'd begun to really care.

"You're the one who put all the parameters on this being such a big secret. I'd have liked to have gone out and done more." As soon as the words flew from his lips, he regretted saying them. He'd come dangerously close to exposing vulnerability he wasn't honestly ready to admit or accept. Yes, he enjoyed her company more than he did any other woman's, but that didn't mean he shared her ultimate goals of marriage and family.

She wrapped her robe more tightly to her body and stared at him. "Why are you so miffed? This whole thing has gone exactly as you proposed. We had fun together, and now that I've met someone who seems interested in me for more than just sex, I'm going to use your tips and, hopefully, you'll get your hat back." She smiled as if he might find the whole thing funny.

He didn't.

Trip scrubbed his hands over his face to hide his feelings from her. She was right; he had proposed this whole stupid plan when he hadn't foreseen feeling more . . . feeling anything. Now what the hell was he supposed to do with all these damn feelings?

He turned to go find his clothes, but she grasped his arm. Her hopeful golden-brown eyes searched his. "Trip, if something's changed, now would be the time to tell me."

While one selfish part of him wanted to keep seeing her, the bigger part knew he wasn't anywhere near ready to take on the kind of relationship and commitment she really wanted. He cared about her enough not to play games and make promises he couldn't keep.

"You just surprised me, that's all, princess." He kissed her forehead. "If you're happy, I'm happy. Now let me go get dressed."

He yanked his jeans back on, all the while convincing himself that this was for the best. Soon enough they'd be squaring off against each other over Wade's project anyway, which would probably have brought an end to this fling, too. At least now they would make a clean break before things got messier.

On Trip's way out, Cowboy scampered up against his leg. Kelsey stood near the kitchen, chewing on the inside of her cheek, looking conflicted. Trip picked up the kitten and stroked it under its chin. "You take care of our girl now, you hear?"

He set the kitten back on the floor then winked at Kelsey, pretending he didn't ache with regret. "Good luck with your dreamboat, princess."

Chapter Ten

Kelsey slammed the folded newspaper down on the counter at Backtrax and skewered Grey with the most heated glare she could muster. "Where's your partner?"

"Steer clear of him, Kelsey. He's been grouchy ever since he got back from Denver." Grey unwrapped a grape Tootsie Pop and stuck it in his mouth, apparently unfazed by her death stare.

For one millisecond, she wondered if Trip's foul mood had anything to do with her ending their trysts. Then she considered the waitlist of women hungry to warm his bed, and brushed aside her little fantasy.

"Well, I've got a bone to pick with Mr. 'Concerned Citizen'."

"Oh." Grey's brows rose along with both hands, indicating she'd guessed right. Trip *was* the man behind the open letter to the Copeland family featured on the front page of the local paper's Lifestyle section.

"Is he here?" She picked up the newspaper roll and tucked it under her arm.

"Upstairs."

As she marched toward the interior stairwell, she glanced over her shoulder. "Unless you own earplugs, it's probably best if you stay down here until I leave."

"I've got some work to do in the back office." He waved her off. "Try not to break anything."

"Hmph." She tromped up the steps, her platform snakeskin pumps pounding a warning against the wood treads.

Fueled by the anticipation of a showdown, she barely knocked on the back door before pushing it open and barging into the kitchen. "Trip!"

"Right here, princess," he drawled, standing in front of the open refrigerator wearing nothing but a towel wrapped around his waist.

His skin was still damp from a shower, his thick, black hair glossy and wet, with water droplets rolling down his neck. The defined muscles in his chest and arms flexed as he closed the refrigerator door and faced her.

Kelsey's mouth opened and closed, her well-rehearsed tirade temporarily forgotten thanks to her dirty mind imagining him in the shower.

His gaze traveled from her head to her toes, which made her body flush with unwelcome desire. It had been nine days since she'd seen him. Nine days since she'd felt this rush. Nine long days since her heart had soared.

He cocked his head. "I'd be flattered by the way you're staring at my towel, but after our last discussion, I'm guessing you're not here looking for love."

The smirk on his face doused her desire like cold mountain spring water, reminding her of why she'd come.

"Darn straight, I'm not. And if I were looking for love, I sure wouldn't find it with you!" She thrust the paper toward him. "Obviously you don't care about me at all, or you wouldn't go out of your way to screw up this project I'm counting on."

He snatched the paper from her hand and tossed it on the floor. "I've warned you more than once *not* to count on that deal."

"So that makes what you're doing okay?"

"Yes." He crossed his arms.

It took concentrated effort to keep her gaze above his neck. Apparently he wasn't the least bit interested in getting dressed and having a serious discussion. God, she wanted to poke those cool green eyes out of his smug face.

"Just when I was convinced there was more to you, you prove me wrong." She shook her head. "You're as selfish as I first believed."

"Me?" His eyes narrowed. "You think *I'm* selfish for trying to stop an unnecessary and detrimental development from wrecking this community? If anyone's being selfish, it's you, Miss Moneygrubber."

"Oh, please. You expect me to believe you're doing this for the good of the community?" When he shrugged, she rolled her eyes. "If you're so passionate about this cause, why don't you use your real name?"

"I've got my reasons, not the least of which is keeping a decent relationship going between Backtrax and Wade." He rested his butt against the edge of the kitchen counter, ankles casually crossed, apparently waiting for her to make the next move.

As always, he seemed to maintain his calm demeanor while managing to push all her buttons. Her skin itched from sheer irritation.

"Trip, if you succeed in killing this deal, I'll lose several hundred thousand dollars in commissions and won't be able to buy the small apartment building I've had my eye on. Meanwhile, you'll gain nothing from your win . . . other than hurting me, that is. Please reconsider. If you walk away, you lose nothing."

"Not true, Kelsey. I've told you already, I've made an investment in Backtrax and a commitment to living here, so I *do* have something to lose if the Wade Kesslers of the world come in and change everything. I'm sorry if this might cause a temporary setback in your personal plans, but I've got to do what I think is right."

"I've lived here my whole life. Do you really think I'd promote development that I didn't think would benefit the town?" When he didn't soften, she sniped, "And you'll excuse me if I have a hard time buying into your commitment to our town, since commitment isn't exactly your strong suit."

Trip's face turned bright red as he crossed the kitchen in two long strides and got right in her face, speaking in a quiet yet terse tone. "Careful, princess. I've been a decent friend to you, so how about you show me the same respect?" Then he raised one brow. "Besides, you're hardly objective about this deal."

He stood there looking more confident and hotter than any man should look, while her insides churned.

"You really don't feel bad about doing this to me, do you?" Rather than stomp her foot like Fee might do, she shoved at his chest. Another tactical error, which he proved when he caught her hands before she pulled away.

"I'm not doing this 'to you,' Kelsey. I'm doing this for the people in the town who feel like I do. For the small retailers who'll lose money when fancy upscale stores take over. For the wildlife and habitats that'll be bulldozed to pave the property."

"Oh, yes, you made your *many* concerns very clear in your letter." Kelsey tugged her hands free from his grip. "There are pros and cons to every development, but that doesn't mean you should stop progress. Now I've got to convince Nick Copeland and his siblings not to get cold feet, and persuade Wade not to take his business elsewhere. Clearly I don't matter to you, but know this much: I'm not going to let you kill this deal."

Trip softened his voice, but stepped even closer, throwing her further off balance. "I haven't done anything but raise legitimate questions. Has Wade even done any kind of impact study to show how his ideas will affect groundwater, traffic, or any other number of factors?"

Kelsey didn't have an answer. All she knew was how much she wanted to secure at least one part of her future. If Trip couldn't make her the kinds of promises she really wanted, why couldn't he at least stand aside and let her expand her business?

A swell of confusion and embarrassment tightened her throat and made her eyes start to water. She bent over to retrieve the paper from the floor and hide her emotions, then she turned toward the door, muttering, "I don't know why I bothered coming here."

"Maybe it's got nothing to do with Wade's deal." His words were soft-spoken but as sharp as an arrow.

She placed her hand on the doorknob, unwilling to look at him or engage in further conversation about her motives. "I don't have time for this."

But before she escaped, his hand grasped her waist. "Maybe subconsciously you want me to stop you from going out on your big date tonight." His mouth was suddenly at her ear, his chest against her back. "Tell the truth, Kelsey. Does this other guy knock you so off balance you don't know whether to slap him or kiss him? Does he make you tremble this way? Does he crave your touch?"

When she hesitated, he pushed her hair aside and kissed her neck. Like every other time he held her, she melted against him, needy and restless. He pounced on her weakness, spun her around and kissed her. Hot, hungry kisses that had them both breathing heavily in mere seconds. But once he started loosening her shirt from her skirt, she stopped him.

"No, Trip. I meant what I said before. I'm not like you. I can't be with you and see other people at the same time."

"I haven't seen anyone else since we got together." He kept pulling her in to kiss her, as if that tidbit of information was merely incidental instead of earth-shattering.

"You haven't?" She inhaled sharply and held her breath, leaning away to look in his eyes.

He ran his fingers through her hair and kissed her forehead. "No."

"Why not?"

He shrugged, suddenly looking uncomfortable. "Guess I haven't wanted to be with anyone but you." Then he kissed her again, possibly just to stop her questions. But she had more and needed answers before she went out with Mason.

"But you said no strings. You signed on to help me with another guy. I just assumed you were with other women whenever we weren't together."

"You assumed wrong." He stroked her hips and tried to kiss her, but she turned her cheek before she reached out to touch his.

"So what does this mean?"

"Why does it have to mean something?" He sighed and released her. "Why can't it just be what it is?"

"And what is it?" She stared at him, trying but failing to read his expression.

"I don't know." He raked his hand through the front of his hair. "I don't project or plan or plot. I take life one day at a time. And today, I like hanging out with you, talking to you, making love with you."

"But you still don't want the same things I want, do you?" She chewed the inside of her cheek, her heart stretching wide with yearning.

"This is the part where you fast-forward all the way to marriage and kids, right?" He rolled his eyes, which insulted her and left her heart aching. How could she have been foolish enough to hope for a miracle?

"You spit those words out like stale beer."

"My doubts about the institution are better than you settling for some random guy who probably doesn't even turn you on just because he *might* make good husband material." When she looked away, he chuckled. "And you think I'm screwed up."

Her head snapped back in his direction. Anger ebbed as disappointment and resignation rushed in to take its place. Kelsey sighed. "Maybe we're both screwed up, but I'm not going to argue with you, and I'm not going to give up on my dreams just because you think they're stupid."

Trip took two steps backward, the heat in his eyes cooling. "Well, then, I guess I'll look forward to reclaiming my grandfather's hat soon."

"From your lips to God's ears."

◆ ◆ ◆

Kelsey fidgeted with her napkin while Mason paid the tab. He'd been a perfect gentleman all night, but she couldn't get Trip or his accusations out of her head.

"Have I sufficiently bored you with too many stories about my girls?" Mason's chagrined smile deluged Kelsey in guilt.

"Not unless my tales of Fee and Ty bored you." A deflection to be sure, but she could barely concentrate. A ridiculous part of her resented Mason for not being able to rouse her more. She'd desperately wanted tonight to be a first step toward something real—and to prove Trip wrong—but the truth had only grown clearer with each conversation.

Mason was smart, nice-looking, and respectful, but he didn't excite her. Not even the candlelit tables had helped, although the man did know his fine wines. That was a plus. Trip always chugged them like beer, the beast.

"Of course not," he replied, intently staring at her while finishing what remained in his wineglass. "Thanks for agreeing to come out tonight, but if I had to guess, you're hung up on some other guy, aren't you?"

Add perceptive to Mason's list of good traits, she thought. "I'm not hung up. Maybe I'm a little . . . I don't know, stupid, probably."

"If anyone's stupid, it's him." Mason sat back in his chair. "Let me guess. He's got loads of charisma. He's athletic and fun to be around. Lives for today with no thought to tomorrow or next year. Attentive enough to keep you on the hook without making a real commitment. Am I close?"

Kelsey tried to mask her discomfort at his direct hit and shove away nagging doubts about Mason's heightened interest in "the other man" in her life. "Close enough."

"You think he might change, that maybe you'll be the one to make a difference. Well, I don't know everything, but rarely do adults change much. Just be careful not to waste too much time wishing for something that might never be."

"Speaking of wasting time, let's not spend any more talking about this particular topic." Discussing Trip with Mason felt weirdly like a betrayal. Maybe she could salvage this date by introducing a little activity. "Would you like to go down the street to On The Rocks and play darts?"

Mason wrinkled his nose and chuckled. "Crowded bars aren't really my scene."

"Oh, come on. It's only ten o'clock. It's not ski season yet, so it shouldn't be a zoo. If it's awful, we'll leave."

"How can I resist an offer like that?" Mason pulled out her chair for her and followed her out of the restaurant.

Trip threw back his fifth or sixth shot of tequila, he couldn't be sure. Then he took a long swallow from another cold bottle of beer.

"Hey, man, you might want to slow down." Grey shook his head. "What demons are you drowning? I've never seen you as grumpy as you've been since you got back from Denver. Does this have something to do with Kelsey storming our offices today?"

Trip defiantly swallowed another long gulp of beer. "I'm just blowing off a little steam. But if I want a babysitter, I'll be sure to hire you."

"On that note, I'll think I'll head over to Avery's for the night." When Trip waved him off, Grey hesitated. "You gonna make it home all right?"

"Home?" Trip chuckled. "Not sure that's where I'll land, but I'll be all right, don't worry."

Grey scanned the bar and shook his head. "All these poor women are at risk now, aren't they?"

"At risk of having an awesome time, maybe." Trip laughed, but it rang hollow in his chest. When Grey merely rolled his eyes, Trip nodded. "I'll see you tomorrow."

Trip glanced around the bar after Grey left. Not even the prettiest girls captured his interest tonight. His mind kept wandering to Kelsey.

Where was she, who was she with, what was she doing? An image of some other guy's hand tangled in her hair flashed through his mind. He chugged the rest of his beer and slammed the empty bottle on the bar before pressing the heels of his hands against his eyes, as if to rub away the image.

She'd promised to follow his advice, which included the all-important final tip about not sleeping with a guy too soon. But Kelsey would have trouble playing it cool from the get-go. Restraint went against every one of her instincts. That sexy bundle of fire and emotions believed if she just loved someone enough then he'd automatically love her right back. Well, she'd better not *love* this other guy tonight.

He clutched his stomach when it lurched. What the hell had he been thinking letting her go off with some stranger without getting the details? She might not be safe with this dude. Worse, what if the guy wouldn't take no for an answer?

In fact, maybe Trip should go stake out her house to make sure she was okay. Even if she weren't in danger, he'd be doing her a giant favor, actually, by making her stick to his tips. Yeah, a *giant* favor.

He wasn't interested in seeing who this guy was, *that's* for sure. Nope. That other guy didn't matter, 'cause she couldn't even like him, whoever he was. What *did* matter was making sure she listened to him so he'd win back his hat. Dammit, she still had his hat. Why had he let her hold on to it?

Didn't matter. He needed to stop her from doing something stupid. So what if she got a little mad tonight? She'd thank him tomorrow. Thank him, yessir. No doubt about it.

Yeah, the more he considered the idea, the better it sounded. Really, he couldn't think of a single good reason *not* to go.

He tossed twenty bucks on the bar and waved good-bye to the bartender before sliding off the stool.

Whoa. He braced one hand against the bar to steady himself, then shook his head and blinked twice before crossing the bar. After staggering through the door, he straightened his Stetson and zipped up his fleece.

When he finally looked up, the entire sidewalk seemed to rise and fall beneath him as he watched Mason and Kelsey, arm in arm, crossing the street.

He stopped, swaying slightly, and squeezed his eyes shut in confusion. But they popped open as soon as he heard Kelsey giggle and he realized he wasn't just having a nightmare.

"Get the hell away from her!" Trip's voice exploded from his throat. Then outrage tore through his veins like barbed wire when he noticed the tight dress she'd worn for her date.

Kelsey stumbled in shock, or from yet another pair of sky-high shoes. But Mason merely cocked an amused eyebrow.

"I'm sorry, Mason." Kelsey glared at Trip and snapped, "Go home, cowboy, before you cause a scene."

Trip shook his head, his gaze locked on Mason's mocking stare. "Trust me, Kelsey. He's using you to get to me."

"This may be hard for a man whose ego spans the entire galaxy to comprehend, but everything that happens isn't about you." She tugged at Mason's arm to proceed, but Trip stepped in front of her.

"Maybe not, but this," he gestured between Mason and her, "is definitely about me." Trip nodded at Mason, the weight of his own head tipping him off balance. "Tell her."

"You're wasted!" Kelsey poked his chest. "Go sleep it off before you embarrass yourself further."

"Kelsey, my brother is using you to fuck with me." The streetlights swirled in Trip's peripheral vision, the sidewalk shook like skis cutting through crud. He blinked and focused on Kelsey's face.

"Your brother? You've lost your mind." Kelsey shook her head while Mason remained silent. "He's not a Lexington. This is Mason *Cutler*."

"I'm not so drunk I can't ID my own brother. I'm a Cutler even if I kept my mom's name."

"Don't remind me," Mason finally chimed in, his tone cold enough to cause frostbite.

"Wait, it's true?" Kelsey released Mason's arm and pressed her fingertips against her temple. "You're brothers?"

"Aren't you listening?" Trip thrust his arms outward and let them fall against his sides. What he really wanted was to toss her over his shoulder and run. "The fact he asked you out is no coincidence. He's doing this to get to me. I knew when he arrived here weeks ago something like this would happen. Kelsey, he's been doing this to me my whole damn life."

"But how could he have known about us?" Kelsey's confused gaze drifted back and forth between the brothers. "We've been discreet."

"Tell her the truth, Mason," Trip demanded.

"What truth, Gunner?" Mason crossed his arms, feigning ignorance and innocence at the same time. Alarms went off, but in his altered state, Trip couldn't work fast enough to shut down the conversation. "By the way, it's quite an insult to assume my interest in Kelsey has to do with you instead of the fact she's a beautiful, kind woman."

"Did you know about Trip and me?" Kelsey's eyes widened; her voice turned thready.

"Yes, but I didn't come after you to hurt him. My mother mentioned your name before I first arrived in town." Mason had perfected phony sincerity, and it made Trip want to kick him in the ass. First he had to get Kelsey away from his brother.

"Let's go, princess." Trip motioned for Kelsey to follow him.

"But you don't confide in your stepmom, do you?" Kelsey stood still, waiting for an explanation.

"Hell no!" Trip scowled, then turned on Mason, desperate to end this discussion before his brother repeated the dismissive words Trip had used in Denver to try to throw Deb off his trail. Although it humiliated him to do so, he groveled. "If you need to mess with me, come at me directly. Don't hurt her to do it."

But the gleam in Mason's eye torpedoed any hope Trip might've had of calling a truce.

"I'm honestly shocked by your reaction." Mason held his hands up, shrugging. "You told Mom 'Boomerang' wasn't anyone special, so I assumed you wouldn't care *who* she dated."

Trip squeezed his eyes shut again, heat flashing through his body. When he opened them and turned to Kelsey, her watery eyes pierced his heart, sobering him up a bit. "I only said that to protect you from this ass. I knew if he thought you meant anything to me, he'd pull a stunt like this. You believe me, right?"

"What's 'Boomerang'?" The gentle, hurt tone of her voice, coupled with her lifeless expression, twisted his gut.

"Nothing." He reached toward her but she stepped back.

Mason scoffed. "Liar."

Kelsey turned on Mason, a bit of fire in her eyes. "Don't look so self-righteous. How dare you use me just to play out some juvenile sibling rivalry? If this is how you treat people, your wife's decision to bail makes a lot of sense."

"I didn't pretend anything, Kelsey. What's not to like about you?" Mason's smooth voice sounded too convincing to Trip. "And besides, I didn't coin that derogatory nickname."

She whirled on Trip. "What's that nickname even mean?"

"It's just a stupid name Grey came up with last year when you kept chasing after him." The humiliation in her eyes nearly brought him to his knees. He reached out to embrace her but she shoved him away. "I'm sorry."

"You shared it with your parents?" Her lower lip trembled when she spoke, and the betrayal in her voice scraped against his skin worse than any rough rock he'd ever climbed. Everything Trip had said in the past five minutes had made things worse instead of better, while Mason had yet another front row seat to witness the damage he'd set out to cause.

"I made an offhand comment to my dad before anything happened between us. It slipped out, but I swear I didn't use it to be cruel."

He watched her put on a brave face despite the unflattering and heartless revelations, but she couldn't hide the tear trailing down her cheek. She squared her shoulders. "I'm going home."

"I'll walk you." Trip started toward her, but she stuck her hand out.

"You stay away from me, Trip Lexington." Then she spun on Mason. "That goes for you, too. What a pair you two make. Your parents must be so proud." She looked right at Trip. "You should be glad your mom's not around to see how you turned out."

Although she'd hit a bull's-eye with her last retort, seeing Kelsey's spirit broken snapped something inside Trip. His hat went flying as he lunged at Mason. His fist connected with his brother's face, sending him reeling backward. Kelsey yelped and Trip vaguely registered the small crowd that had formed to watch the spectacle, yet nothing would stop him.

He gripped Mason by the shirt and pushed him to the ground, straddled him, and started punching.

"Stop it!" Kelsey cried. "Trip, stop!"

But fury blinded him. Trip rained his fists down on Mason, who tried desperately to shield his face and body from the force of Trip's blows.

A cop finally pulled Trip off his brother, who lay bloody and beaten on the sidewalk. Trip's heart was racing, his skin damp with sweat. Red and blue lights reflected off the plate-glass windows of the bar, and a dull murmur from the crowds grew louder. Wooziness gripped him as he struggled to catch his breath and fight against the shock setting in. He'd never lost control of his temper like that.

He glanced around the crowd, but couldn't find Kelsey in the melee.

One cop handcuffed Trip while another tended to Mason's injuries. A wave of relief washed through him when Mason stood up despite the pummeling he'd endured. In a matter of minutes, Trip had physically beaten his brother, and inflicted damage far worse on Kelsey.

Shame and guilt converged with all the tequila he'd drunk and, before he could stop himself, he threw up next to the police car.

The cop dabbed his chin with a handful of wadded-up tissues and tossed Trip's hat in the back of the car. "At least you'll have time to sober up in the tank."

The cop then guided Trip into the backseat. The last thing Trip noticed as the car pulled away was Kelsey walking alone on the sidewalk, crying.

Chapter Eleven

"I hope you feel as lousy as you look." Grey shook his head as he strode out of the jailhouse ahead of Trip. "Honestly, Trip. Kelsey? I begged you to stay away from Avery's friends. Instead, you ignore me *and* throw me under the bus with the Boomerang thing."

"Sorry." Trip tucked his hands in his jacket pockets and tipped his hat forward to shield his eyes from the sunlight's sting. If only the dusty streets had been this empty last night, things would look a little better for him this morning.

Grey stooped over to untie his golden lab, Shaman, from the public bench, then glanced up over his shoulder and sighed. "What are you, twelve? Sorry's all you've got to say?"

Grey had been a good friend—Trip hated having disappointed and deceived him.

"What else should I say?" Trip cleared his throat, wishing for some water and ibuprofen. "Can't change the past, but I'll pay you back the bail money."

Shaman trotted over and sniffed around Trip's boots, then wandered ahead of the two men toward an elderly couple strolling out of Higher Grounds coffee shop. The woman's crinkly eyes radiated warmth as she bent down to pet Shaman, her husband lovingly supporting her by holding her elbow. Trip found himself rubbing his chest, as if struck by the tender scene.

"You know I don't give a shit about the bail money. I'm concerned about Avery and our business. Not that you remember, but you were supposed to take a group climbing today." When Trip winced, Grey waved him off. "I already called them and offered a major discount to reschedule. I just hope your arrest doesn't cost us clients. What's your plan if your brother presses charges?" Grey tipped his head sideways and scanned Trip's face. "Doesn't look like the guy landed a single punch. You must've really kicked the shit out of him."

"Don't remind me." Trip rubbed his face with his hands and looked east, toward Kelsey's condo. "I'll make some kind of public apology and do community service work to clean up my image. But first I need to take care of something."

Grey followed Trip's gaze and then shook his head. "I think you should leave Kelsey alone today. According to Avery, she doesn't want anything to do with you right now." He whistled for Shaman, who trotted back to them. "The girls leave for Mexico on Friday, which gives everyone time to cool down. Wait until they get back before you go talk to her."

"Can't do that. You didn't see her face last night. I have to talk to her today."

Grey stuck his hand out, stopping Trip's progression. "I'm serious, Trip. She's not in the mood to hear you right now."

"I'm gonna do what I'm gonna do, and you can't stop me." He very deliberately removed Grey's hand from his chest. "I don't want to fight with you, too."

"Wow." Grey's brows rose and then he narrowed his gaze. "Answer me this: is Kelsey the reason you've been so moody lately? Are you in love with her or something?"

Trip wasn't going to talk about Kelsey with Grey or anyone else. How could he when he didn't even know how he felt? "I haven't been moody. I've been *busy* trying to stop that land deal, cope with my dad's heart attack, and come to terms with the fact that my brother's living in town."

"Last night Kelsey told Avery a little about your family. Given how you overreacted, I'm guessing there's a lot more history there. How come you told Kelsey about it, but you've never talked to me?"

"You know I'm not one for heart-to-hearts, Grey. For the most part, I've put my past behind me." Trip held up a finger. "I opened up to Kelsey a little the first night my brother blindsided me by showing up at our office. If I'd mentioned his name, he couldn't have duped her. I was stupid, but I won't make that same mistake again."

"Are you sure you're not being a little paranoid? He met Kelsey through Wade." Grey held his hands out in question. "Kelsey's an attractive woman. Isn't it possible his interest in her has nothing to do with you?"

"Except that it does." Trip crossed his arms, looked at his feet, and kicked the toe of his boot against the pavement. "I'm sure he likes her fine, but Mason's primary goal was to needle me. It's his favorite pastime."

"Maybe, maybe not. Interesting, though, that you reacted that way to a single date." Grey whistled for Shaman, who'd run far ahead again. Then he grinned and mocked Trip. "Of course, if you're in love with Kelsey, then maybe you couldn't help yourself."

Leave it to Grey to toss around the L-word over and over, as if every guy wanted hearts and flowers like he did.

"Can't I *care* about Kelsey without you labeling it love? We're friends, and I feel shitty that she's hurt because of the way I handled this whole situation."

"Friends don't normally have sex." Grey raised one brow. "A friend doesn't usually get so jealous he pummels a guy with his fists."

"I've had sex with plenty of friends." Trip scowled, needing to dismiss the innuendo in Grey's remarks. "And I wasn't jealous, I was angry. Don't make more of this than it is."

"Fine, don't talk to me. But before you go over there to see Kelsey, you better know why you're going. Don't compound the lousy decisions you've made to date. And, Trip? If you have to see her today, I suggest you go home and shower first."

Trip lifted his arm and sniffed. "Maybe you've got a point about the shower."

"Pathetic." Grey shook his head and tossed a doggy treat at Shaman. "Since you ignored my request about staying away from Kelsey, can you at least promise me there won't be any surprises involving Emma?"

Trip cracked his first grin of the day. "That's a promise I can keep."

The lilies in his hand were beginning to wilt. Trip peered through the windows of Kelsey's office. No lights, no signs of life—just like her condo. He pulled his phone out of his pocket. She still hadn't returned his texts, voice mails, or emails. After checking to make sure the sound wasn't muted, he returned it to his pocket and wiped his sweaty forehead.

The massive hangover and lack of sleep slowed his reflexes and stiffened his muscles. This hide-and-seek game wasn't helping his headache, either.

Grey had sworn Kelsey wasn't camped out at Avery's. Emma had practically chased him from her inn with a broom. The only place he hadn't yet tried was Maura's house. He sighed, closing his eyes.

Maura would probably be at least as angry as Emma, if not worse. But he had to face the music, and he had to see Kelsey before her hot anger cooled to hatred.

Trip lugged himself toward Maura's, slowing down as he rounded the corner and the familiar porch and picket fence came into view. Doubt niggled. Was he making a mistake? Maybe waiting until she returned from Mexico *would* be smarter.

As he drew nearer, he saw little Fee playing with Cowboy in the grass. Kelsey *was* here. The fact neither she nor Maura were on the porch watching over Fee surprised him.

He must've been frowning, because when Fee looked up, she asked, "Are you mad, too? Everyone's in a bad mood today."

Trip remained on the sidewalk side of the fence. "I'm not mad. But I am looking for your Aunt Kelsey. Is she here?"

Fee nodded. "She's eating all our ice cream. My mom keeps saying 'told you so' and then Aunt Kelsey just eats more scoops. So I sneaked out here to play."

The image Fee had painted made Trip smile despite knowing nothing about the situation was funny. "Ah, I was wondering why you were out here alone."

Fee approached the gate with Cowboy in hand, her baby-blues twinkling above a cheery grin. She pointed at the lilies. "Are those for me?"

"No, sweetheart. These are for your Aunt Kelsey."

"Are you going to marry her today?" Fee bounced on her toes. "That will make her happy."

"No, no." He had to smile at how strong the marriage-crazed gene ran through the Callihan family. And contrary to Fee's opinion, he doubted very much that Kelsey would accept any proposal from him today, let alone a marriage proposal. Not that he'd ever take that vow. "These are to say I'm sorry."

Fee scowled. "What'd you do?"

"Well, it's complicated. But I'd like to apologize." He knelt down and ruffled Fee's hair. "Would you run inside and ask her to come out here?"

Fee wrinkled her nose, appearing to consider the pros and cons of helping him. "Okay, but I'm taking Cowboy with me."

"Good idea." Trip stood up and watched Fee scamper up the porch stairs and into the house, carrying the kitten in both hands.

His stomach burned a little, so he started pacing in front of the gate while he waited for Kelsey. He noticed movement on the porch and turned to face her with a smile, only to be confronted by her angry sister instead.

Maura was a pretty woman, although not a bombshell like Kelsey. She looked a little wiped out, which made sense given the fact she was pregnant and caring for two small kids, and now an angry sister, too. Why was Kelsey in such a rush to be like her sister when her own life—free and financially independent—seemed like so much more fun?

Maura marched down the walkway with her arms crossed. "If you think a few flowers are going to make a difference, you're sadly mistaken."

"I take it Kelsey sent you to shoo me away." Trip aimed for a contrite yet jovial tone, hoping to loosen up Maura's scowl.

No dice.

"Yep." Maura stopped a few feet before the gate, which she did not open.

Trip straightened his hat and rubbed the back of his neck. "I get that everyone's upset, but I'd really like to speak with her. What are my chances of getting you to convince her to come out here?"

"Oh, um, about zero." Maura's face wore the same fierce expression he'd seen on Kelsey from time to time. "After last night, I'm not sure she's safe around you."

Trip briefly closed his eyes. "I've never started a fight in my life before last night. I was drunk and my brother has just pushed me one too many times, I guess. That aside, I promise I'm no threat to you or your sister, or anyone else, for that matter."

"Maybe not physically." She shook her head. "I warned her not to get tangled up in your stupid sex plan. I told her she'd end up hurt or worse. But no, she had it all figured out. Had *you* all figured out. Now she's humiliated and hurt thanks to you, your partner, and your idiot brother."

"And I feel awful about that." Really awful. Couldn't she see it? "It's why I'm here. I need to explain everything, so please get her to come talk to me."

"No. You might be able to smooth-talk all the other women in town, but I don't want you and your silver tongue within ten miles of my sister." Then Maura pointed her finger at him, like some old schoolmarm. "She's too good for you. You don't deserve her forgiveness, especially after creating a public spectacle that people will talk about for weeks."

Trip could take his lumps, but he was reaching his limit as to how much dressing-down he could endure in one day.

"This is silly, Maura. She can't avoid me forever. Please. I just want to apologize." When Maura hesitated, Trip started to open the gate. Maura grasped it, eyes flashing hot with disbelief.

"I said no. You're not welcome here."

Trip saw a curtain move in one of the upstairs windows. Kelsey was barely fifty feet away, watching him tap-dance with her sister on the sidewalk. Well, if either of these two women thought they were going to stop him from making sure Kelsey knew he didn't think of her as some kind of joke, *they* were the ones sadly mistaken.

"Do you want another public 'spectacle'? Because I'm about five seconds away from calling her name over and over until she talks to me. So will you help me or not?"

"Even you wouldn't be that big of an ass." Maura scoffed.

"Oh, Maura. You underestimate me." Trip winked and then put one hand at the side of his mouth and bellowed, "Kelsey Callihan! I'm not leaving until you talk to me."

"Ohmigod, you've got no shame. Shush!" Maura whipped her head left and right to see if any of the neighbors had taken an interest in the scene at her house. She opened the gate and waved Trip into the yard. "Wait here on the porch. I'll see if she'll speak with you, but you have to promise you'll leave as soon as you finish whatever you have to say."

Trip noticed Fee's face pressed against the storm door, smiling. Apparently she appreciated his dramatic flair. He knew he liked that kid.

Finally Kelsey appeared behind Fee, kissed the top of her little blond head, and then came through the door, staying within arm's reach of the knob. "Once again, you win. So make it fast, because I have nothing to say."

Trip extended the bouquet toward her. He watched her brow furrow with concern when she noticed his bruised knuckles, but she quickly wiped her expression clean and tossed the flowers on the porch swing.

"Princess—"

"Oh, so you're back to princess, now? Guess Boomerang got *boring*." She looked away, nose tipped upward.

He deserved that, but he didn't like it. "Kelsey, please stop. Just look at me for two minutes."

To his surprise, she snapped her gaze to meet his, her tawny eyes looking as gray as the thickest ice on any cornice he'd ever skied.

It seemed the most natural thing in the world to reach out to touch her, yet unlike every other time, today she recoiled. He sighed. "I can't tell you how sorry I am that you got caught in the middle between my brother and me. I should've done a better job of protecting you. Should've warned you as soon as I knew he was in town. I thought I had it under control."

"Yes, by making sure your entire family thought of me as some kind of joke, or bimbo, or both. Thanks for that awesome protection."

She'd almost managed the entire sentence without her voice cracking, but he heard it waver, which made him want to gather her up in his arms and whisper something soothing in her ear. Only her serious back-off vibes kept him from trying.

"Deb caught me off guard with her questions. I wasn't thinking straight with everything happening at the hospital. I'm really sorry, except at least now you know to stay away from Mason so he can't hurt you again."

Kelsey laughed in his face. "*Mason* can't hurt me? That's rich!"

"What's with the sarcasm?"

"*He* didn't hurt me, Trip. You did. All Mason did was ask me out after learning you didn't care about me. You, on the other hand, have been using me for weeks while joking about me behind my back."

"Is that what he's trying to make you believe?" Chaotic thoughts and a touch of panic danced through his mind wearing sharp heels. "Kelsey, please stay away from Mason. He's not a good person. He's not trustworthy."

"Unlike you?"

"Damn right, unlike me." Trip edged closer to her, determined to bust through the invisible wall she'd constructed, and tipped her chin up with his forefingers. He stared directly into her eyes while unfamiliar feelings and awkward words forced their way out of his mouth. "Look at me. I'm sick about the fact that you got hurt last night. I hate that what happened made you think for one second that I don't care about you. Nothing is further from the truth." He stroked her jaw with his thumb, like he was calming a skittish horse. "I care very much about you and how you feel. If you'd just take a deep breath and remember everything we've done and said to each other these past several weeks, you'll believe me."

And then, because he was only inches from her mouth and couldn't help himself, he kissed her. Instead of kissing him back like always, she pushed away from him and wiped her mouth with the back of her hand, which wrung out a little corner of his heart. "Don't kiss me again. I told you already—whatever this was, it's over. So is this conversation."

"Hang on." He rubbed his temple as he glanced around, groping for the right words. "Can't we just rewind a week or two and start over? Especially now that you know Mason's not going to be your future husband."

"Oh, really? How do I know that? Because you say so? Because you've got some conspiracy theory drummed up instead of considering that maybe he actually likes me for who I am? That maybe, unlike you, he sees me as more than a friend with benefits?"

Whether it was her screwed-up thoughts, the bright sun, or the remnants of alcohol still swimming in his veins that had his body flashing hot and cold, he couldn't quite say. He wiped his forehead with his shirtsleeve and tried to slow his heart rate.

"I sure hope you're saying all this just to get my goat, because if you're actually considering going out with my brother after the things I've told you about him—past and present—well, I'm just . . . I'm . . ." When he couldn't think of something better to say, he finished with, "That's just not going to happen, I can promise you that much."

Instead of getting mad like he expected, Kelsey waved dismissively. "Pffft. Then I'm not too worried, because your promises don't mean much, do they, cowboy?"

"What the hell does that mean? I keep all my promises."

"No, you don't." She held up her fingers and started ticking them off, one by one. "You promised to keep our fling a secret, but you sure screwed that up last night with the public boxing match. You promised to help me make a relationship work, but you're doing everything you can to mess that up, too. You promised to be a good friend, but you've been intent on messing with my business and now you're threatening me."

"I haven't threatened you, despite the fact you seem determined to push me against a wall." He stepped closer, leaned in, and spoke slowly and firmly. "I know right now you think I'm full of shit, but weeks ago I told you about how Mason treats me. You believed me that night, so believe me now. He's not the man for you. You need to steer clear of him."

"Or what?" She stuck out her little chin.

"Or else!" He thrust his arms wide open.

"I see we've reached the really grown-up part of the conversation. Are you going to start beating *me* up now?"

"Dammit, Kelsey, why won't you accept my apology and agree to stay away from Mason?" Then a horrible thought burned a hole in his gut. He withdrew from her and narrowed his gaze, wooziness and nausea mixing together. "Do you actually like him?"

Kelsey averted her gaze for a moment, refusing to answer. Holy shit, could she actually prefer Mason to him? His chest burned as if he were running stairs at thirteen thousand feet.

When she finally spoke, she cocked her head and stared at him like a hunter with a deer in her sights. "Why do you care who I'm with anyway?"

"What?" Another wave of heat radiated through his body.

"You heard me, why do you care who I date?"

"Because . . ."

She waited, tapping her toe. He frowned, unable to offer an answer. Did he care who she dated, or did it only matter because it was Mason? Well, hell, he couldn't answer if he didn't know. What he did know was that he'd never accept her and Mason as a couple.

How could she even consider being with his brother, anyway? It was gross. And how had he lost control of this entire situation? Trip wasn't used to losing control, especially not to a woman.

"Promise me, princess, no Mason."

"You know what? When you're ready to be honest with me, then maybe we can talk. Until then, stay out of my way." She spun on her heel and slammed the storm door closed in his face.

Trip stood on the porch, staring at the closed door. *That went well.*

A breeze rustled some nearby leaves, while others fell and drifted to the ground. He turned and picked up the discarded flowers, then set them by the front door and walked down the steps.

When he glanced back over his shoulder, he noticed Fee standing on the porch with his flowers. She waved before running back inside.

Trip sighed and started walking toward Backtrax. His head throbbed with thoughts about Mason, the clients he'd let down, the damage control he needed to do with his image, and Kelsey.

Today had been the first time she hadn't succumbed to him at all, which he didn't like one bit. What he liked less was realizing how deeply she'd been hurt by his carelessness.

Maybe Maura had a point about his stupid proposition. Now both he and Kelsey felt like hell, and he had no idea how to fix it for either of them.

About a block before he got home, his phone rang, sparking a little hope. Maybe she'd reconsidered her harsh position.

He snatched the phone from his pocket and glanced at the screen, at which point hope turned to dread. "Hey, Dad. How are you?"

Chapter Twelve

An ocean breeze rustled the lush greenery surrounding the terrace, wafting the tropical flowers' perfume into the warm, salty air.

"Waking up to this view is amazing, Kelsey. Thanks a million for this trip. Yesterday was so much fun." Emma spun around on the terrace of the three-bedroom villa, with the Sea of Cortez crashing against the rocky promontories behind her in the distance. "I wish you felt better, though."

Kelsey gulped some bottled water, having just thrown up ten minutes earlier. "I must've eaten the wrong food last night. Or maybe had one too many margaritas."

"We did knock back a lot of margaritas last night, but you were queasy yesterday morning, too," Avery reminded her. "And we didn't have anything but chips and guac—and margaritas—the night we arrived."

Emma sat on the edge of Kelsey's cushioned outdoor chaise. "That's true. I ate everything you did yesterday and I feel great."

"I'll be fine with a little more water and some sun." Kelsey chugged the rest of the water and stood up. "Let's hit the pool before our spa appointments."

"Sounds good to me." Avery led them through the sliders and back inside the grand villa, with its stucco walls, oversize furnishings, and Mexican pottery. She grabbed the stack of plush beach towels provided by the hotel. "All set."

Although eager to return to the tiered, infinity-edge pool overlooking the sea, another wave of nausea roiled in Kelsey's stomach. "Hang on a second. I need to find my sunglasses."

As Emma and Avery began gathering their beach bags and books, Kelsey trotted to her bathroom and fell to her knees in front of the toilet. She didn't know which was worse, throwing up or suffering nausea without the relief of throwing up.

After a minute, she gave up and went to the vanity to grab sunscreen and sunglasses. As she fished through the drawer where she'd stashed all her toiletries, she came across her unopened box of tampons. Technically, she should've finished her period before this trip, but it still hadn't started.

Her stomach gurgled again and, wide-eyed, she glanced at the toilet as if in slow motion.

Oh. No. Way.

No *way*!

The unopened blue box taunted her from inside the drawer. She wiped the thin line of perspiration from her forehead and retrieved the box. Grabbing her stomach in awe and wonder, her mind fought against the most reasonable explanation for her nausea and those unused tampons.

She and Trip had been careful—except when they hadn't been. There had been that one spontaneous night when he'd come unprepared and then stayed until dawn. Twice they'd had sex without protection. But he'd been careful to pull out at the crucial moments. So how did this happen, if, in fact, this had happened?

Dazedly, she wandered into the bedroom and collapsed on the edge of her unmade bed, all the while staring at the tampon box.

Could she even get a pregnancy test down here? Maybe she should she wait until she got home. Yeah, right. Like she could wait another forty-eight hours to find out if she was pregnant. An involuntary shiver passed through her body.

Oh, God. She might be pregnant. A mother-to-be.

A dream come true, except not like this. Not before marriage. Not by a man who didn't love her.

"Kelsey, is everything okay?" Avery called out from the living room.

Tears sprang to Kelsey's eyes. How could she have let this happen? How would she tell her friends? And why on earth was some part of her thrilled by the idea even though she knew Trip would rather kiss his brother's ass than become a father?

A light rap at the door startled her just before Emma popped her head in. "Let's go!" Emma's smile faded the instant she saw Kelsey. Her forehead creased and she rushed across the room. "What's wrong, Kels?"

Words wouldn't come out, so Kelsey held up the unopened box of tampons and wiped her eyes.

Emma studied the box and turned her confused expression on Kelsey. "I don't get it. Why are you crying about a box of tampons?"

Avery wandered into the room at that point, eyeing them and listening.

"A box of *unopened* tampons," Kelsey corrected, mumbling through her tears.

Emma remained perplexed, but Avery gasped. "Oh, no."

Kelsey nodded, sniffling. "I might be pregnant."

"Oh!" Emma dropped the box and covered her mouth with both hands.

"That damn idiot!" Avery barked. "First the big fight in town and now this?"

Kelsey held up her hand. "Stop, Ave. It takes two. Trip didn't force me into anything I didn't want to do."

"You and Trip are having a baby?" Emma started pacing in small circles, muttering, "A baby."

Avery walked over to sit beside Kelsey. She hesitated, then brushed Kelsey's hair off her shoulder. "We don't know anything for sure, yet." She placed one hand on Kelsey's thigh and gave a reassuring squeeze. "You've been under a lot of stress, which could delay your period. And you wouldn't be the first person to get queasy in Mexico."

Kelsey nodded, unsure which option she hoped was true. "You're right. It could be both of those things."

"Do you want to get a pregnancy test, or would you rather wait until you get back home?" Emma asked once she'd stopped pacing.

"I don't think I can wait," Kelsey admitted.

"Good, because I don't think I can, either." Avery sighed before springing up off the bed. "You two wait here. I'll see if they sell home pregnancy tests in the boutique. If not, I'll grab a cab to a local pharmacy and see what I can find."

"We should probably cancel our reservations at the tequila tasting tonight, too," Emma said to no one in particular, her gaze bouncing all around the room as if she might hit upon some magic solution if she looked hard enough.

Kelsey began crying again. "I'm sorry I'm ruining this trip for you guys."

"Don't be silly." Emma sat down and hugged her. Her gentle voice, full of sincerity and concern, made Kelsey cry harder. "We wouldn't even be here if it weren't for you. And anyway, is this really such terrible news? You've always wanted to be a mother. If you are pregnant, we will look at the bright side and celebrate together."

"Thanks, Em." Kelsey wiped her eyes and squeezed Emma. "You always want everyone to be happy."

Of course, Avery wasn't talking sunshine and rainbows. She smoothed her ponytail and then set her hands on her hips. "First things first. Let's get the facts. Then we'll celebrate, one way or the other, I guess. Though the idea of Trip being your baby daddy doesn't exactly make me want to throw a party."

Avery had always been a bit wary of Trip, worried about his influence over Grey. Not shocking, considering Trip hadn't been exactly supportive of how Grey had let his feelings for Avery influence certain business and financial decisions this past year.

But while Trip may have projected a certain carefree attitude about life and women, Kelsey knew there was more to him.

She'd spent the past two days thinking about the way he'd wanted to kick the ass of whoever made her cry, how he'd bought her Cowboy and the beautiful hair combs, and all the nice things he'd said to her during the past several weeks. Now she twisted the ends of her hair in her finger and stared at the ground, speaking softly. "He's not so bad. There's more to him than what he shows most of the world."

"I thought you hated him after the whole Mason debacle?" Avery cocked her head.

"I was embarrassed and confused and angry." Kelsey looked from Avery to Emma, who continued to offer an understanding smile. "But he hunted me down to apologize the next day. He told me he cares about me . . . a lot."

"So you're going to forgive him, just like that?" Avery's mouth hung open in dismay.

"I think he beat up his brother because he thought Mason would hurt me. And I think those accusations Mason made about what Trip told his parents were taken out of context to make it all sound worse than Trip meant them. I guess, yes, I believe Trip's explanation." Kelsey looked from Avery to Emma and back again. "And if I'm pregnant, he and I are going to have to talk. At the very least, we need to be friends."

"Oh, no. I see you spinning dangerous fantasies, Kelsey." Avery shook her head in frustration. "You think he's going to embrace this news and marry you now?"

Embrace it? Hardly. At first he'd probably freak out. Worse, he might even blame her, or accuse her of trapping him. The dark thoughts caused a shudder to travel down her spine.

No. He'd always been fair and up-front. For whatever reason, she had faith in him to be reasonable.

With that thought, she met Avery's skeptical gaze. "I know you think I'm always a fool when it comes to men, but Trip gets me and likes me anyway. I believe I matter to him, even if I know he'd hesitate to make a major commitment."

"Hesitate?" Avery crossed her arms. "That's a nice euphemism."

"Like Grey's so perfect, Avery?" Kelsey shot a cool stare at her friend, then noticed Emma wince. "It's true, Em. Grey was the one who coined that ugly nickname."

"I know." Avery blushed. "I'm sorry. That was awful. Grey has a terrible habit of giving nicknames without thinking about it."

Kelsey waved her hand in the air. "*Boomerang* is the least of my worries right now. Let's just find a test so I can know, one way or the other, if I'm having a baby."

◆ ◆ ◆

"Mason, you're not pressing charges against your brother." Ross Cutler's tone brooked no defiance as he sat at the dining table between his two sons. "I don't want to hear another word about it."

For the most part, Trip had been keeping his eyes downcast, which was just as well. He seethed while sitting in the condo Kelsey had picked for Mason, staring at the pricey furniture and high-end kitchen. The condo she might have figured she'd be spending more time in with Mason, which was at least five times nicer than the dumpy apartment Trip and Grey currently shared out of necessity.

"He broke my nose, Dad," Mason complained. "Why should he get away with it?"

"Because you provoked him by going after Kelsey."

Mason sat back in his chair and crossed his arms like a petulant kid. "He said he didn't care about her."

"Mason, I'm not stupid. It's more than a coincidence you ended up on a date with that poor girl. Aren't you ashamed of using her as a pawn just to needle Gunner?" Their dad shook his head. "Honestly, I can't believe you two. It's like you're trying to give me another heart attack."

At least this time, with Kelsey nowhere in sight, Mason didn't deny the real motive for that "date."

Then his Dad turned his ire on him. "Gunner, at the very least you owe Mason, Deb, and me an apology. You're lucky those cops pulled you off your brother before something worse happened."

Trip tensed his fists. Heat raced to his face. He couldn't deny the truth. He'd been like a wild animal that night.

"I know, Dad." He looked across the table at Mason. "I'm sorry I roughed you up. I was pretty shitfaced when I ran into you and Kelsey. I snapped. I just snapped."

"Mason," their dad interrupted. "When you were younger, I was battling a lot of guilt over what I'd done, so I empathized with your struggle to accept the changes in our family, to accept your brother. But why the hell haven't you outgrown it? This taunting and bullshit has got to stop." Then he looked at Trip. "And isn't it time *you* started making some effort to be part of this family?"

Trip abruptly pushed back from the table and walked into the living room, running his hands through his hair. This conversation had been put off too long, but he hated having it in front of Mason.

"Where are you going?" his dad asked.

Trip inhaled slowly, his throat tightening in anticipation of offending his father, his eyes stinging like a sissy, making him feel like that ten-year-old boy again.

"Look, I'm sorry I beat him up, but I won't lie. It was a long time coming. And unlike you, I don't have empathy for poor little Mason's imperfect family." He gripped the back of a random chair in the living room, squeezing it until his knuckles turned white. His gaze shifted from Mason's smug expression to his father's flabbergasted one. "You all talk about how *you* were affected back then. *My* mother died. I got yanked away from my friends and grandfather and then plopped into a house with two people who resented me, and a father who considered me an obligation." Despite hearing his voice crack, he forced himself to continue, although now he averted his gaze. "I did everything I could to fit in, then to be invisible, and then when I finally walked away, you all gave me shit about that, too." A sense of defeat made his legs feel heavy as he walked back to the table. "Dad, if you hadn't sent Mason here in some attempt to force a family bond that's never going to exist, none of this would've happened."

"So this is my fault?" His dad scoffed.

"I don't mean it like that, but why can't you just accept that this," Trip circled his hand among the three men, "isn't meant to be?"

"Because it *is* meant to be. Like it or not, you're my son, and you two are brothers. Maybe you weren't planned, but there's a reason you're *my* son." His dad stood and looked at Mason. "I need a few minutes alone with your brother. Can you go in your bedroom or take a walk?"

"Even when he's a jerk, you treat him with kid gloves." Mason slammed his fist on the table before shoving away and rising from his chair. "What the hell, Dad? This is my house."

"Mason, sometimes you're as obstinate as your mother." Then their dad turned to Trip. "Take a walk out on the deck with me."

Once they were sitting outside with the slider closed, his father spoke with a steady, clear voice. "You and I need to finally clear the air. I don't mean to speak ill of the dead, but I can't help it if your mother chose to keep me out of your life until she got sick. If I had known she was pregnant, maybe things would have been different for all of us. So instead of only blaming me or Mason or Deb for this chronic distance between us, maybe you could remember that your mom had a hand in how this all turned out, too."

Trip's blood ignited; his chest tightened. He locked his hands behind his head and closed his elbows together while he counted to ten. The last thing he wanted was to cause his father to have another heart attack, but his thoughts were boiling.

Rather than trigger another disaster, he slowly blew out his breath. "Tread lightly, Dad. My mother chose to be a single mom rather than disrupt your family."

"She made a tough choice, and maybe you see it as unselfish. But no matter what you say, she kept my son from me for almost ten years. She robbed me of time I'll never get back, and that decision has affected our entire relationship."

A September breeze sent a shiver down Trip's spine. He looked across the rooftops in town, toward the San Juan mountains. Memories of his mother rushed forward and lodged themselves in his throat. Maybe his dad had a point, but Trip wasn't ready to admit his mother's decisions had negative consequences.

"My mom was loving and warm and worked her ass off to raise me, so I'm not going to sit here and let you badmouth her when she's not even here to defend herself." Trip leaned forward and looked his dad in the eye, remembering all the things he'd overheard while living under Deb's roof. "When I first moved in, I thought maybe you were happy to have me there. Maybe you started to love me. But then I heard you tell Mason that I wasn't wanted like him, and that you took me in because you couldn't be a man who didn't take care of his mistakes."

"I never said that!" His father's adamant expression and tone caught Trip by surprise.

"Yes, you did. It was after my eighth grade football championship game. I'd snuck back down to the kitchen for a snack late at night and you were consoling Mason because he was whining about me again."

"Then you misheard or misunderstood what I said, Gunner." His dad leaned forward and reached across the table to lay his hand on Trip's forearm.

Trip sat back, hands rubbing his thighs, eyes downcast, emotional exhaustion making his body ten times heavier. "I don't blame you, you know. You didn't plan for me. You never loved my mom or wanted a kid with her. And still you took me in, gave me every opportunity, and we had fun together when it was just the two of us." He met his father's gaze. "I respect and love you for all of it, 'cause I know it wasn't easy. But let's just be honest and admit that we'll never be father and son the way you and Mason are, and Mason and I will never see eye to eye."

His dad seized his hand and squeezed it tight, his voice determined. "You're right about *one* thing, it wasn't easy. I was ashamed to face my wife, to face Mason after setting such a bad example. But your conclusions are all wrong. My shame had nothing to do with *you*. It didn't detract from the thrill of meeting you. You think I don't look at you and love seeing the things we have in common? You think I'm not proud when I talk about you to my friends? I've done and said everything I could think of to let you know that you are as much my son as Mason is. I love both my boys, even if you are as different as night and day."

Trip's nose tingled and his eyes burned. His skin itched and he wanted to run far and fast, away from this conversation, away from his brother, and away from his past. His dad released his hand and raked his own through his hair.

"Gunner, what's the deal with this girl? Do you care about her, or do you just want to keep her from Mason?" He raised one brow. "I hear you've got the sellers of some land asking for all kinds of studies from Wade, which Mason said could screw up the deal Kelsey's been putting together. And you were pretty convincing when you told me you weren't interested in her."

"Kelsey knows my position on that deal. We don't see eye to eye, but it's not personal. When I told you about Kelsey, I didn't think I was interested, but then I got to know her better." Trip shifted in his seat and looked across the street, shrugging. "I'm not looking for a lifetime commitment with anyone, but she matters to me."

"No lifetime commitments with anyone, eh? I've never thought of you as a coward, son."

"I'm not a coward!" Trip scowled. "You think I don't see how much I'm like you? I don't want to make promises I'm not sure I can keep. One woman for the rest of my life sounds like an impossible vow, so I'd rather steer clear so no one gets hurt."

"Huh. And how's that working so far? Is Kelsey hurt? Mason? You?" His dad stood up and gripped the railing of the deck. "I've already admitted I'm not proud of how I betrayed Deb, but I can't say I regret it, either, 'cause I got you. People are human, Gunner. We make mistakes. The best you can do is own them, try to make up for them, and try not to repeat them. But if you live your whole life trying to avoid them, you'll never be happy."

Trip scrubbed his face with both hands, emotionally wrung out. "Maybe."

"No maybes about it." Then his dad started walking to the slider. "I think I've said all I can to you for one day. Let's go inside and see if I can't find some way to get Mason to back off these assault charges."

Trip stood and began to follow his dad inside when his phone beeped. "I'll be in in a sec."

Once his dad disappeared inside, Trip looked at his phone and his heart sped up.

```
I'll be home tomorrow. Have something
important to discuss. Can you come over
at 5?
```

Trip stared at the cryptic message, his heart in his throat. He typed:

```
C U @ 5.
```

After hitting Send, he sighed, knowing he'd spend the next twenty-four hours eagerly awaiting the chance to see Kelsey again, while wondering what she wanted to discuss.

Chapter Thirteen

Trip approached Kelsey's building, his breath foggy in the dusky evening air. El Niño had the weathermen predicting the first snow could fall any day. Yet before he could start getting excited about long days skiing knee-deep in powder, he needed to set things right with Kelsey.

He had no idea what to expect this evening, but he had hopes. First and foremost: forgiveness. He'd be stuck in a mental prison until she pardoned his bad behavior. Secondly, he hoped she had no interest in Mason. A shiver danced down his spine at the thought of how he'd deal with the opposite scenario. Third, he wanted a chance to pick up where they'd left off. That would be trickiest of all, and probably the least likely. But he'd never shied away from anything he'd wanted in his life, and he sure wouldn't start tonight.

Gripping the bottle of Brunello di Montalcino in his left hand, he drew a deep breath before pressing her door buzzer. He'd bungled his apology last week, so this time he'd brought her something he knew she'd love, unlike the lilies she'd tossed aside.

"Trip?" Her even tone rang through the intercom, offering no hint of her mood.

He slid a finger back and forth inside his collar and then cleared his dry throat. "The one and only."

"Come on up."

He grasped the knob before the latch clicked open, his muscles twitching with nervous anticipation. Trotting up the stairs to her unit, Trip smoothed his hair before rapping on the door.

"Hey," she said, waving him inside while Cowboy squirmed in her other hand.

Upon first sight of her, his body hummed like an engine forced to idle. Any other day, he would've lifted her off her feet and kissed her. Today he resisted the pull, knowing they needed to settle things first.

Her gaze flitted around the room, apparently uncomfortable making eye contact. His stomach knotted a bit, knowing her uneasiness wasn't the best sign. Then he noticed something about her looked different—a lot of things, actually. No makeup, loose-fitted loungewear, knitted slippers, and paleness that didn't make sense for someone who just spent four days on the coast of Mexico.

Rather than risk offending her by remarking on her uncharacteristic appearance, he presented the wine. "A peace offering."

"Oh." Her brows pinched together before she set her kitten down. "Thanks." She hesitated before taking the bottle—not exactly the enthusiastic response he'd wanted. "Nice Brunello. For a guy who doesn't know wine, you picked a good one."

Her uncertain grin merely emphasized the tension between them. Like two positive magnet poles being forced together, the tangible energy between their bodies seemed determined to keep them apart.

"Want me to open it?" He started walking toward the kitchen to look for wineglasses. Maybe acting like things were normal would make them so.

While he stood glancing at her cabinets, trying to recall where she kept her glasses, she set the bottle on the counter. Her gaze wandered as she tapped her fingernails against the granite. "Not now."

What? He tilted his head, resting his hands on his hips. "Since when do you turn down wine after five?"

"Well . . ." She tossed a hank of hair behind her shoulder. With her head slightly bowed, she looked up at Trip through pale brown lashes. "This isn't really a social call."

Her subdued behavior threw him, as did her stillness and the lack of the soft music he'd grown accustomed to in her home. A quick survey of the living area revealed a pair of shoes kicked off in the corner, two small paper bags set on the dining table beside a pile of unread mail, and a sweater haphazardly draped over the back of a chair.

She and her apartment both looked as if she'd just given up on caring about anything. Even with his monster ego, he had a hard time believing his and Mason's recent behavior had completely killed her spirit. Time to stop dancing around the subject.

Trip tucked his hands in his jeans pockets. "Kelsey, I know I hurt you. I can't go back and do things differently, but I'll keep apologizing until I convince you how sorry I am."

Kelsey waved him off, a wan smile tugging at the corners of her mouth. "I know you're sorry, Trip."

For the first time in ten days, his lungs didn't feel compressed. If anything, he might've sworn they'd filled with helium and his toes were leaving the ground. "You do?"

She nodded, then added, "I don't like what you did, or agree with how you handled things, but I believe you meant well."

Despite the admonishment, he couldn't help but smile. Stepping closer, he reached out to playfully tug on the ends of her hair. "So have you forgiven me?"

She hesitated again, her expression unreadable, then gestured toward the sofa. "Maybe we should sit."

His momentary weightlessness died, feet now firmly on the ground. Something was still wrong. Really wrong.

He scanned her face, once again noting its pasty hue and anxious expression. Her averted gaze, the nibbling of her lip, the way she kept wringing her hands—all of it caused flashbacks to the day his mother first told him she had cancer.

Trip's stomach churned. He gently placed his fingers under her chin and tipped up her head so he could study her eyes. "You're worrying me, princess. Are you sick or something?"

Through a nervous chuckle, she said, "Or something."

He released her and rubbed the back of his neck. His radar detected a major problem, but for the life of him, he remained clueless. "How 'bout we deal with stuff head-on? Whatever you're fretting about, just spit it out. I bet it won't be as bad as you think."

"Don't make that bet, cowboy." Her heavy sigh hung in the air.

"I'm here like you asked, so if this isn't about Mason, and you're not sick, then what? Is this about Wade's proposed development? 'Cause as far as I know they haven't finished the impact study yet."

Kelsey's widened eyes made her look as if she'd completely forgotten about the deal, then a quirk of her brow seemed to dismiss the whole matter as if it were inconsequential. "It's got nothing to do with that."

"Kels, I'd rather not play twenty questions." Trip narrowed his eyes and engaged in a game of chicken, which he won the second she averted her gaze.

"Sorry. You're right." She tipped up her chin and stared directly in his eyes, revealing the first spark of *his* princess he'd seen since he'd arrived. "There isn't an easy way to say this, so here goes: I'm pregnant."

He blinked. His facial muscles—hell, every muscle in his body—froze. Pregnant?

He blinked again. Pregnant!

Breathe. Keep breathing.

Suddenly her silent apartment came alive with sounds, like the ticking of the mantel clock in the living room, and the playful thud of Cowboy's tiny paws against the wood floor as he pranced around Kelsey's feet.

Had the lights flickered? The room didn't spin so much as the fine details of the lamps and curtains and artwork blurred together. Having retreated so far inside his own head, he couldn't distinguish Kelsey's words, which buzzed in his ears like an active beehive.

A baby. His baby.

His baby.

How the hell could he be anybody's father? And how the hell had this even happened? Every hair on his body stood on end as if he'd been struck by static electricity after shuffling across a carpet while wearing socks.

"Trip, are you okay?" Kelsey touched his arm.

He inadvertently flinched. A chaotic whirl of memories spun through his mind as he tried to answer his own questions until one broke free and struck him like a baseball bat to the head. He stood and without forethought uttered, "The broken condom."

Kelsey straightened her spine, her voice distant and questioning. "What broken condom?"

"That first night." Trip bent at the waist, gripped his knees, and sucked in some air. He then glanced up at her stunned expression. "I'd figured I ripped it while removing it, but maybe it happened earlier."

"Why didn't you tell me?" Kelsey's brows drooped. She looked more hurt than angry.

"I don't know." Adrenaline pulsed through his veins, spreading tingling sensations throughout his limbs. He began pacing in a tight circle, shaking his hands out as if they were wet. "I got distracted because you were so busy kicking me out." Immediately he regretted his snappy tone and halted for a second. "Sorry, I'm not . . . I'm . . . just ignore me."

He didn't want to make a distressing situation worse by saying the wrong thing, so he continued pacing in an effort to collect his scattered thoughts. When he finally managed to look her in the eyes, he noticed her shoulders were slumped.

"Based on the timing, it's more likely that night we rolled the dice without condoms," she reminded him, her soft voice dripping with guilt.

Trip closed his eyes.

He'd never before taken that risk, yet that night he'd let overwhelming desire defeat good sense. Not just desire. Need. He'd needed her comfort and kindness. Was that how things had unfolded between his own parents?

Did it matter? As he'd always feared, he was his father's son.

"I can't believe I've made the same mistake as my dad." He shook his head at no one in particular. "Exactly what I've always wanted to avoid."

"Mistake." Her deadened tone alerted him that he'd stuck his big black boot in his mouth.

Sighing, he gave in to a moment of self-pity. "You know my history."

Kelsey's nostrils flared. "I don't *ever* want this baby to feel like a mistake."

"You think I do? I've spent twenty-plus years trying to outrun those very feelings myself. I wouldn't wish it on anyone, least of all my own child." He scrubbed a hand over his face. "My own child. Three words I never imagined saying." *Was this really happening?* "You're sure about this? Did a doctor confirm it?"

"I have an appointment tomorrow afternoon, but two home pregnancy tests came back positive." She smoothed her hair again while small red patches bloomed on her cheeks. "Look, Trip, this isn't how I envisioned starting my family—unmarried and pregnant! But I won't pretend I'm not glad *one* of my dreams is coming true. Still, I know this is your worst nightmare, so I don't expect anything from you. I just thought I owed you the truth."

Her words stung like the snap of a wet towel against bare skin. Insulted, he bugged his eyes. "You think I'd ignore my child? That I'd let him hurt like I did? Not gonna happen as long as I'm walking this earth."

He blew out a breath and looked around Kelsey's perfectly decorated condo—a nice home for a child, unlike his apartment. Her soft, caring heart much more suited to parenting than his flawed one.

Hell. Before she'd gone to Mexico he'd botched his apology, and now he was making a hash out of this situation, too. "You must be sorry this kid is stuck with me as a dad, aren't you?"

Kelsey sniffled, her eyes filling with tears, her chin trembling.

"Trust me, I'm no mother of the year. I've been drinking wine all month and just guzzled margaritas in Cabo before figuring out why I felt so sick." Behind the wall of hair partially hiding her face, Trip saw tears trailing down her cheek. "I've probably already caused some kind of brain damage or something."

Instinctively, he stepped forward and wrapped her in a bear hug. "You haven't damaged anything, princess. And no baby could ask for a better mother. You're warm and sweet, yet tough and sassy. You'll be a great mom. Everything will be fine."

He held her, his cheek resting on top of her head, and stroked her back. His entire sense of world order was crumbling around him, yet, in that moment, all he thought about was how he'd missed the curves of her body, the scent of her hair, her playful banter. He'd missed her. Now she nestled against his chest, calming his throbbing nerves, so he held on and just breathed in and out.

If he had known, when he first propositioned her, where things would lead, would he have gone for it? Probably not. He'd always resisted the idea of being tied down and making commitments. Funny how, right now, holding on to Kelsey was the only thing keeping him from losing his mind. He wanted her, and not just for sex.

"I'm so nervous." Kelsey sniffled, wiping her tears against his shirt before snuggling tighter into his arms, seeking security, solace, or God knows what else. "Thinking about this baby and the future is scarier than I'd ever expected. So much to plan. So much to do. I don't even know how to get started."

He kissed the top of her head, glad she seemed content to stay locked in his embrace. Yesterday he'd survived opening up to his father, so perhaps he could also open up to Kelsey.

He groped for words, unable to articulate his thoughts and emotions, mostly because he hadn't quite gotten ahold of them. Yet he knew that his child needed two parents, and that, while marriage wasn't something he might ever want, he needed more from Kelsey than the occasional night together. "Maybe we start like this."

"Like what?" She eased out of his arms and wiped her final tear away.

He swallowed hard, fighting to force words through his dry mouth. "Together."

Kelsey pressed her lips together and gazed at him. Once again, it seemed as if time stood still in the confines of her apartment. He could hear her breathing, see the cogs in her mind trying to work out his meaning.

Her round eyes looked skeptical. "Together how?"

"I know you never wanted people to know about us, but there's no hiding from this now. So maybe we should try dating . . . like . . . you know, for real."

She appeared vaguely disappointed by his response. "I'm pregnant. I'm going to be hormonal and nesting and getting fat. Why would you want to start a relationship with me now, when you've never wanted to date anyone—ever?"

"You mean, aside from the fact that we're having a baby?" He crossed his arms in front of his chest, discouraged by her question. Why did the girl who'd been longing for a relationship show so little enthusiasm for his suggestion? "Not long ago, we were good together. If we're both being totally honest, our little no-strings bargain developed into something deeper, even if we didn't admit it to each other because of doubts or egos."

"Considerable ego on your part," she teased.

"To match my considerable charm." He winked, taking her little joke as a positive sign. "Come on. I already told you, I haven't been with anyone since we got together. Let's see if we can make this work. Don't we owe it to junior to at least try?"

"So you're doing this for the baby," she said, more like a statement than a question. Lowering her gaze, she smoothed one hand over her stomach.

"Not just for the baby." He raised her hand to his lips and kissed it, then covered it with his other hand. "I know you wanted the whole ball of wax in the right order—husband, house, kids—but that's not how life played out. Forget about your fairy tales. Let's take things at our own pace, one day at a time. What have you got to lose?"

"Not the most romantic plea." She cocked one brow and twisted her lips. He wished he could make the grand declarations she dreamed of, but he couldn't be someone he wasn't, or make promises he couldn't keep.

"But it's honest." He rested his hands on her waist, happy she let him touch her without pushing him away. Her nearness kept him grounded, enabled him to block out the panic blooming in the back of his mind. Like any other time he'd hurled his body off a cliff, he knew the only way to land safely was to own the move. "I really like you, Kels, which is more than I can say about any other woman I've been involved with in the past several years. I know I'm no Prince Charming, despite Fee's opinion. I can't promise I'll be romantic or live up to your expectations or even be a great boyfriend. But I can promise I'll always be honest, respectful, and will never abandon this child."

He held his breath, waiting for her answer. After several agonizing seconds, she draped her arms over his shoulders, a dash of color returning to her cheeks. "Okay, cowboy. But you still haven't earned back your hat."

"Hmph." He brushed his knuckles over her cheek and kissed her forehead. "So tell me, how did your family take the news? Should I be watching over my shoulder for your sister to come at me with a pitchfork?"

"I haven't told them yet." She crinkled her nose and eased out of his arms. "I wanted to talk to you first so you didn't hear it from anyone else."

"Something tells me you were grateful for the excuse to procrastinate."

Kelsey went to the sink to fill a glass of water. "My parents won't be proud of me for getting pregnant before being married."

He didn't miss the fact she'd mentioned marriage twice in this conversation. "Maybe you should wait a few weeks and see what happens. Lots of people don't tell until later in case something goes wrong."

Kelsey shook her head. "Avery and Emma were with me when I put everything together. I can't have them know and not tell my own sister or parents. Besides, my family doesn't keep secrets from each other. Everyone is in everyone's business, and we like it that way. Makes us feel loved and cared about."

Trip couldn't relate to that feeling at all. He momentarily wondered how his father would react to the irony of Trip's new reality. Then he thought of his arrest. Kelsey's family probably wished her well rid of him. He'd have to work hard to mend fences, starting now. "I'll come with you to talk to them."

"No." She set her empty glass on the counter. "They'll prefer not to have to weigh their words in front of a stranger."

"That sounds like you expect a browbeating." Trip rubbed his forehead to alleviate the dull headache that had settled behind his eyes. "I don't like that idea. Let me come. I bet they'll be less upset if we present a united front."

Kelsey shook her head. "I want to handle this on my own, although I am relieved to be able to say we're doing this together."

"Okay." Trip reached for her. Once he had her back in his arms again, he kissed her. Unlike at Maura's house, she didn't resist him when he cradled her jaw in his big hands. As he slipped his tongue past her warm, full lips, he realized this kiss differed from their others—powered less by lust, and laced with a bit of wonder.

He steadied himself, remembering the seriousness of their conversation. "When do you plan to tell them?"

She shrugged, sighing. "They're expecting me in about thirty minutes."

Trip glanced out the window at the darkening sky. "Don't walk over there now. Drive, okay?"

"Oh, stop." Kelsey waved him off. "I told you before, I've been making that trek for years on my own."

He placed his hand on her stomach and looked into her eyes. "But it's not just you anymore. Now you have to protect the baby. You need to be safe."

She appeared almost as surprised as he was by his protective instinct, but at least he got his way. "Fine. I'll drive."

By the time Kelsey arrived at her sister's house, her parents were already seated at the dining table enjoying coffee and pie. Coffee, another beverage crossed off the menu for the next eight months. But apple pie? It was filled with fruit—practically a health food.

"Aunt Kelsey!" Fee ran over and clasped Kelsey's legs. "What'd you bring me from Mexico?"

Kelsey's eyes filled with joyful tears upon the sudden recognition that, this time next year, she'd have her own son or daughter to love. She held the tears at bay and stroked Fee's back.

"You little stinker." Kelsey grinned and tweaked Fee's nose. "At least pretend to have missed me before demanding your gift."

"Sorry." Fee's hands clapped together and she craned her neck and tried to look inside Kelsey's giant purse. "But what *did* you bring me?"

Kelsey laughed at her mini-me, although Maura looked mortified. She reached into her bag and pulled out a colorful, embroidered cotton dress and hair comb embellished with a large silk flower. "What do you think of these pretty things? Now you can dress up and make believe you're in Mexico."

"Yay!" Fee tore the items from Kelsey's hands and ran off, presumably to change her clothes, while shouting an obligatory thanks over her shoulder.

Kelsey retrieved a petite pair of painted maracas from her bag and waved them in the air. "These are for Ty."

"Thanks, sis." Maura took them from Kelsey and then went to sit beside her husband at the table. "Now that Fee's gone, come tell us your big news. Does it have to do with that real estate sale you were hoping to close?"

"No, it's not a work thing." Four pairs of eyes fixed on her face, their scrutiny making her feel like she was buck naked on the sidewalk. She took a deep breath. God, she dreaded saying the words again, but maybe her family would surprise her with their reaction, like Trip had. "Let me sit. And pass the pie."

Kelsey opted for the empty chair at the far end of the table and delayed the inevitable by filling her plate and taking her first bite. Her heart pounded, which only made her mad at herself. She hated feeling like a coward. *Just begin.*

Setting down her fork, she glanced at everyone as she drew in a deep breath. "So, I know this will be unexpected, and maybe not anything you'll consider good news at first, but I just want you to know ahead of time, I'm happy." She watched her family exchange worried glances. "With that said, I guess I'll just blurt it out: I'm pregnant."

All at once, her mother gasped, Maura dropped her fork, and Bill donned a "holy shit" expression.

Kelsey forced a broad smile—her defense shield against the anticipated barrage of questions.

Her dad fired the first shot.

"Who's the father?" His concerned tone reassured her until she caught a glimpse of Maura silently mouthing "not him, not him."

"Trip Lexington, whom you met here, at my birthday dinner." She kept her voice as even as possible, despite her rising body temperature and rocketing pulse.

"Didn't he just get arrested the other week?" her mother asked, one hand raised to her mouth in surprise.

"Those charges will be dropped. It was a fight between brothers. I'm not defending him, but there's a lot about their history that people don't know or understand."

"You were dating brothers?" Her father's horrified expression reminded her of the time she, Emma, and Avery had been picked up for vandalism in the spring of their senior year for painting their graduation year on the high school parking lot. Just like back then, his disapproval made her stomach twist.

"I didn't know they were brothers. They have different last names." Her response appeared to heighten her dad's dismay. "It sounds worse than it was, Dad. It was just a first date with Mason. Trip and I weren't exclusive at that point. *Shoot, not helping. Now Dad thinks I'm promiscuous and stupid.* "It's complicated."

Maura then sank her forehead into her palm. "Oh, boy."

Trying to lighten the mood, Kelsey joked, "Not necessarily. It could be a girl." She then shoveled another giant bite of pie into her mouth, hoping the sugary goodness would calm her roiling stomach.

"Babies aren't a joke, Kelsey." Maura shook her head, while their mother and dad sat in some kind of crestfallen state. "I can't believe I couldn't talk you out of your crazy arrangement when I knew, *knew* it would end in disaster."

"Maura!" Thankfully her dad cut off Maura's tirade. After collecting himself, he turned back toward Kelsey with hope in his eyes. "So you're dating this Trip character now . . . *exclusively*, I presume?"

"Yes—" Kelsey began at the exact same time Maura scoffed, "Ha." Maura shot Kelsey a surprised stare. "Oh?"

"Trip and I are planning to raise this child together. *Together* together." She stared at her sister, pretending to feel triumph while knowing Maura had watched her inhale a gallon or more of ice cream at that very table while crying about him the other week. But he did want to be with her, and he said it wasn't just because of the baby. He'd never lied before, and she desperately wanted to believe him.

"So if you're together and planning to raise this baby, will you be getting married soon?" Her mother's gentle voice caught Kelsey off guard.

"No." Kelsey noticed her mother's struggle not to cry. "This has caught us both by surprise. We'd never planned on this baby or talked about the future. For now, we're just taking things one day at a time."

It killed her to disappoint her parents. If she'd come with an engagement announcement, everyone in this room would've been happier, including her.

Ruthlessly she shoved that thought aside. Dwelling on what wasn't just wasted time and energy. Instead she'd embrace what was: impending motherhood, and a real relationship with a man she found exceedingly attractive and exciting, if sometimes exasperating. Weren't those worth celebrating?

"Mom, Dad, please be happy for me. I know this isn't the best way for me to start a family, but I'm thirty-one, not sixteen, and I'm thrilled about becoming a mother. Now Maura and I can be pregnant together and our kids will be close. It may not be ideal, but it can still be a blessing."

"Why didn't he come here and face me?" Her dad's disdain had never been a good sign.

"He offered, but I thought it would be better if I broke the news on my own." Kelsey stretched out her arms and planted her palms on the tabletop. "Please don't come down on Trip. He's always been honest with me, and thoughtful. Despite being a bit of a bull in a china shop, he's sensitive to my feelings. He's fun, he really likes me as I am and not just because of this baby, and I think he'll be a loving father."

"Do you?" Maura asked. "Based on what?"

"Based on how he interacts with Fee, and on things he's told me in confidence. Reasons it's really important to him that any kid of his knows he's loved." She looked around the table. "We may not be engaged *yet*, but I wouldn't bother dating him if I didn't believe we had a good chance of ending up together. As you're all pointing out, I've got a tough road ahead. Please don't make it harder for me. Just love me and support me now, okay?"

Maura sighed. After exchanging some silent mind-reading message with Bill, she rose from her chair and came around the table to hug Kelsey. "Congratulations, Kels. It will be nice to go through our pregnancies together."

Kelsey clung to her sister as she noticed her parents exchange a resigned look.

"Guess there's not much more to say. What's done is done," her mother finally said through a strained smile. "And we certainly can't be sad about another grandbaby."

Kelsey had hoped for a little more enthusiasm, but she knew her parents weren't looking forward to the gossip within their church group. She'd have to give them time to come around.

"Hey, Kels," Bill interrupted. "Think Trip will give me an in-law discount on some backcountry action?"

Kelsey smiled, grateful for Bill's attempt to lift the weight from the room with a little levity. "I've skied with you. Stick to the corduroy so we don't have to dig you out of an avalanche."

Bill chuckled and the tension ebbed from the room. As Kelsey answered more questions about her recent trip and her pregnancy, she couldn't help but wonder about how Trip was feeling and whether he'd told his family.

Chapter Fourteen

Kelsey sat at her desk with the phone pressed to her ear, rubbing the creases from her forehead with two fingers. "Just because Wade's still waiting on the completed impact study doesn't mean we should halt all negotiations, Nick. Let's hammer out the major deal points with an option agreement so we're ready to go once we learn that, overall, the development project will be a boon for town and for your family."

She tapped the eraser of her pencil against her desk while listening to Nick Copeland hem and haw on the phone. This deal mattered more than ever now. Raising a child would be an expensive undertaking. Trip said he'd help, but his business was never going to be a cash cow. Kelsey knew she'd have to be the breadwinner. If this commission mattered to her future before, it meant even more now.

"I don't want to spend time and money with lawyers if it's going to be moot, Kelsey," Nick replied. "Just hold off until Mr. Kessler gets his hands on that study."

"I understand." Kelsey managed to hide her massive disappointment and remain pleasant and professional. "I'll be in touch soon."

Setting the phone on her desk, she checked her calendar. Fall wasn't her busiest time of year, but things would ramp up soon, as skiers from all over the country would come to town, be struck with mountain fever, and decide to plunk down a wad of money on a vacation home.

Wade's retail project would make the town that much more appealing to potential buyers. God, she really wanted this deal to go through. If only Trip hadn't stirred up the town and forced the idea of that darn impact study. If she didn't like him so much, she'd wring his neck. The delay he'd caused was costing Wade time and money and giving the sellers cold feet.

Trip. Such a contradiction. A womanizer, a *former* womanizer, but with a gentle heart. Bigger than life. Sexy as hell, but just as frustrating and intractable. So why did the very thought of him make her smile inside and out?

Sitting back, she sipped her orange juice and popped a strawberry in her mouth. Folic acid—check. Satisfaction? Not so much. Why weren't mochas and cinnamon muffins good for fetal development?

The bell above her door jingled. She looked up just as Mason strolled through her door looking suitably humble, a faded yellow-green bruise beneath his eye the sole evidence of his fight.

So much had happened since that night, it already seemed a lifetime ago. Dormant humiliation shot a blast of heat to her cheeks. Kelsey brazened ahead, resting her chin atop steepled fingers while Mason politely smiled and cleared his throat.

"Sorry for the intrusion," he began, "but I was afraid you'd tell me to go to hell if I'd called first."

For an instant, she considered saying it then and there, but part of her wanted to hear why he'd come.

When she didn't give him the boot, he continued. "I remembered you were getting back yesterday, so I thought I'd take a chance. May I sit for a minute?"

Despite everything she knew about him, something about Mason garnered her empathy. Maybe it was his fierce loyalty to his mother, or his own disappointment over his divorce, or the fact that today he looked dejected. Or maybe her current "baby brain" had chased away whatever animosity she'd harbored the other week.

Of all the ways she could look at things, one inescapable fact existed. Mason would be her baby's uncle, for better or worse. Maybe he and Trip didn't see it yet, but Kelsey knew blood mattered. Family mattered. She'd always been optimistic about the power of love. So if, by some miracle, she might be able to broker peace in the Cutler family, by God she would try.

"You look better than I would've expected. I'm glad Trip didn't cause any permanent damage." She gestured toward the chairs on the other side of her desk. "So, what can I do for you today?"

"Accept my apology." He flashed a hopeful grin before sitting back and flicking nonexistent lint from his slacks. "I'm sorry I wasn't completely aboveboard with you when we met. I promise, I didn't intend to hurt or embarrass you."

"But you did."

"And I regret it. As I tried to explain before, I knew you had some kind of relationship with Gunner, but needling him wasn't my sole interest once I actually met you. I'm going through a divorce and am lonely living in a town with no friends. You're quite pretty, and I admire your ambition and directness. I'd thought offering you an alternative— someone mature and stable—might've been what you wanted, too."

His expression and tone sounded earnest, but given his long history of trying to outwit Trip, she had a hard time believing him. "Thank you for the apology. You'll understand if I need a little time to accept your sincerity."

"Of course." He edged forward in his seat, staring directly at her. "Now that everything is out in the open, perhaps in time you'll let me start over?"

Kelsey cocked her head. "You haven't spoken with Trip this morning, have you?"

"No." Mason's shoulders stiffened. "Why?"

If the brothers had ever been close, she'd have told Mason to ask Trip. Under the circumstances, however, she decided it might be better he hear it from her. "I'm pregnant."

"Oh." His brows rose high on his forehead. "How long have you known?"

"Figured it out in Mexico. I told Trip last night. He and I are going to raise this child together, so while I'm not holding a grudge, I think you realize we can't be more than friends. Even that will be difficult unless you work things out with your brother."

Mason blinked, and, for a second, she saw the passing resemblance between him and Trip. How had she missed it before?

Shrugging, he admitted, "Of course, you're right."

He appeared a bit dazed before he finally rose from the chair. "Congratulations, Kelsey. I hope you'll be happy, and I hope my brother is up to the task of parenthood."

"You don't give him enough credit, Mason. I offered him the out, but he insisted not only on being involved with our child, but also with me."

"He hasn't shown much use for family or relationships these past ten years, so you'll forgive me for my doubts."

"Mason, do me a favor." She stood up to meet him eye to eye. "Remember that this baby is your blood, too. Kids need tons of love, and I want my child to have a good relationship with both sides of his or her family." Kelsey kept talking, even after Mason stared at the ground. "Maybe I'm crossing a line here, and I know I don't have the whole story, but whatever your dad did, and however your family changed after Trip's arrival, it wasn't Trip's fault he was born. Just like *this* baby is coming into the world innocent. Maybe it's time for peace?"

Mason's flushed cheeks warned Kelsey that he didn't see it her way, nor did he appreciate her point of view.

"This is a subject I suggest you steer clear of, Kelsey. I came to apologize, and don't want to argue or defend myself anymore."

"Mason, he's your brother. Doesn't that mean anything to you at all? Aren't you even a little curious about what could happen if you two stopped fighting and tried to be friends?"

Mason studied her as if she were some strange zoo exhibit he'd never seen. "I wish I could tell you what you want to hear, but I don't share your faith in Gunner. He's never sustained a friendship beyond five years or an adult relationship with any woman beyond a few encounters. He's always been happiest skimming the surface, having a good time, not caring about others' expectations. Nothing in his past points toward him being a good partner or father." Mason rocked back and forth on his heels before crossing to the door. He placed his hand on the knob, then paused and glanced back over his shoulder. "I hope, for your sake, he proves me wrong."

Kelsey hid the chilling effect of his warning behind a blank expression.

After he disappeared, she slouched into her chair and laid her hand over her stomach. Trip's history didn't bode well for her future, but her gut urged her not to give up on him. People could change when motivated, when they met the right person.

All this time she'd been holding herself back, following Trip's stupid tips. No more. She would be herself, show her feelings, and shower him with affection. And, in her heart, she just knew it would be exactly what he needed.

Leaning her head down low, she whispered to her little bean, "Don't you worry. Your daddy will prove everyone wrong."

Trip held the phone away from his ear in anticipation of his father's reaction to the life-altering news. He couldn't help but feel like the world's biggest hypocrite after the way he'd argued with his dad two days ago. Hell, after the way he'd felt for most of his life.

Silence reigned for several seconds before Ross Cutler spoke.

"I'm delighted, son." His father's surprising blessing eased some of Trip's fears. "For you and for me."

"Why for you?" Trip grinned. "Because now you've got a shot at a grand*son*?"

"Partly," his dad said through a chuckle. "More because you'll learn exactly how much I love you even though *you* weren't planned. Maybe this baby will finally convince you of that and unite us as a family."

Trip considered the swell of emotion that had arisen since Kelsey dropped the bombshell. The protectiveness he already felt toward her and junior, the connection he'd felt by the time he'd left her house. Was that how love began? Was that what his father had experienced when they'd first met?

"I hadn't thought about it that way." In a moment of discomfort, he rushed his dad off the phone. "Listen, I've got to take Kelsey to the doctor now. Thanks for being supportive. I'll talk to you soon."

He actually had a little time before he was to meet Kelsey. He grabbed a jacket and closed his bedroom door behind him as he strode through the apartment.

"Thought you had another hour before your appointment?" Grey called out as he came around the breakfast bar and approached Trip, lollipop in hand.

"Need to make a quick stop first." Trip zipped up his fleece, grateful for a nonjudgmental friend who hadn't questioned his ability to handle parenthood. Maybe that made Grey foolish, but it had helped lessen Trip's own doubts.

Grey slapped him on the shoulder. "Good luck. Tell Kelsey I said congrats."

"Will do." Trip nodded and headed toward the door.

"Will you be back tonight?"

"Not sure, 'Mom.'" He snickered. "Didn't know I had a curfew."

"Does anyone other than you laugh at your jokes?" Grey tucked his hands under his armpits, smirking. "With all this baby business, I'm just making sure you don't forget about tomorrow's climb. Group of four. Eight o'clock meet up downstairs."

"I'll be there." Trip grabbed one of his hats. "See you later."

Within minutes, Trip was browsing the pregnancy book section in Mind Matters bookstore, a place he didn't frequent often. There were several such books, including a couple specifically geared toward expectant fathers. Flipping through them, Trip had some kind of out-of-body experience, like he was looking at himself through an ever-expanding tunnel.

This time next year, he'd be carrying a child around town, changing diapers, going to the doctor's office for checkups—generally being exhausted and overwhelmed.

No more women. No more going where he wanted when he wanted. No more putting his needs first.

He shoved the book back on the shelf, a thin line of perspiration dampening his brow. *Take a deep breath.*

What the hell was wrong with him? He'd scaled mountains, skied off cliffs, even skydived a time or two. How could one little baby scare the shit out of him?

At thirty-two, he was more than mature enough to raise a child. He had money, even if he didn't want to use it for himself. He had a warm, sensual woman who'd be a terrific mom and was more than capable of holding his interest.

He blew out another breath and selected two books, one for himself and one for Kelsey.

On his way to the register, he saw Mason enter the store. *Shit.* He hadn't thought about his brother for a blissful twenty-four hours. The last thing he needed to worry about today was protecting himself, Kelsey, or this baby from his brother.

He tucked the books under his arm, hoping Mason didn't see them, and proceeded toward the register.

No such luck.

"Trip, I just saw Kelsey." He stood a few feet away—outside Trip's reach. Apparently Mason didn't quite trust Trip to keep his fists to himself. "I hear congratulations are in order."

Despite his benign words, Mason had a way of keeping Trip on the defensive. Trip's heart started beating a little too fast. Why had Mason been with Kelsey? What had he done to screw this up for Trip now?

For his father's sake, he willed himself to relax and be civil. Kelsey knew the truth about Mason, and she was pregnant with Trip's child. She was smart enough not to fall for Mason's schemes again.

"It's true." Trip eyed him warily. "I just told Dad a few minutes ago."

Mason hesitated, appearing to study Trip while weighing his words. "I'm sure he's happy. He loves being a granddaddy. Probably hoping you'll give him a grandson, seeing as my girls aren't much into football."

No snide remarks. No smirking. Only the tiniest hint of envy in the grandson comment. Good God, this version of Mason might be scarier than the combative one.

"Dad's always adored your girls," Trip replied awkwardly, feeling uneasy in a conversation with his brother that wasn't loaded with anger and accusation.

"Yes, he has." Mason rolled his shoulders back. "Anyway, Kelsey tells me you promised to see this through with her, as a partner and a parent. I hope you didn't give her false hope only to let her down later."

"I didn't." Mason's condescension annoyed Trip, but he thought of his dad's wishes and clamped down the resentment boiling in his gut. "We agreed to take it one day at a time."

"Hmpf." Mason shook his head. "Once again, you're so cocksure of yourself, just like Dad. Kelsey's pregnant, Gunner. One day at a time? Don't you think you should count your lucky stars that she wants you back and just man up? Make a commitment, or you'll be sorry when she gives up on you and then you have to watch some other guy step in and help raise your kid. Trust me, *nothing* is harder than that."

For the first time, the bitterness in his brother's eyes wasn't directed at Trip. Beneath the anger, Trip saw his hurt, too, which deflated whatever irritation he felt at being lectured to by Mason. If it had been Grey, Trip might've patted his shoulder. But despite the tentative tone of truce in this discussion, he couldn't quite bring himself to make such a gesture to his brother. "I'll keep that in mind."

The mere thought of having to share his kid with some other guy, let alone having Kelsey in the arms of another man, gave Trip an instant headache. He wondered if Mason walked around shouldering that agony all day. "Mason, we both know why Dad sent you here. But you should be in Denver, close to your girls. Tell him to get someone else to oversee Wade's project."

"Dad's counting on me." Mason swallowed whatever he was about to say next. Probably something sarcastic about how Trip wouldn't understand. But hey, his silence was progress.

"I know you've never liked to disappoint Dad, but don't you think your daughters need you more than he does? And maybe you need them just as much." Trip hoped his remarks sounded supportive instead of judgmental. "Now, if you'll excuse me, I've got to pay for these and get to an appointment."

Mason waved Trip toward the counter and then strolled over to the new release shelves.

Trip squirmed in his waiting room seat, surrounded by pastel-colored art and a bunch of women. Across from him sat a middle-aged mother with a teen daughter who looked even more uncomfortable than Trip felt. The woman to his right looked like her baby should've been born months ago, her stomach was so enormous. Kelsey sat to his left, browsing the pregnancy book he'd bought her earlier. Another pregnant woman sat in the corner.

The high concentration of estrogen in the stuffy, windowless room was giving him more vertigo than an expert-only rated climb.

"Kelsey?" A nurse called out.

"Right here." Kelsey's sunny smile helped him settle. Knowing he'd helped put that smile on her face was deeply satisfying, too. "Ready?"

"Yep," he lied. He didn't know exactly what happened inside this kind of doctor's office, but he guessed it wasn't anything a man should have to see.

Dr. Davis, a pleasant, plump woman in her midfifties, helped put Trip at ease with her friendly, but matter-of-fact, approach to the visit. After asking a laundry list of questions, and performing a pelvic exam that made Trip very glad Kelsey's doctor wasn't a guy, she turned on some equipment and squeezed blue gel over the tip of some kind of probe.

Kelsey didn't look bothered, but Trip felt his eyebrows scale his forehead and his thighs squeeze together when he watched it disappear under the paper drape over Kelsey's legs. Then he heard Kelsey gasp. He followed her gaze toward the screen, where he saw a whole lot of black and gray and not much else.

"See that little sac?" Dr. Davis extended her finger toward the screen. Trip strained to discern the sac from the rest of the photo, but he finally saw it. "That's the yolk sac and that tiny pea is the baby."

His breath stuck in his lungs. His baby might not be any bigger than a sesame seed, but there it was, safe and warm inside this beautiful creature to his right.

"I don't hear a heartbeat." Kelsey's anxious voice and pinched forehead caused Trip to hold her hand while he looked at the doctor, praying for a non-devastating explanation. He could handle almost anything except seeing Kelsey hurt.

"You're not quite six weeks along, so it's a little early for the heart-beat." The doctor kept wiggling that probe and studying the screen while she spoke. "At your next appointment you'll hear it and see more than this tiny speck."

Kelsey's face glowed once more. She craned her neck and squinted, concentrating on trying to see a baby instead of a dot. Then she pried Trip's fingers from her hand. "Ouch."

He hadn't realized he'd been squeezing her hand. He looked at the little spot and back at Kelsey.

No doubts now. This was all real. A baby. A family. Hopefully one like he'd had with his mom and grandfather. Thinking of them, he wondered if they could see this somehow, from above. His mother would've doted on her grandchild.

His nose tingled and he felt his eyes begin to water. Overwhelmed by emotions he couldn't name, he leaned forward, kissed Kelsey's temple, and smoothed her hair. He might not be one hundred percent sure he could handle these changes, but he didn't want her to doubt him.

She broke into another smile before turning to the doctor. "So what's the due date?"

"May ninth, give or take." The doctor handed Kelsey a printed picture of the ultrasound. "Let's schedule your next visit in four weeks. In the meantime, fill this prenatal vitamin prescription, eat healthy, get lots of rest, and stay hydrated."

Trip doubted Kelsey even heard the doctor's last remark, she'd been so focused on the photo in her hand. Radiant—the only word that came to mind when he looked at her face. Seeing her full of joy and love and excitement made his heart beat a little faster. She looked gorgeous and sexy and, best of all, she was all his. That thought stirred a different part of his anatomy.

"Hey, Doc." Trip's one and only question might be indelicate, but he had to ask. "So, are there any restrictions on other activities, like, you know . . . sex?"

Kelsey covered her face, but Dr. Davis chuckled. "Normal sexual activity is perfectly safe and healthy."

Relief washed through Trip, because the very next thing he wanted to do with his day was get Kelsey into bed. It'd been three weeks since she'd called quits on all physical contact, and he was more than eager to resume that part of this relationship.

As soon as the doctor left the office, Trip turned to Kelsey.

She sat up, cheeks as red as apples, and motioned toward her clothes for his help. "I can't believe the only question you asked this whole time was about sex."

"Really?" He handed her the dress and gave her a peck on the lips before joking, "I think anyone who knows me would expect that to be the only question I'd ask."

At least she snickered before putting her clothes back on while still seated on the table. "I'm hungry."

He stepped in between her legs and tugged her against his body. "Me too."

"I'm serious!" But she kissed him.

"Me too." He cupped the back of her head and sucked her lower lip into his mouth.

"Feed me first." She let out a happy sigh and hopped off the table. "I just realized, now I have a legitimate excuse to eat for two."

Trip smacked her curvy behind on their way out the door. "Eat whatever you want, 'cause you'll be getting plenty of exercise tonight."

Chapter Fifteen

Kelsey tossed her keys on the end table when they entered her home. Before she could remove her jacket, Trip came up behind her and looped his arms around her stomach. A perfect ending to an amazing afternoon.

Two days ago, she'd feared a Texas-size tantrum in response to her news. Nothing had shocked her more than Trip's willingness to not only embrace the baby but also her. Now she prayed he wasn't hiding doubts or regrets.

"We've had dinner," he murmured in her ear. "Time for dessert."

"You have a one-track mind." Not that she minded the direction of his thoughts. She'd been distracted by the same thing ever since they'd left the doctor's office.

"Come on, princess." He spun her around, removed her jacket, and flung it on a nearby chair before tugging her close. His sexy voice coaxed, "Admit that you've missed me."

"My God, if we have a son, I hope he's more humble than you," she teased, slapping his shoulder.

"*If* we have a son?" He smirked, as if the idea of a baby girl were pure whimsy.

"Trip, not even the almighty *you* can decide the baby's gender."

"Au contraire. The father totally controls it based on whether his X or Y chromosome gets there first." He nodded in that smug way that still managed to be cute. "I've done my research."

"But you can't control which sperm swims faster."

He released her for a second and swept his hand from his head down the length of his torso. "Do I look or act like a guy with *any* X chromosomes in his body?" He shook his head, grinning, then grabbed her into his arms again. "Trust me, this baby is a boy."

He was so ridiculously sure of himself, and not even the least bit embarrassed by his caveman attitude, she could do nothing but laugh.

His green eyes twinkled, and the little dimple in his chin deepened, when he smiled in response to her laughter. Then, quick as a brisk wind, he turned serious. He lifted her chin and looked in her eyes. "But if, by some miracle, it is a girl, I hope she's exactly like you."

Just like that, her knees weakened and her heart swelled. She threaded her hands through his hair and kissed him with her entire soul. Everything she'd wanted for so long lay at the tips of her fingers, and she'd be damned if she wouldn't dig in and hold on.

Within two seconds, he'd lifted her into his arms and begun to walk to her bedroom. Cowboy tried to follow them, but Trip nudged the door closed with his knee before the kitten could slip inside. He then set Kelsey on her feet, near the bed, facing away from him. After brushing her hair to the side, he kissed the back of her neck and shoulders as he slowly unzipped her dress.

She loved the sound of his breath growing heavy, the little hum in the back of his throat, the hard ridge of his erection pressing against her butt.

Her silky dress slid down her body and puddled around her ankles, but before she could step out of it, he ran his hands down her arms to her hips. His hot mouth latched on to the base of her neck as he caressed her abdomen before reaching for her breast.

He sank his other hand inside the elastic of her lace panties to where she was already wet and ready for him.

"Oh." She reached up behind herself in search of his silky hair while he continued his tender ministrations. "Wait. You're still dressed."

She felt him smile against her neck. He held his hands above his head, silently instructing her to undress him at her leisure.

At her leisure, indeed. She savored the chance to admire all six feet three inches of his rock-solid frame.

As she began to remove his pullover, she reveled in every flinch of muscle under her fingertips, every sharp inhale as she feathered kisses over his chest, the tension in his abdomen as she dropped to her knees and unzipped his pants.

He sprang out of his boxers, so she removed them and took him into her mouth. His head fell back with a groan and his hands immediately threaded in her hair. "Sweet Jesus, princess."

She used her hands and mouth to work him until his knees began to buckle, at which point he pulled free, lifted her up, and laid her on her bed. Standing at the edge of the mattress, he raised one of her legs up to his shoulder and unfastened the brass clasp of her blue velvet platform heels. He dropped the shoe, kissed her ankle, then slowly lowered her leg before repeating the routine with her other shoe.

Her heart galloped inside her chest thanks to the gleam in his eye and the tenderness of his touch.

"I thought you liked my sexy shoes," she said, as he bent over and slowly removed her underpants.

"I like how they look. But let's not risk any bruises tonight." Then he crawled onto the mattress and pulled her across his body to straddle his lap. He reached around to unfasten her bra and then tossed it aside. His lusty gaze and rasped voice made her insides clench with anticipation. "No more talk."

He sat up to kiss her, fastening her against his body with one arm while caressing her back and neck with his free hand. His passionate, hot, hungry kissing shot tingles through her limbs, like always. Her heart soared when he acted like he couldn't get enough.

But when he grabbed her hair like reins, Kelsey had other ideas. She shoved at his chest and pinned his arms above his head. Rather than resist, he caught her breast in his mouth, seeming quite content with her plans.

She remained lowered to his mouth while she began grinding against his erection without taking him inside her body.

"Kelsey!" He bucked his hips against her, seeking entrance, but she continued the slow torment while he sucked harder at her nipples until she felt like she might come.

In a weak moment, she loosened her grip on his arms. He immediately wrested free, gripped her hips, and entered her.

Both of them groaned as he thrust himself inside. She thought he'd flip her over, but he seemed to enjoy watching her ride his body. He brought her hands up to her breasts then returned his to her hips. When she fondled herself per his unspoken request, he moaned. His gaze darted from her face to her breasts and back until he finally closed his eyes and pressed the back of his head into the mattress.

She rotated her hips in quick circles, loving each and every growl and grunt she heard. Then she leaned forward to kiss him while meeting each thrust of his pelvis.

He kissed her back, his tongue probing her mouth with as much heat as the other part of his body moving inside hers. Without breaking free, his hands traveled from her head, down her back, and then gripped her hips.

He slammed into her with such force it nearly took her breath away. "Baby, you feel so good. Just. Like. That."

Everything in her body tightened, like a wave cresting, until it broke open and she came apart in his arms. As her body's convulsions slowed, his took over and he shouted her name.

Her head fell against his neck as they both panted while their trembling bodies absorbed the force of their orgasms. Trip's fingertips ran up and down her spine and then he toyed with her hair. Although her body went limp with satiation, her mind raced in several directions. Being wrapped up with Trip gave her such pleasure, such a sense of physical comfort and security.

She could easily picture a future like this, with a man like him. A man who could turn her on, make her laugh, challenge her, touch her heart, and even make her want to pull her hair out and scream. Did he feel the same about her? She thought he might, but whatever tenderness he showed or promises he made, he never uttered the L-word.

Although she'd been enjoying a near-blissful afternoon, Mason's warnings and her own insecurity nipped at the contentedness blooming in Kelsey's chest, causing an involuntary shiver to travel through her body.

"You're cold?" Trip craned his neck to look at her, then hugged her and rubbed her arms for warmth. "I'm sweating like a pig."

"I'm not cold." She wrapped one arm around his waist. "This is nice. I'm glad we're doing this together."

"Even if you never get any baby girls out of the deal?" He teased, his ready smile showing no signs of regret.

Kelsey knew him well enough at this point to recognize his habit of deflecting a serious conversation with a lighthearted joke. But she also noticed he'd said "girls"—plural—implying he was already thinking long-term. More kids. Her heart squeezed with hope. Hope gave her courage to explore his feelings.

"Humor me, okay?" she replied. "If we do have a girl—"

"Which we've already agreed would be kinda like the second coming of Christ in terms of miracle births," he interrupted.

"Yes, fine. What would you want to name her?"

That shut him up. He probably hadn't even started daydreaming about fun details like names, but she had. She watched different emotions play over his face, but had no idea what he was thinking. Rather than wait for his answer, she led him toward her own. An answer that should show him how much he meant to her.

"What was your mother's name?" she asked, praying it wasn't something awful or old-fashioned.

He stilled and stared at her, blinking the same dazed way he did when she first told him about the baby.

"Danielle." His throat worked while he watched for her reaction. "But my grandfather called her Dani."

When she smiled, she felt his muscles slacken.

"I like that." She kissed his chest and fingered his bangs, hoping her decision would please him. "If we have a miracle daughter, I think we should name her for your mother."

Without a word, he pulled her into a kiss. It started out firm but then softened into something gentle and loving. Something that melted her very core. He eased away and stroked her cheek with his thumb.

"You take my breath away," he said, his eyes locked on hers. "I can only hope to be worthy of your kind heart."

You are. Her heart longed to shout the words. To tell him he was the most captivating, sexy, stimulating, tender, infuriating man she'd ever known. To tell him she'd fallen for him, heart and soul. But the baby had been more than enough shock for him to handle. She'd hold her feelings inside until she knew they wouldn't send him running away.

Trip tugged her back against his chest and into the vise of his muscular arms. His steady heartbeat pounded beneath her ear. They laid together in silence for another minute before he kissed the top of her head. "If it's a boy, we shouldn't name him after me."

"Really?" She'd have expected his ego to demand that he and his beloved grandfather be the baby's namesake. "Why not?"

After a brief hesitation, Trip joked. "'Cause I can live with being called Trip, but 'Quad' doesn't quite have the same ring to it."

Kelsey chuckled, but sensed more to the remark, knowing his joke was probably just another deflection. "We could skip the nicknames and call him Gunner."

"Maybe." His dismissive tone only increased her curiosity. His arms tightened around her, making her warm inside and out. "Or maybe our son should get his own identity."

Whether Trip was attempting to distance their child from his reputation, his family history, or something else, Kelsey wasn't sure. Rather than press him, she changed the subject.

"Will you be bummed if it is a girl?" She bit her lip, awaiting his answer.

"No. But unless she's the world's biggest tomboy, I'll be clueless about how to handle her."

"You're good with Fee."

Trip chuckled aloud. "Oh, boy. If I father a girly girl with that big a personality, she'll give me a heart attack. She won't date until she's thirty, I can promise that much."

"It's always womanizers like you who never want their daughters to date." Kelsey pinched his chest.

He grabbed her fingers and kissed them. "You think I want my daughter to end up with someone like me?" Rolling her onto her back, he playfully pinned her beneath his body, wrestling her until she stopped squirming. "Now let's change the subject." He kissed her breastbone and then her stomach as he worked his way down her body. "I've got a better way to spend the rest of the night."

"You do?"

"Mm hmm."

Then his face disappeared between her legs and even she stopped caring about baby names.

Trip set the pregnancy journal and fancy body creams he'd picked for Kelsey on the counter where Jessie—one of his former flings—was working. Her sandy-colored, wavy hair, not nearly as shiny or thick as Kelsey's golden locks, hung wild around her shoulders. A snug sweater revealed full C-cups and a small waist. Skintight jeans completed her walking advertisement for sex-on-the-go.

The kind of ad he'd usually answered, but not anymore.

She'd been a party girl looking for a good time, and they'd shared a few. No complications. No regrets. Still, this particular purchase presented an awkward moment.

"I heard karma caught up to you." She chuckled while scanning the items. "Guess you're off the market now, or for a while, anyway."

"Breaks your heart, I know," he teased before patting down his jacket to locate his wallet. *Ah, left-hand pocket.* When he fished around for it, he discovered a folded piece of paper tucked in the pocket, too.

After handing his credit card to Jessie, he scanned the handwritten note:

I hope I make you as happy as you've made me, cowboy. XOXO, K

He reread it, grinning, and then tucked it in his pocket before Jessie noticed. Two weeks ago, his entire world had turned on its axis. Aside from an occasional doubt, he'd been coping with his new reality just fine. More than coping. If he were being completely honest with himself, he liked his growing closeness with Kelsey.

"You know," Jessie began while she finished bagging the items, "people are taking bets on how long you and Kelsey will stick it out."

"Excuse me?" Trip set his hands on the counter, heat rising to his neck.

"Basic stuff, like whether you'll still be together by the time the baby comes." She pushed the bag of goodies toward him, smiling like she hadn't insulted both him and Kelsey. "Based on your conquests during your first eight months in town, odds are long on that one."

He drummed his fingers against the counter, trying to maintain an unaffected air. "Guess gossip is a pitfall of my legendary reputation. But if people spent more time worrying about their own sex lives instead of analyzing mine, they'd be more . . . satisfied."

"Since when have you been touchy?" She laughed, which told him he'd failed to hide his feelings. "In a town this small, you had to know news of the most desperate romantic snagging the most notorious play-boy with an 'accidental' pregnancy would set tongues wagging."

Trip's nerves caught fire at her tone and accusation. He glared at her. "Watch it, Jessie. There's nothing desperate about Kelsey."

"Sorry, Trip." Jessie's eyes widened, as if surprised he'd rushed to Kelsey's defense. "Just joking around."

"It's no joke to imply she tried to trap me. That's not what hap-pened. And, by the way, I feel damn lucky, so consider that before you place your next bet." He turned without looking back and marched out the door into the first snowfall of the year.

Normally giant snowflakes boosted his mood. Right now, they weren't even helping to cool him down. Jessie's disbelieving expres-sion still lingered in his mind, pissing him off. He'd walked two blocks before the muscles in his neck and shoulders finally loosened.

Couldn't Jessie see he was happy, dammit? Calling Kelsey desperate. *Please!* Kelsey was sweet and sexy and sassy all rolled into one.

Thinking of Kelsey reminded him of the message she'd snuck into his wallet. The last time he got surprise love notes had to have been tenth grade, when they were stuffed through the slats of his high school locker.

Those had usually been anonymous, which had been fun because he would spend the next day or two trying to figure out which girl had a crush on him.

Now there were no questions about who had the crush. For all the casual indifference she'd shown prior to the pregnancy, Kelsey's behavior had now returned to the woman he'd met last year. The one who'd had her heart set on Grey.

That memory brought an instant scowl to his face. Not only had Kelsey chosen Grey over him that night so many months ago, but she'd gone on to pursue Grey for months afterward.

Luckily Grey hadn't been interested, Trip thought, as he breezed into the back office at Backtrax and brushed the snow from his hat.

"That's the first pout I've seen on your face in a while." Grey crossed his arms and shot Trip a smug smile. "You have a fight with 'the little woman'?"

"No." Trip had talked smack for so long, he knew he had to suffer whatever digs Grey took now that he'd succumbed to being in a relationship. Still, he didn't have to endure too much if he could change the subject. "Have you been outside? Another little snowfall. I spoke with Jon yesterday. He's available to help out this year until you're cleared to ski."

"Jumping the gun, aren't you? It's only October fourth, and we're only expecting three inches today." Grey unwrapped a grape lollipop and shoved it into his mouth. "Such a tease."

"It won't be long now. El Niño, baby." Trip sank into his chair and crossed his legs at the ankles. "When do you think you'll be ready to ski?"

"I promised Avery I'd wait until the resort opened and do a first run down a groomer, but I'm thinking I may not be able to keep that promise." Grey sighed. "Seven weeks seems like forever away."

Trip didn't want Grey to push too hard, but being restricted to groomers? For God's sake, that seemed extremely cautious for such a strong athlete. Surely there was a better compromise. "The forecast is predicting a huge storm this weekend. Maybe Sunday you and I can hike up the inbounds trails and rip up deep pow, maybe dodge some trees in the glades?"

"Technically that would be 'resort' skiing." Grey smiled, but Trip knew his friend was likely a little anxious about testing his knee. In any case, Grey shifted gears. "I've got something planned this afternoon, so if the 'Concerned Citizens' are still meeting here at four to plan the next steps in scuttling Wade's project, count me out."

"That's fine. I'm good to go." Trip set his hand atop a thick paper report sitting on his desk. "Got a copy of the impact study right here."

"How'd you get that?" Grey craned his neck to look at the papers. "Shouldn't it only have gone to Wade and the Copelands?"

"Does it matter?" Trip leaned forward. "I thought you supported doing whatever it takes to make sure this deal doesn't happen."

"I don't want to see anyone come in and upset the balance of town, but you gotta know, your leading the charge is going to get you in trouble with Kelsey."

"Neither of us has made a secret of our opposing views or promised to back off. One of us won't be satisfied with the outcome, but it's not personal."

Grey shook his head. "I know you aren't that dumb."

"Just 'cause I'm not pussy-whipped into backing off my own principles so Kelsey can get her way, doesn't make me dumb." Trip tossed a frustrated wave at Grey. "She's got no right to be angry. I'm not mad at *her* for not backing off and giving me my way, am I?"

"Not the same thing because Kelsey has a bigger stake in this than you."

"Bullshit. Money isn't the most important thing at stake." Trip poked the document with his index finger. "This study shows potential adverse impact to the surrounding residential properties, surface and groundwater risks, displaced wildlife, and other issues. I'm not saying the sky is falling, but there's got to be a better use for that property than luxury shops and office buildings."

Grey shrugged one shoulder, his desk chair creaking as he shifted his weight. "I'm sure Wade will offer solutions or compromises to deal with the stuff in that report."

"Maybe, but we don't have to make it easy." Trip eased back into his seat. "Current zoning height restrictions might pose a problem for him. If he needs town's approval for a special exception permit, that's another place we can make some noise."

"When you get so fired up, it seems personal. Don't piss Wade off so much he cuts off our access over his hotel property."

"We've got a recorded easement. As long as we meet the terms of that agreement, we're safe. Besides, I'm not sticking my name on everything. I'm merely coordinating the efforts. The retailers are way more vocal at this point." Trip smirked and grabbed one of Grey's suckers from the jar. "After the meeting tonight, Bob Russell's going to get together with the youngest Copeland and try to persuade him to hold out for another opportunity. Something better will come along. That should help Kelsey get over whatever disappointment she feels when this deal falls through."

Grey's expression revealed doubts. "For your sake, I hope she sees it that way."

Chapter Sixteen

Trip knocked on the window of Kelsey's office before he breezed in through the front door, whistling. The entire room smelled faintly of her flowery perfume, which caused him to smile.

Kelsey remained seated behind her desk, pen in hand. He noticed she'd pulled her hair away from her face with the antique hair combs he'd bought her in Denver. Her silken locks flowed over her shoulders and hugged her chest. As always, she looked feminine and delicious, despite her absorption in her work. If she weren't eating for two, he'd probably suggest skipping their dinner plans altogether and going straight to bed.

"Hey, gorgeous. Ready to go?"

"Is it six thirty already?" She glanced at her phone. "Why don't you go across the street to The Mineshaft and get us a table? I'll be there in ten minutes, promise."

"I never say no to ribs." Trip leaned across her desk to give her a quick kiss, then set the bag containing the lotions and journal he'd picked up earlier today in front of the keyboard. Jessie's smart-ass remarks about local bets zipped through his mind, but he brushed them aside. "By the way, I got you some more little surprises."

Her face lit with a smile as she peered inside the bag and pulled out its contents. She thumbed through the pregnancy journal, her eyes growing misty. "I love this!"

"Good. Now finish up your work so we can eat and go home." He kissed her once more for good measure. "See you soon."

Knowing Kelsey's tendency to get lost in her work, he figured ten minutes could easily turn into twenty or thirty, so he opted to sit at the bar rather than wait alone at a table.

He was chugging from an icy mug of beer when a pretty brunette sidled up to him. Although she was petite, he could discern her athletic build from the fit of her clothing. Her hazel eyes scanned him quickly before crinkling above her broad smile.

"Trip, right?" She smiled at him expectantly.

"That's me." Dimly lit bar or not, normally he remembered faces, but he didn't recognize hers. "I'm sorry, have we met?"

"You don't remember me?" Her sly expression warned of an intention to toy with him.

Surely he'd remember if he'd had sex with her. Then again, there had been a few nights last ski season when he'd been drunk enough not to remember much of anything. He needed to deliver a smooth line to wiggle out of this pickle. "Well, my bad memory is certainly no reflection on your pretty face."

"Still a flatterer, I see. Guess it takes more than sweat-soaked skin and ropes to retain your attention." Her eyes twinkled with good humor.

Sweat and ropes? How in the hell could he forget a night like that? His face must have revealed his confusion, because she finally chuckled aloud and let him off the hook. "You led my buddies and me on a climb this summer. Seems all that attention you showered on me was more about business than anything personal."

"Now I remember. You were with three guys. We all crack climbed a chimney." Trip raised his glass in a toast, relieved he hadn't actually forgotten having had sex with a woman. "If I recall correctly, you had natural skill. Ellie, right?"

"Ali, and thanks." She leaned close, her thigh brushing against his, humor now replaced with genuine flirtation. "If *I* recall correctly, you promised to show me a good time next time I saw you."

That he had. Of course, now he couldn't make good on that promise. More importantly—and somewhat shockingly—he wasn't even interested. Unfortunately, Kelsey walked in just at that moment, looking none too pleased to see him at the bar with another woman practically sitting in his lap.

He waved Kelsey over while replying to Ali. "Well, my circumstances have changed, but we can still have a good time up on the big mountain."

Kelsey stopped beside him, wearing the phoniest smile he'd ever seen on her face. Her misty gaze barely met his before darting to Ali. Was she about to cry? He stood and kissed her cheek and draped his arm around her shoulder to reassure her. "Hey, princess. This here is Ali."

"Hi!" Ali extended her hand to Kelsey. "Trip and I were reminiscing about our summer climbing excursion."

"Nice to meet you." She briefly glanced at Trip, her demeanor almost as chilly as his draft beer. "With ski season on the horizon, I suppose you two can hook up on the mountain again soon."

He didn't know if Ali caught the wordplay, but he certainly hadn't missed the hook-up remark. Kelsey may have been on the verge of tears, but his princess still knew how to push back on him, God love her.

"That's right." Ali touched his arm. "We talked about a backcountry tour, didn't we?"

"We did. So give us a call once some serious snow falls." Trip tossed ten bucks on the bar. "Now if you'll excuse us, we've got dinner plans."

Once he and Kelsey were settled at a table with menus, he gave her a questioning look. "Okay, what's going on with you? You don't expect me not to talk to clients, do you?"

"You can do whatever you want." She barely looked at him, pretending instead to be studying a menu he suspected she knew inside and out. "In fact, I'm quite sure you will regardless of how I feel about it."

Trip grabbed the top of her menu and pushed it down on the table. "Jealousy can be cute to a point, but don't go overboard. I didn't do anything today except buy you some gifts."

"I'm not jealous, but for the record, buying gifts doesn't excuse you from being insensitive." She sat back, betrayal written all over her face. On closer inspection, she looked more defeated than jealous. He didn't know why until she spoke again with a quivering voice. "I got a call from Nick Copeland on my way out of the office. Surely you have an idea of how that conversation went, don't you?"

"Based on your mood, I'd guess it didn't go as you and Wade had hoped." He swallowed the rest of his beer along with a tiny dose of guilt. Apparently Bob Russell hadn't wasted a single moment after their afternoon meeting. Who knew he'd be so efficient?

"Based on my mood? Please don't play dumb with me or I'll reach across this table, grab that Stetson, and stomp all over it." She sat forward, her voice tight. "I don't know how you and your posse got a copy of that study so easily, but I do know you're screwing with a deal that will benefit the Copeland heirs and this whole town."

"And you," he added, irked by the pretense her anger had any altruistic basis. "If we're putting all our cards on the table, the least you could do is be honest about what's really got you upset. This is about what *you* could gain."

"Darn straight, that's a big part of it!" Defiance flickered in her eyes. Her cheeks glowed as red as summer strawberries. If she could have shot lasers from her eyes, he'd be dead, no doubt.

Better he face her anger than her tears. But rather than match her high emotion, he beat back his irritation and calmly nodded. "And you blame me."

She rolled her eyes. "You've already admitted to being the 'Concerned Citizen,' and I know you've been stirring up all the local retailers."

"You've got that wrong. Wade and his big project stirred up the local retailers. All I did was make sure everyone was fully informed of the impact of Wade's plans *before* things went too far. Apparently my concerns were on the mark."

"That study barely skims all the benefits of the project on tourism, on tax revenue, and a bunch of other stuff." She sat back, shaking her head, eyes brimming with fresh tears. "You know that commission money will come in handy now more than ever. I really thought, once we officially got together, you'd stop working against me. Honestly, I thought you cared about me. That we were a team now."

"I do care, dammit. But I never promised to back down from my plans to stop this development." He reached across the table for her hand, but she withdrew it. "I haven't asked you to back off as some kind of proof of your feelings for me, have I? Besides, if this deal falls apart, it's just a delay for you, not a loss. You'll get a commission whenever the Copelands sell that land to someone who has a better project in mind."

"You have no idea how rare it is to be the *sole* broker in a deal. Plus, Wade is willing to pay top dollar for that land. Neither of those things are likely to happen again if this deal dies." She pinched the bridge of her nose to stave off her tears. In an embittered voice, she said, "I'm sure every other offer on that property is going to meet with the same attack from your group, so don't pacify me with this false hope of some better use. There is none."

"Not true. Someone could come up with an idea that benefits the town. In fact, that spot would be a great place for a sports park, with unpaved parking, a football field, baseball diamond, a playground, and maybe even a skateboard park. None of that would destroy existing businesses or the environment. And those would be great resources for kids, teens, and families."

Kelsey's mouth opened and then closed while she considered his suggestion. "That's a beautiful idea, but since there's little to no return on that investment for a developer, it's unlikely." She sunk her chin into her palm and stared at the candle between them. Despite believing he was doing the right thing for the community, her frustrated dreams nipped at his conscience. "The bottom line is that you know how much this deal means to me. You know I'm counting on it so I can afford to buy that apartment building for our future. The fact our future means so little to you tells me maybe *this*—" she gestured between them, "isn't what I'd thought."

Her soft-spoken words tore through his chest with the force of an ice pick. "Princess, *this* is important to me, but I said at the outset I wouldn't be perfect. It's going to take us more than a few weeks or months to come to know and understand each other. But let me tell you, if you think being in a relationship means I've got to always back down when you want your way, well, *no* man will ever live up to that expectation. You've got to trust me when I say I'm invested in our future, and I promise I'm going to help raise this child, which includes paying for everything."

Kelsey fiddled with her fork, glancing up at him from beneath her lashes. "I admire you and Grey making a go of your business, so no offense intended here, but Backtrax isn't raking in the cash. Babies are expensive. School, clothes, lessons, college . . ."

"Trust me, Kelsey, our baby won't have any money worries." Trip shifted in his seat, as uncomfortable as ever when thinking about his giant trust fund.

"Good intentions won't bring in the *serious* money I could clear on Wade's latest proposal." She sipped her lemon water, her emotions fading as she swung into business mode.

"I have money." He crossed his arms and stretched out his legs. "Serious money."

Kelsey narrowed her eyes. "From what? Gigolo services on the side?"

His body heat jumped ten degrees thanks to her sarcasm. "I didn't say billions, princess." He immediately regretted his snide remark. "It doesn't matter why I have it, I just do."

She sat back, her lips twitching.

"So you won't tell me more? Don't you trust me?" Now she had the audacity to look hurt, like she hadn't just insulted him six ways to Sunday. He couldn't help but laugh at the whole situation: him trying and failing to understand this frustrating, sexy woman.

"You're a handful in more ways than one, you know that?" When she cocked a brow, he leaned forward and took hold of her hand. His muscles relaxed, his pulse slowed.

She shrugged and sat back in her seat, pulling away from him. "Guess we've both got to take the good with the bad. Is that a problem?"

"Not for me." He polished off his beer and nodded at the waitress to bring another.

The weight of Kelsey's scrutiny hung on his shoulders. She pressed her lips together while she creased her napkin like a fan. "Trip, tell me about where you got this money." She playfully smirked. "Otherwise I'm going to worry about having to bring our baby to visit you in jail."

He sighed, knowing he'd have to tell the truth sooner or later. "My dad set up a substantial trust fund when he adopted me." He shifted in his seat again, glancing around the restaurant looking for the waitress who should be bringing him his much-needed next drink.

"So you've had money for most of your life?" Kelsey's forehead wrinkled in confusion. "Then why do you drive that beater van and share that dingy little apartment with Grey?"

"I don't touch the money." Wincing, he sighed. "At least I never did until recently, when I needed a little to buy into Backtrax."

"Why not?" Her bewilderment softened the probing question, but it still pricked at the base of his skull.

He rubbed the back of his neck. "Because I always thought of it as bribe money. Like my dad thought he could buy his way out of his mistakes, or buy my love or something. I don't know exactly. I only knew I couldn't be a hypocrite and take the money while keeping my distance."

Kelsey drummed her fingers against the table, apparently deep in thought. Her compassionate eyes studied him as she reached across the table to touch his hand. "I'm sorry you've had such a hard time with your family. Makes me realize how much I take my own situation for granted. But do you really think he's trying to buy your love? Maybe he just wanted to give you a sense of security."

"Or save on taxes," Trip scoffed. It occurred to him Kelsey had better understand he had no interest in living the high life. "Listen, I've never been, and will never be, interested in being part of that moneyed world. My life was happier poor than it ever was with my rich family. And from what I observed among my parents' friends, wealth can be a booby trap of stress, competition, and paranoia."

"I wouldn't know." She grinned and sipped her water.

"In all seriousness, I'm happy with simple things. And I don't want my kids to define themselves by any kind of price tag." He stared at her, making sure she understood the importance of that value.

"Neither do I, Trip. And I hope you know, my feelings for you have nothing to do with your money or how you can make my life easier."

"I know." Not only hadn't Kelsey known about his wealth until five minutes ago, she also still hadn't asked him how much he had, which proved she had no plans to take him to the cleaners. "Let's drop the whole thing, except for the fact that now you can relax about whether or not you end up with that big commission."

Her nose wrinkled. "Not really. It's great that you're willing to draw from your trust for our child, but it's *your* money. You throw yourself off cliffs for a living, so what if something happens to you? My career—and deals like Wade's—are still important to me, and I'm going to fight you on this one until the bitter end. I have to be able to provide for myself and this baby because, bottom line, you and I aren't married."

The melancholy tone of her voice at the end of her diatribe sank in his gut like an anchor, making him ache. Married. It was what she'd most wanted. What, originally, he'd promised to help her achieve. And what he could not give her now.

Maybe not ever.

If only he could convince her that marriage wasn't a panacea. That they could be great together without a piece of paper forcing them to be a couple. That, even if their relationship didn't last forever, he'd make sure she was always taken care of.

"If something happens to me, then my trust funds will go directly to any and all of my children." He squeezed her hand, unable to make more than a promise he *knew* he could keep. "I promise you, you'll never have to worry about needing money to raise our child, okay?"

She barely looked at him as she forced a lame grin on her face. "Okay."

Without saying more, she lifted the menu and hid her face. This time he didn't make her put it down, because he couldn't bear to see her so dejected.

"Do you know why Avery wanted us to all meet at my office before work?" Kelsey asked Emma while handing her a cup of coffee.

"Nope." She shook her head. "But she sounded excited."

Kelsey slid into her chair and sipped her decaffeinated drink, missing the high-octane version. To her right sat a copy of the blasted impact study that threatened her sale. She hated the possibility of losing the battle, but had worked all night to convince herself that being with Trip and having this baby were ultimately the more important prize. She was so close to having the life she'd dreamed about for so long. If only he'd put a ring on her finger and promise to love her forever.

"I hope, at eight weeks into this pregnancy, you're not still experiencing morning sickness for too much longer." Emma leaned forward, apparently interested in discussing the baby situation.

"At least it goes away by midday." Kelsey rubbed her temple. "Lately it's these headaches that are killing me. I think it must be caffeine withdrawal."

"Maybe you should check with your doctor," Emma suggested, then bit her lip before speaking again, her voice somewhat tentative. "Is Trip being helpful?"

Sure, if you don't count him screwing up my career goals.

"He's been surprisingly cute about everything. Making sure I'm eating right, helping do things around my house so I don't have to stress or strain, buying all kinds of pregnancy stuff, acting excited about 'junior' instead of terrified or resentful, like I first expected."

"So you're happy?" Emma edged forward, her eyes wide with hope. "I mean, I know you've always wanted to be a mom, but I also know how much you really want to be a wife."

"I'm not overthinking that part, at least not yet." Kelsey took a long sip of coffee and avoided Emma's gaze. Her friends knew her too well. Being a wife *had* been a lifelong priority, so of course she wanted to marry Trip, especially now that they were having a baby.

First, however, he'd actually have to declare his love for her—a milestone they hadn't yet reached. And considering the way he was attacking the Copeland deal, maybe he didn't care quite as much as she'd hoped. Maybe she'd never be able to read any man's intentions right, not even Trip's. Was she foolish to believe a freewheeler like Trip could commit? Maybe she shouldn't go borrowing trouble. "I think all Trip needs is more time to adjust to all the changes."

At that moment, Avery swept into the office wearing a smile as broad as the Grand Canyon. Without a word, she held her left hand up in the air and wiggled her ring finger.

"Oh my God!" Emma jumped up, her gaze fixed on the sparkling diamond ring now at home on Avery's hand, and rocked Avery back and forth in a hug. "Oh my God, congratulations!"

Kelsey schooled her features, rose from her chair, and walked around her desk to join in the group hug. After easing away, Kelsey grabbed Avery's hand, studying the ring: a round-cut diamond simply set in platinum. Probably somewhere between one-half and one carat in size. Very classic. Very Grey.

"I didn't even know you guys were talking about marriage." Kelsey mentally ripped apart the envy lacing her happiness for Avery. She smiled, although she couldn't lie to herself and pretend it didn't gall her that Avery, the girl who never wanted to be anyone's wife, would be married before her. Avery, who'd kept Grey at arm's length for months, was living out Kelsey's dream of perfect romantic love and *she* wasn't even pregnant!

"We weren't. He totally surprised me yesterday afternoon." Avery beamed as she recounted the details of Grey's proposal. "We took Shaman on a hike, back to the place where we had our first official date. Then, out of the blue, Grey bent down on his good knee, all traditional, and asked me to be his wife."

"And you said yes!" Kelsey shoved aside her petty envy and grabbed Avery again, bouncing a bit on her toes. After all, she'd always been a sucker for romance. "Finally you've joined the rest of the world in believing in love. This calls for a big celebration! Jeez, Ave, why in the heck did you choose now to share this news? I've got a full plate today."

"Sorry! I was just so excited, and I didn't want to risk you guys hearing it on the street before I had a chance to tell you." Avery smiled and looked at her own hand again before clasping it in the other and bringing them to her chest.

Avery had succumbed to love. If *Avery* could be swayed, then so could Trip. That thought prompted a little jolt of excitement.

"Can I ask what changed your mind about marriage?" Kelsey leaned against the edge of her desk and crossed her arms, waiting for the key she needed to unlock Trip's heart and drive out his reservations. "You pretty much swore you'd never be anyone's wife."

Avery shrugged. "I don't know. Grey's different. He lets me be who I am without trying to change me. I trust him."

Kelsey frowned. Avery's answers were too darn generic to be helpful. "When did you know that you wanted *only him* for the rest of your life?"

Avery cocked her head, looking thoughtful. She tapped a finger to her lips before glancing at Emma and Kelsey. "Maybe when he helped Andy with the prosecutor even after my family and I hurt him? I don't really know. It's not like something suddenly hit me over the head. I didn't even expect the proposal, but I also didn't hesitate to say yes. "

"You two make an awesome couple. I can't wait for the wedding." Emma clapped excitedly. "Can I bake the wedding cake?"

"Of course!" Avery laughed.

"Chocolate hazelnut cake with buttercream icing, right?" Emma smiled, knowing Avery's favorite dessert.

"Perfect." Avery glanced at her watch, then her ring finger, then her friends. "Well, hate to dash, but I've got a patient in ten minutes. Maybe we can get together for dinner this week?"

"Sounds great," Kelsey replied.

The friends hugged again before Avery exited the office. Kelsey wistfully watched Avery jog down the street and then sighed.

"Are you okay?" Emma approached and placed her arm around Kelsey's shoulder.

"Of course." Kelsey patted Emma's hand before shrugging out of her grasp.

Emma tipped her head. "You can be honest with me, you know. I've known you my whole life. Don't tell me some part of you doesn't wish you were in Avery's shoes now, especially with a baby on the way."

"Naturally I'd prefer being married to being a single mom. But I'm happy for Avery and Grey. I swear I am." She really was, despite the brief appearance of the green-eyed monster.

"I know. I only hope their engagement doesn't have some negative impact on you and Trip, especially since you two are doing well."

"No worries. If anything, Avery's news makes me more optimistic, not less." When Emma frowned at Kelsey in confusion, she continued. "If Grey could convince Avery to get married, surely I can convince Trip. No one was less romantic than Avery. Not even Trip!"

Emma shot Kelsey a concerned look. "Oh, Kelsey. Don't get your hopes up. Trip may be accepting responsibility for you and the baby, but that doesn't mean he'll do an about-face on his whole life's philosophy. You can't expect that, especially not so soon."

"Life philosophy? No. I think he's just afraid of love." She nodded, as if convincing Emma somehow meant she'd win the war for his heart. "Afraid of getting hurt because he hasn't experienced a lot of unconditional love. Once I prove that I won't hurt him, he'll propose."

"And is that what you want?" Emma pinned her with an openly questioning gaze. "You always talk in the abstract about babies and family and marriage, but do you *love* Trip? Because, honestly, that's the only reason you should want to marry him."

Kelsey's skin tightened under Emma's scrutiny. She closed her eyes, embarrassed. "I know I'm probably foolish to have fallen for him, but I have. He's sexy and surprisingly sweet, strong and willful, fun and sentimental, even if he doesn't see it. But I haven't shared my feelings with him yet, at least, not in so many words."

"So I take it he hasn't told you he loves you, either." Emma's face filled with empathy.

"He hasn't, but he acts like he loves me. He's always buying me little gifts, which means he's thinking about me a lot. He worships me in bed. He'd already given up other women before he even knew about the baby. And he beat Mason to a pulp over me." Kelsey looked at Emma, seeking confirmation. "Don't those sound like the actions of a man in love?"

Emma's skeptical expression spoke volumes. "Well, it sounds like he's got volatile emotions. Maybe he loves you, but shouldn't it be easier for both of you to talk about it? I mean, isn't that what healthy couples do?"

"Heck if I know, Emma. When's the last time you saw me in a healthy relationship?"

Emma reached for Kelsey's hands and squeezed them. "Even if he loves you, Kels, that doesn't mean he'll ever believe in marriage. I know you think he can be turned around, like Avery. But what if you're wrong?"

Kelsey's brain shut down. Honestly, she couldn't conceive of any person intentionally pushing away love. Surely Trip had convinced himself of this "marriage never works" attitude in order to make sense of the circumstances of his own messed up family . . . his very existence. Once he spent time around loving families and couples, his silly fears would fade.

Kelsey nodded to herself, and then met Emma's sympathetic gaze. "I'm not wrong."

Chapter Seventeen

Dusk settled as Trip followed Kelsey onto Maura's front porch, where he could hear muted conversation and melodies emanating from behind the closed door. The last time he'd climbed these steps carrying a bouquet of flowers, things hadn't gone so well.

Tonight could be worse.

Across the threshold he'd be facing her parents' closest friends and family, all of whom had been invited to celebrate their thirty-fifth wedding anniversary. He'd bet his entire trust fund that his and Kelsey's "situation" would draw unwanted attention and questions, especially now that Avery and Grey had gotten engaged. Nervous anticipation curdled in his stomach, making him wish they could ditch the party altogether.

At least they'd managed to set aside their differences about Wade's plans since Tuesday rather than fight while awaiting the outcome. But that part of her future was less critical to her, and to her family, than this part—the family part. Trouble here could make everything between Kelsey and him fall to pieces.

"Ready?" Kelsey brushed her hand along his arm. Her golden hair glowed beneath the soft porch light, the tip of her nose rosy from the bite of cold air. She looked stunning, dressed up in a plum-colored ensemble and a brave smile. It still surprised him; the way his heart stuttered each time their eyes met. Her grace under pressure, however, didn't surprise him.

After taking an extra second to admire her, he followed her lead and faked a smile despite entering the gauntlet. "Let's go."

They'd barely stepped into the entry when a petite, blond Tasmanian devil in a ruffled yellow dress and white tights galloped toward them, shoeless.

"Aunt Kelsey!" Fee skidded before colliding with Kelsey's legs, hugging them until her little face turned crimson. Then she turned her wide eyes up at Trip. "Hi!"

He squatted and tweaked her chin. "Hey there, pretty girl. Twirl around so I can see the whole dress." Her tiny-toothed smile perked him up, as did the quick spin she excitedly performed. "Well, it's *almost* as lovely as you."

She giggled and grabbed Kelsey's hand. "Meemaw and Pops get all the presents tonight, huh?"

"Yes, they do. Thirty-five years of marriage is a big deal, right?"

Fee shrugged, clearly unimpressed by the milestone. "As long as I get cake."

"Don't worry," Kelsey assured. "I'll make sure you get the biggest piece."

Just then Maura spotted Kelsey and Trip still standing near the front door, where Fee had them cornered. She beelined toward them and placed her hands on Fee's shoulders. "Well, hello, you two." She kissed Kelsey's cheek and offered Trip a look he could only describe as resigned. "Welcome, Trip. Guess congratulations are in order for you, too, right?"

"Thanks." He wrapped his arm around Kelsey's shoulders, partly because he wanted to touch her, and partly because he wanted to show her family their solidarity. "We're real excited."

"About what?" Fee asked.

"About the baby," Trip answered. When Kelsey's elbow poked his side, he realized too late that the family had intentionally withheld the information from Fee.

"What baby?" Fee asked, turning her face up toward her mom. "What baby, Mommy?"

Maura sent a sharp glance in Trip's direction before faking a smile at her daughter. "Aunt Kelsey is having a baby."

"Like you?" Fee's eyes widened in shock, then, when turning toward Kelsey, her pale brows pulled together. "But how can you be a mommy if you're not married?"

"I . . . uh." Kelsey cringed. Under other circumstances, the sheer astonishment of seeing Kelsey at a loss for words might've made Trip chuckle. He stifled the urge in order to avoid a consequence more painful than a simple elbow to the ribs.

"Fee, honey, we can talk about all that later. Let's let Aunt Kelsey and Trip come in and enjoy the party." After exchanging a quick glance with her sister, Maura gestured toward the rear of the home. "Mom and Dad are in the living room."

"Thanks." Kelsey took two steps and scanned the candlelit home, her gaze moving from the gleaming silver trays lining the dining table to the fresh flowers scattered in glass vases throughout the space. Frank Sinatra's indelible crooning enhanced the nostalgic mood of the party.

Cozy, like a lot of things Trip noticed about the Callihan clan. A marked difference from the crystal-laden reception Deb had thrown for her and his father's thirtieth anniversary, complete with eight-piece band, Beluga caviar, and one hundred of their "closest friends."

However, the ambience also suggested the entire Callihan family indulged romantic sentiments just like Kelsey, as if they could make their real life as enchanting as a Hollywood love story. It worried Trip—Kelsey's illusions of love—making him question her ability to be happy in a less-than-perfect relationship with a notoriously less-than-perfect man.

Kelsey grasped Maura's forearm. "Looks great, sis. Don't forget to tell me my share of the catering bill."

"I will, don't worry." Maura turned toward Trip, her polite smile almost masking her annoyance with his recent gaffe. "The bar is in the dining room. I've got to go check on the caterers, if you'll excuse me." She tugged on Fee's curls. "Come help Mommy, okay?"

"Can I have a cookie from that big tray in the kitchen?" Fee clapped her hands together in prayer.

"After dinner," Maura said.

Fee frowned but dutifully followed her mother, skating along the wood floor in her tights.

"Well, that was awkward." Kelsey wrinkled her nose while Trip took her purse and coat to hang in the hall closet.

"One down, many to go." Trip sighed. "Guess we can't avoid the firing squad forever."

Kelsey slapped his arm. "Who knew a guy who defies death on a daily basis could be so fearful of my parents and their old cronies?"

Who knew, indeed?

Feigning the confidence that had deserted him on the front porch, he smirked. "Lead on, princess."

When she stepped ahead of him, he pinched her behind. She swatted his hand. "Honestly, I think we both know this isn't the time or place for your games. Can you stop acting like a teenage boy and please help me convince my parents we aren't making the biggest mistake of our lives?"

Remorse twisted through him with the sharp sting of a paper cut. He should've pushed Kelsey to get them all together *before* this big party. He'd been so consumed with his own discomfort, he hadn't given much thought to hers, or theirs, until that moment.

As they breezed past the dining room, he looked longingly at the makeshift bar.

"Let's say hi to my folks, first," Kelsey said when she noticed him hesitate. "Then you can run back here for liquid courage."

"I don't need courage," he grumbled. Yet his mouth did feel damn dry.

At the far corner of the living room, just beyond the archway, Mr. and Mrs. Callihan stood, surrounded by several older people. Mrs.

Callihan, an attractive blonde like her daughters, was telling a story when Mr. Callihan glanced over and noticed Trip and Kelsey's arrival. Although Trip had met the man months ago at Kelsey's birthday dinner, his broad chest and dark brows looked more menacing than Trip recalled.

The older man's faltering smile suggested he was almost as uncomfortable greeting Trip as Trip felt about seeing him. And now both had to playact in front of an audience.

The swelling pressure at the base of Trip's skull intensified with each step toward the group until Kelsey grabbed his hand and squeezed. Like a warm bath after a cold day on the slopes, her gentle touch soothed.

When they reached the circle of adults, Kelsey excused their intrusion before hugging her parents. "Congratulations, Mom and Dad. You set a high bar for the rest of us."

Trip maintained a friendly smile despite being raked by a dozen curious eyes. He extended the bouquet toward Mrs. Callihan. "Happy anniversary, Mrs. Callihan."

Unlike Kelsey's dad, her mother's natural warmth shone through her stilted demeanor as she accepted his small gift. "Thank you. It's nice to see you again."

"You, too. You look lovely tonight." Trip then turned and extended his hand toward Kelsey's dad. "Mr. Callihan, congratulations."

Mr. Callihan's tight-lipped expression and firm handshake confirmed Trip's suspicions. The man didn't trust him. In fact, he probably resented the hell out of him, considering Kelsey was knocked up and Trip hadn't proposed.

"Trip," Kelsey began, in a valiant effort to act perfectly normal, "this is my Aunt Winnie and Uncle Lou, my parents' neighbors, Jim and Sally, and my dad's longtime colleague and his wife, Bill and Pat. Everyone, this is Trip."

Trip shook everyone's hands, then snaked an arm around Kelsey's waist and braced for a bunch of questions.

"Nice to meet you, son." Uncle Lou sipped what appeared to be whiskey. "So where are you from?"

"I grew up in Denver, then spent my twenties working in various resorts across the northwest up to Alaska."

Jim interrupted, "Our son, Tim, worked at Alyeska in 2010 and 2011. Know him?"

Seriously? "I actually worked for a heli-ski outfit up there, not at a resort. I was already gone by 2011, sorry."

"Surely you won't do that dangerous kind of skiing now, with the baby coming?" Kelsey's aunt asked once she'd quit gaping.

Mr. Callihan's gaze homed in on Trip, making him wish he'd stopped at the bar before facing his executioners. Perhaps it was better to address the elephant in the room sooner rather than later. But the nervous cone of silence that enveloped their little group pushed him center stage, transforming him into a young kid who suddenly forgot all the lines of the school play.

Mrs. Callihan tossed a perturbed glance at Aunt Winnie.

Kelsey gently rubbed Trip's back, reassuring him while pleasantly smiling at the group. Hell, if she could brazen through, so could he. After clearing his throat, he finally replied, "Gotta work so I can help support Kelsey and our baby."

"Don't mind Winnie." Uncle Lou swirled his glass, ice cubes clinking against its sides. "She's just looking out for her niece, and eager for any excuse to talk about babies . . . and weddings."

Trip hadn't noticed his ever-tightening hold on Kelsey's waist until she wedged her thumb inside his grip. "Uncle Lou, we're here to celebrate Mom and Dad, not talk about me. Now, if you'll excuse us, we haven't had a chance to say hi to Bill, or grab any of the yummy apps."

Thank God she'd rescued him.

Weddings!

Winnie's remark made a total of two unwed pregnancy comments within ten minutes of his arrival. He'd expected a couple of unsubtle hints, considering they were attending a milestone anniversary party. But at this rate, he'd be tarred and feathered by eight o'clock.

Once they'd ducked into the dining room and out of her parents' sight, he gave Kelsey a quick peck on the cheek. "I need a drink. What can I get you?"

She sighed, and only then did he notice both the strain and distance in her eyes. "Seltzer, please. I'm going to see how I can help Maura. Be right back."

When she meandered toward the kitchen, his stomach started to burn.

"Hey, Trip. Hiding out from the preacher?" Bill stood behind the bar, cutting extra lemons and limes.

Preacher? A cold sweat broke out beneath Trip's clothes. His muscles seized up, his throat tightened. "Pardon me?"

"Just kiddin'!" Bill chuckled and then poured himself a drink. "You oughta see your face right now."

Embarrassed and annoyed, Trip drew a deep breath. Tonight he couldn't offend Kelsey's family or stick his foot in his mouth with his typical sarcasm. For better or worse, he had to forge relationships with these folks for junior's sake, and for Kelsey's.

"You got me," Trip conceded. He glanced at the grandfather clock in the entry. Only seven twenty. Good Lord, it would be a long night.

By nine thirty, Trip gulped down his third scotch of the evening, weary from the duck-and-cover game he'd been playing to avoid direct questions about his and Kelsey's plans for the future. "Hell if I know" probably wouldn't have gone over very well with this crowd.

He stared into the bottom of his empty glass, frowning. What he *did* know was precious little. A, Kelsey enthralled him like no other woman ever had. B, no doubt he couldn't have lucked into a better mother for his child. C, he'd never planned on having children, and although he had every intention of being the best father he could, he wasn't all that convinced his best would be good enough. D, sooner or later Kelsey would start pressuring him for a more permanent commitment, and then what?

Tonight he'd observed a dozen or so happy couples of various ages engage with each other. All but one seemed genuinely happy. He'd noted affectionate touches, loving glances, gentlemanly gestures, secret whispers—all the while questioning the truth behind their actions. Like an alien plopped into the middle of a culture he'd never much experienced, he couldn't quite believe what he saw.

Although his mother had casually dated, she hadn't brought men into their home, so he'd never seen her in a serious romantic relationship. His father's marriage wasn't openly affectionate, although he suspected his dad and Deb shared an active sex life, if for no other reason than Deb's determination that he not stray from her bed again. Mason and his wife, well, he'd barely been around them enough to make a fair judgment, but the divorce confirmed his suspicions.

Even if Trip *were* certain he was falling in love with Kelsey, did it follow that marriage would make them happier? Seemed to him half of all married couples divorced, and the other half mostly complained about each other and had less sex than when they'd been dating. With stats like that, why muck up a good thing?

Just then he heard Kelsey's feminine giggle from across the room. She'd been a perfect cohost for her sister, balancing her time between entertaining guests, helping to direct the caterers, and looking after Fee and Ty when needed.

A force of nature at times, yet tender and soft at others—a five-thousand-piece puzzle with no picture for guidance.

He looked up to catch her, standing in the archway with Ty on her hip, accepting the child's sloppy kisses before wiping the slobber from her cheek. She hugged the baby, swaying to the music with her tiny dance partner, her eyes lit with adoration.

In an instant, Trip envisioned her cuddling *their* infant. That beautiful, loving woman would be the mother of his child. One way or another, they'd forever be intertwined. She'd shower him with all her warmth if he'd let her, and that reality snatched the breath from his lungs.

A pang—an ache for something he didn't even know he wanted—pressed on his heart.

He set his glass down and crossed the mostly empty room. "Can I cut in?"

Kelsey glanced around for a second and spotted her mom in the dining room. "Mom, can you take Ty?"

"Oh, please." Her mom approached with open arms. "Come here, love bug."

Once the exchange had been made and Mrs. Callihan walked away, Trip pulled Kelsey into his arms for a private slow dance in the entry. Ed Sheeran's "Thinking Out Loud" wasn't a country song, but it was close enough for Trip's liking.

He wrapped one arm firmly behind her back, and took her hand in his other and placed it against his chest. He merely needed to tilt his head a bit in order to be cheek to cheek, thanks to her spiky heels.

Neither of them said a word as he led her around the little space. Peace took root and spread through him. This kind of tender moment . . . it was enough for him. He didn't need to complicate things with promises about a future he couldn't predict.

Kelsey's earlier tension seemed to melt once he held her in his arms. Her lips brushed his neck before she whispered, "Maybe this will be us one day, thirty-five years from now."

If she noticed his misstep as every muscle in his body contracted, she didn't let on. Instead, she laid her head on his shoulder and hummed along with the melody.

Kelsey stared into the mirror, brushing her teeth without seeing her reflection. Her mind was too lost in thoughts about the party and Trip to register much of anything else.

The blinds in the bedroom rattled, probably from him pushing them aside to look out the window at the snowfall. The major storm predicted—uncharacteristic for this early in October—had started up around nine o'clock. If they woke to the anticipated foot of fresh snow, no doubt he'd be pulling out his skis tomorrow and hiking up the mountain.

Not that he'd mentioned it on their way home. He'd been unusually quiet ever since their spontaneous dance in Maura's entry.

When he'd asked to cut in, with his sexy bedroom voice, his eyes had shone with affection. He'd taken her in his arms and held her close—gently, *lovingly.* A perfect moment: one that had nearly convinced her of his love, until her wistful comment had sent him fleeing.

One moment she wished she could retract it, the next moment she resented him for not even allowing her to hope for anything beyond the here and now.

Emma's probing questions about healthy relationships and love kept poking at her conscience. Maybe *they* were the reason for all the headaches she'd been experiencing this past week.

After rinsing her mouth, she grabbed her silk robe and walked into the bedroom. Trip lay sprawled out on her bed, eyes closed, wearing nothing but his boxer briefs. His athletic body—its gorgeous slopes and ridges of muscle—momentarily distracted her.

As if sensing her gaze scouring him, he popped one eyelid open and grinned. "Like what you see?"

"Most of the time." All of the time, really, but his ego needed no encouragement.

Trip propped himself up on his elbows and tipped his head. "But not tonight?"

Kelsey sighed and sat in the chair across from the bed. She placed her hands on her knees, her gaze drawn to her fingernails while she groped for words.

"Uh-oh. This little scene is reminding me of our first night together." Trip sat upright. "You're not about to kick me to the curb again, are you?"

She looked up, surprised by his careful tone and perturbed recollection of that hot July night. So much had changed since then it seemed like much longer than ten weeks ago. The bargain they'd struck hadn't turned out as either of them had planned.

Trip had thundered into her world bringing an avalanche of thrills, chaos, comfort, and one of her heart's dearest desires—a baby. Like any natural disaster, his presence had upended her life. Now, despite all of her early efforts to control her heart, it lay exposed and yearning and not at all safe from harm.

His dating tips flashed through her mind like a blinking traffic light, urging caution. Yet her need for reassurance overwhelmed her restraint.

Her skin grew clammy, her stomach cramped, but she pushed forward.

"You were uncomfortable tonight, weren't you?" She glanced away and then back at him. "I mean, you were pleasant with my family, but you weren't yourself."

"That's probably a good thing, right?" he teased. Another deflection, like always. She stared expectantly without smiling, forcing him to answer her question with something more than a glib remark. He rolled his shoulders back. "Did I do or say something wrong earlier, aside from the Fee thing?"

"No. In fact, I doubt anyone but me noticed your itch to bolt . . . like the place was on fire." Kelsey sighed. "Why were so you eager to leave? Don't you like my family?"

Trip reached out for her to come to him and, reluctantly, she did. He pulled her onto his lap, hugging her close and resting his chin on her shoulder. "I think you've got that backward, princess. I like them just fine, but I doubt right now that's a two-way street—not that I blame them, exactly."

He was insecure? Inching closer to the heart of the matter, she said, "Why do you say that?"

Trip placed a hand on her stomach. "Because they love you. They want all your dreams to come true, but I'm in the way. I've messed with the life they wanted you to have. The kind of life they have."

"A married life, you mean." She noticed he'd conveniently left out how it was also the life she wanted.

He hesitated, avoiding her gaze but keeping a firm hold on her. "Yes."

"And marriage will never be for you, will it?" She kept her eyes down, unable to face him, or face the truth.

She felt him shrug, but he said nothing. Tension poured off his body in waves, rocking her emotions like a small rowboat adrift in a stormy sea.

In the ensuing silence, the bedroom seemed to shrink and become stuffy. A thousand unspoken words clogged her throat, making it impossible for Kelsey to catch her breath.

I love you.

Will you ever love me?

Will you ever need *me?*

"Kels?" He raised his hand to her face and forced her to look at him. "It's not you."

Despite her best efforts to be strong, she could feel tears stinging her eyes. "So you say."

"It's *not* you. You're perfect. This—us—it's incredible, too. Why can't this be enough . . . one day at a time? No piece of paper pressuring us to stick it out if things turn sour." He tightened his embrace and spoke enthusiastically, as if he might actually persuade her to see things from his skewed viewpoint. "Isn't it better to wake up every day and make the choice to be together? Aren't we less likely to take each other for granted that way? Less likely to be disappointed because we're not setting up too many expectations? And let's face it, in many ways we're still getting to know each other."

Insecure thoughts and doubts mushroomed like storm clouds, intensifying her headache. Couldn't he understand that the freedom to walk away at any moment was exactly what she didn't like about his perspective? When she tried to pry herself from his arms, he strengthened his hold.

"Kelsey, tell me why this hurts you. You know I've never wanted another woman as much, never felt as safe being myself, never been as content. That's all because of you. Can't we just embrace the journey?"

Kelsey couldn't argue with all of his points. And sure, this whole thing had started less than three months ago, but she'd fallen in love. She could make a promise. She was ready.

Unfortunately, she couldn't force him to feel what he didn't.

She eased off his lap, and this time he didn't stop her. "Let's just drop it. My head is killing me."

Kelsey turned down the covers and crawled under the sheets, her body exhausted from working the party.

Trip stood and faced her. "Do you want me to go?"

"If that's what you want." Her flagging energy and churning stomach stole all her fight.

Trip didn't speak for a minute. Then he turned off the lamp and slid between the covers. He gently tugged her against his body, spooning her. Brushing his hands over her head and down her arm, he murmured, "I want you to be happy, not stressed and upset. You deserve nothing but happiness, and that's what you'll get. Trust me, princess. Everything will turn out all right, I promise."

The fact that he'd just broken his rule against making promises he couldn't keep shot a chill down her spine.

Chapter Eighteen

After eight hours locked in Trip's arms, Kelsey felt him slink out of bed. She cracked open her eyes. In the dim room, she watched him cross to the window to peek behind the blinds. When he turned around—his face lit with enthusiasm—she knew the weatherman's predictions had come true.

So much for a lazy Sunday morning in bed.

She pushed up to her elbow, dismissing the stiffness in her limbs. "Sneaking off?"

He clapped his hands together and rubbed them in excitement. "Nothing better than a foot of fresh pow in October—well, except maybe two feet."

As he collected his clothing and dressed, she settled back beneath the covers and glanced at the clock. Six thirty. Her headache drummed on, and her lower back ached. She must've winced, because Trip walked toward her, frowning. He sat on the edge of the mattress and touched the back of his hand to her forehead.

"You don't look so good, princess. Are you sick?"

"No. I'm just achy."

"Maybe you're coming down with the flu. You should go see the doctor." As he studied her with a look of concern, she couldn't help but grin at his overprotective nature. Something few people would ever guess about him.

"It's not the flu." She patted his hand. "My throat is fine. No congestion. A masseuse would be a better prescription than the doctor."

"You've had a lot of headaches lately. And you were groaning in your sleep, like you were in pain." He looked toward the window, scowling to himself. "Maybe I should stay with you . . . get you to the doctor."

"And miss all the 'fresh pow'?" she teased.

He stroked her head and hair. "Seriously, Kelsey. You haven't felt right all week. Your body's telling you something. We shouldn't ignore it." She noticed his gaze drop and linger in the general area of her midsection.

The baby.

Of course. If Trip loved anyone, it was their baby, not her.

That was the main reason he cared about her health. Why he'd offer to skip skiing and shuttle her around. Why he even proposed dating her at all. Had she never been pregnant, things between them would be so different.

A month ago he'd walked away so she could go on a date with another man—clearly not the action of a man in love. Was she a fool to think he would change? To believe he would come around to embrace her ideas about family and marriage?

She curled her knees up to her chest, glancing away. "I'll be fine, cowboy. Go skiing."

"Kels . . . ," he began, but then he dropped it. He squeezed her thigh. "It's Sunday, so stay in bed and rest. Can I get you anything before I go? Water? Herbal tea?"

She shook her head while trying to beat back her insecurities. "I can take care of myself, thanks. I'm going back to sleep as soon as you leave."

His halfhearted smile suggested he felt conflicted. "My phone will be in my pack, so I won't hear it if you try to call—assuming the call even gets through the spotty coverage up in the mountains."

"Okay. Be careful, Trip." Clasping his hand, she met his gaze. "I know you tempt fate all the time, but . . . well, I don't want you to get hurt."

"Don't worry, princess. I know what I'm doing. But thanks for caring." He leaned forward and kissed her. "I'll come back later this afternoon and check on you. If you spike a fever, get to the doctor."

He lifted his hat off the nightstand and winked at her. "See you later."

And then he was gone.

Closing her eyes, she hugged a pillow and drifted into a dream state.

◆ ◆ ◆

The throbbing in her lower back prevented Kelsey from falling into a deep sleep. Following two hours of semiconscious tossing and turning, she gave up. She opened her eyes and sighed, stretching in a vain effort to loosen the tension that had formed a thick knot at the base of her spine.

Moving slowly, she threw back the blanket and stood, yawning. A small mewl caught her attention as Cowboy padded his way across her floor. Smiling, she lifted her kitten—her favorite gift from Trip—and snuggled him against her face and neck.

Together they crossed to the window and peered outside, where a steady, light snow continued to fall. At least twelve inches, maybe more, had piled up. Snowplows had made one pass down her street, but it looked like another would be needed. In the distance she could see the peaks of the San Juan range over the tops of the buildings in town.

Nuzzling Cowboy, she said, "Your daddy's in his glory right now."

Kelsey stood at the window another moment, watching the steady snowfall add to the pile on the street below. She couldn't remember a storm this severe in early October during her lifetime.

The near whiteout in town meant visibility on the mountain would be wretched. Trip had surely encountered these conditions and worse before, especially in Utah and Alaska. Still, concern nagged.

She'd never seen Trip ski, but she'd overheard others in town talk about him and Grey. Unlike Avery, whose competitive nature spurred her to keep up with her brother, Kelsey had never ventured into backcountry skiing. Once the baby arrived, she'd continue that policy. Frowning, she realized she'd have to train herself not to worry about Trip facing danger on the job every day.

When she finally released the blind, it clattered against the window as it fell back in place, shattering the silence of her apartment.

After setting Cowboy on the floor, she twisted left and then right. When that failed to ease the tension in her body, she rubbed her lower back with her hands while arching her spine like a cat. Still, the achiness spread and her lower back muscles began to spasm.

With no appointments or open houses on her agenda, she drew a warm bath, determined to feel better. She slipped into her gorgeous claw-foot tub, closed her eyes, and listened to the soothing sounds of Reneé Michele's music.

The heat instantly eased her body and calmed her mind.

Inhaling the steam, she focused her thoughts on envisioning the future she wanted. The one she prayed a little patience, understanding, and persistence would attain.

A smile curled the corners of her mouth as she pictured Trip at the end of the center aisle in her church. He'd be dashing, with his jet-black hair and fashionable tuxedo.

She fantasized about the look that would be in his eyes when she walked down the aisle—one of adoration and affection. The same look she sometimes thought she noticed when his guard was down.

Amazingly, what had begun as unbridled lust between them had blossomed into a genuine, intimate friendship. If only he could trust it, or her, or love. She desperately wanted to suppress her misgivings and assure herself that someday he would. If not before the baby arrived, then soon afterward.

The baby. Despite Trip's conviction they'd have a boy, Kelsey pictured a girl. One with dark hair, green eyes, and a smile as big as a crescent moon, just like her father.

She imagined strolling through town with Trip on a lazy summer day, their daughter on his shoulders, and her own belly distended with another baby. It all seemed so perfect and real, her heart thumped against her chest.

Then, just as she had begun to embrace hope, her abdomen clenched hard. The sudden stab of pain propelled her upright. She opened her eyes and saw pink-tinged water radiating from between her legs.

Stunned, she kicked, as if trying to get away from danger, sending water sloshing over the edge of the tub. *Please, not the baby. Please, not my baby.* She quickly climbed out of the tub and dried off, reminding herself that a little spotting was nothing to panic about. Then more blood saturated the toilet paper she used to assess the situation.

Oh, God. No!

As if in a daydream, she stumbled into her room. Her limbs prickled with heat, her heart thundered in her ears, her skin broke into a sudden, profuse sweat. The dizzying spike of adrenaline caused her to teeter, so she sank onto her bed and tried to take control of her body.

Calm down. It's okay. It'll be okay.

Another cramp struck while she lay curled on her comforter. Warm tears tracked down her cheeks, screams strangled to silence in her ever-tightening throat.

Move, Kelsey! Save your baby.

She forced herself to sit upright. Taking deep breaths, she called Trip but it went straight to voice mail. She hung up without leaving a message, threw on sweats and a turtleneck, and then called Maura.

"What's up, sis?" Maura's sing-songy voice rang out.

"The baby . . . I'm bleeding," Kelsey choked out, unable to stop her tears or sniffling.

"Oh, Kelsey, I'll be right over! Did you call Trip?"

"He's skiing. I can't reach him." The enormity of what could be happening overwhelmed her once more, and another painful sob escaped her throat.

"I'll be there in five minutes. Call the doctor. I'll drive."

While Trip removed the skins from his skis at the top of his fourth climb that day, he took a minute to soak up the scenery. The snow had finally stopped and the sun was peeking through the clouds. An occasional breeze wafted snowflakes off of fir trees, casting them into the air, where they floated around like glitter.

Grey had quit before lunch, unwilling to push his knee too hard on day one. But he'd been pleased with the joint's stability, so they'd both considered the morning a success. Trip had then met up with his buddy Jon and continued to shred fresh powder for three more hours. Now his thoughts returned to Kelsey.

He should've insisted she go to the doctor earlier this week. But more troubling than her health was the melancholy mood she'd revealed late last night. He'd hated himself for upsetting her. Hated that he couldn't quite trust his own feelings, allowing past ghosts to spook him. Allowing fear and doubt to intrude.

"All set?" Jon called out from the edge of the cornice where he hovered, ready to huck into the gorge.

"One sec." Trip returned the skins to his backpack, locked his bindings, and clicked his boots in place. He couldn't afford to think about Kelsey when avoiding a major accident on his last run of the day required every bit of his concentration.

He edged closer to Jon and gave the thumbs-up. With a quick shout of triumph, Jon shot over the edge. Ten seconds later, Trip followed, a puff of icy powder exploding around him when he landed, snow spray billowing as he descended down the slope, knee-deep in powder.

When they got to the base of the mountain, he declined Jon's offer to stop at the OS for a drink. Waving off his friend, he then pulled his phone from inside his backpack. Kelsey had called earlier in the morning, but hadn't left a message. Bob Russell had called, too. That seemed unusual, but maybe he had more news from the Copeland family.

Much as he wanted to kill Wade's deal, he didn't relish delivering bad news to Kelsey. Hell, if something had happened, she probably already knew it. Best he face the fire head-on.

He sat on a public bench near the gondola, propped up his skies, and dialed Kelsey. When she didn't answer, he hung up and called Bob.

"Hello?" Bob answered.

"Hey, Bob. It's Trip Lexington, returning your call." Trip stretched his legs out. "What's up?"

"The Copelands have pulled the deal to sell their land to Wade Kessler." The man sounded drunk with excitement. Yet somehow Trip's own sense of victory was tempered by the knowledge of Kelsey's defeat.

"So it's dead, for real?" He sat forward, gaze glued to the sidewalk.

"Yessir. Apparently Kelsey and Wade made a last-ditch appeal to the family the other day."

That news surprised Trip, because other than her general vow to pursue this deal to the bitter end, Kelsey hadn't mentioned that meeting. He cracked a smile at his firecracker's determination, one of her most admirable qualities. His thoughts were interrupted when Bob continued speaking.

"Wade tried to downplay the negative aspects of that study, and promised to do a bunch of extra things to address everyone's needs and concerns." Bob chuckled. "Good thing the Copelands have been around the block before and knew enough to realize, once Wade owned their land, they'd have no control over what happened."

Trip knew that wasn't exactly true, either. They could've forced restrictions in the deed or other agreements that would affect the land. Not that he wanted to see Wade build shops and offices, but still.

"So, when did Wade get the bad news? Last night?" Maybe Kelsey had received a text after they'd left her parents' party. That could explain the dip in her mood late last night, and why she wouldn't want to discuss it with him.

"Nick couldn't reach Kelsey, so he called Wade after church this morning."

Trip wondered if Kelsey had turned off her phone this morning to rest without interruption. She probably called him after she got Nick's message, ready to ream him out. Given her discomfort and mood this morning, the timing really sucked.

Bob continued, "Gotta hand it to Kessler, though. He's a class act. Nick said he was polite. Told Nick to please call him if the family changed their minds."

"I've got no personal problem with Kessler. He's fair. But his goal is to make money, period. I honestly believe that development would've been bad, in the long run, for Sterling Canyon."

"Hey, man, you're preaching to the choir!" Bob chuckled once more, but Trip knew his own words had mostly been about convincing himself that hurting Kelsey had been for the greater good.

"Well, I'm sitting out here on a cold bench, so I'm going to hang up and head home." Trip stood and lifted his skis. "Thanks for the update. You have a good day."

Trip stuck the phone in the backpack, hefted his skis over his shoulder, and walked the few blocks to his home. After a quick shower, he called Kelsey again, hoping she was feeling better, and that she didn't hate him for killing her deal. Maybe he'd pick up her favorite takeout for dinner as a peace offering.

"Trip, it's Maura," Maura said when she answered Kelsey's phone.

"Maura?" His heart stuttered. "Why are you answering Kelsey's phone? Did she get sicker today?"

Maura hesitated, as if trying to figure out what to say. "You should come over as soon as possible."

His pulse sped up slightly as he frowned. "I was already on my way. You sound upset. Is this about Wade Kessler?"

"Wade?" Maura's confused tone gave him his answer. "No. Just come, okay."

"Hang on. Tell me what's wrong."

After a pause and a sigh, he heard her sniffle. His stomach dropped to his feet while he waited for an answer. "I'm sorry, Trip. Kelsey miscarried. I'm really, really sorry, for both of you."

Everything went hazy for a second as he processed the news. *Kelsey miscarried.* "I'll be there in five minutes."

He shoved his phone in his pocket and let white-hot anguish consume his body. He shouldn't have gone skiing today. He'd known it this morning, but shoved aside his instincts to satisfy his own selfish need for pleasure.

The image of Kelsey crying all day, depressed and in pain without him by her side, intensified his guilt and self-loathing.

If this news struck him like a lightning bolt, Kelsey must be inconsolable. No woman ever wanted to be a mom as much as she did. The knowledge that she'd lost the thing she'd most wanted in the world hammered his heart.

Hell, on top of that loss, she probably also received Nick Copeland's message. Trip had to get to her and find some way to make it all better. Pacing like a prisoner looking for an escape, he finally kicked his bedroom door, loosening the hinges.

On shaky legs, he trotted down the steps to the street below, then broke into a sprint.

Using his key, he let himself into her apartment. Maura was in the kitchen fixing a cup of tea. He expected to see Avery and Emma, too, but was glad neither was there.

"Where is she?" Trip tossed his keys aside and crossed to the kitchen.

"Resting in bed." Maura blankly stirred cream in the cup. Her red eyes and blotchy face proved she'd spent the day as distraught as her sister.

"What happened?" Trip gripped the back of the kitchen stool to counteract the current instability of his body. "Did she fall or something?"

"No." Maura shook her head, her eyes watering. She wiped them dry. "Doctor Davis says that about twenty percent of pregnancies end in miscarriage and they don't always know why. Most likely this was nature's way of dealing with a genetic defect in the fetus."

"The doc thinks there was a problem with our baby?" Those two words—our baby—stabbed his chest. Their baby no longer existed, a fact he still couldn't quite wrap his head around.

"Most likely." Maura tentatively touched his forearm. "But she examined Kelsey and didn't see anything to prevent her from getting pregnant again, or carrying to full term next time."

Mired in his own grief, Trip didn't respond to Maura. He felt her mood shift before she released him and he saw her hardened expression.

"Of course, you're not married, so maybe that last part isn't your concern." Maura started to turn away, but he grabbed her arm.

In a terse but low tone, he said, "We're all upset right now, but don't think for one second that I don't feel this loss as much as the rest of you. And whatever happens between your sister and me, I know how much being a mother means to her, so it is very much my concern that she still can be one someday."

Maura shrugged out of his grasp and nodded. "Sorry. I was out of line." She rubbed her forehead and heaved a sigh. "Let me take her this tea, then I'll let you two have some privacy."

Five minutes later, Maura returned to the living room with her purse in hand. "She knows you're here and asked me to go home, but please call me if she needs me. And Trip, I am sorry for your loss, too. I hope . . . I hope you two can comfort each other."

After Maura closed the front door, Trip scrubbed his face with his hands and then walked to Kelsey's room. He drew a deep breath before opening the door.

She lay propped up in bed with Cowboy nestled at her side. When she looked up at him, her chin quivered and fresh tears sprang from her eyes. In three strides, he was at her side.

Careful not to crush her or hurt her, her took her in his arms. Her sobs were loud and authentic and filled with raw emotion, just like every other part of her. His got stuck in his throat, strangling him, keeping him from saying things he felt. Things like how much his heart hurt. How much he'd been looking forward to raising that child with her. How maybe they could try again, if she wanted—a wistful wish that shocked him.

Instead, he remained in silent agony, clinging to her to keep from drowning in his own sorrow.

He'd never felt less of a man.

Kelsey hiccupped and eased away from Trip, pressing herself back into a wall of pillows, looking utterly exhausted. She grabbed more tissues from the nightstand and blew her nose.

Avoiding his gaze, she squeaked out, "I'm sorry," and her face began to crumple again.

He kissed her forehead. "Don't you apologize for anything, princess. I'm the one who's sorry. I should've stayed with you today. I knew you weren't well, but I took off, like a selfish bastard, determined to ski."

"You didn't know." She wiped more tears from her cheeks.

"I knew *something* was wrong." He ran his hands through his hair, acid burning its way through his gut. "Still, I couldn't resist the draw of all that snow."

Kelsey glanced out the window. "Well, October ninth will be memorable for more than that freak storm now."

Trip didn't know what to say. His thoughts were racing around his head like a hamster in a wheel. "Do you feel okay? I mean, are you hurting anywhere? What can I do to make you more comfortable?"

"Nothing, Trip. There's nothing you can do." She glanced at her phone, and then up at him. "Turns out losing the baby isn't the only bad news I got today, by the way."

She slid him a sideways glance, as if gauging what he knew.

Damn it. "Kelsey, I—"

"Don't." Kelsey held up her hand while shaking her head. "Our relationship may never have been perfect, but it's always been honest. We both know you wanted to kill Wade's deal, so let's not pretend otherwise now."

"Okay. But this is the truth. I *am* sorry my tactics cost you something you wanted. I wish . . . well, I wish there had been some kind of compromise, I guess."

"Maybe compromise just means no one is happy, and what's the use of that?" She squeezed his hand, and then released it. He didn't like the tone of her voice, or the distant aspect of her gaze.

"What's going on in that head of yours?"

Her eyes got all misty again as she chewed on her lip. A few second later, she tipped up her chin. "Today was a big wake-up call. First the baby, then my business. Somehow I'd been going along fooling myself into thinking I was getting closer to reaching all my goals, when really, I was just getting sidetracked. Now that the baby is gone," her voice cracked, "Well, I think this is the end of the road for us."

"What?" He reached for her hand and kissed it, pretending her words didn't rock him. "I'm not walking out on you now, princess."

She shook her head, wearing a sorrowful grin. "I don't want or need your pity, cowboy."

"It's not about pity." He leaned in to kiss her, but caught only her cheek because she turned her face. He took hold of her chin. "Don't shut me out. I'm right here with you, and I hurt, too."

Her amber eyes glistened as she brushed his cheek with her palm. "I know you do, but the truth is, you were with me mostly because of the baby. We both know the last thing you'd ever planned on, or wanted, was to be saddled with me and a child for the rest of your life. Now there's nothing tying us together." Her voice cracked. "You're free to go back to the carefree life you love without any guilt."

"Didn't we just talk about all this last night?" He rose off the mattress and walked in a circle like a dog chasing its own tail. "I'm not looking to get out. I like the way things are with us. I'm happy, dammit."

Her gaze dropped to her hands, which were folded on her lap. In a quiet voice, she said, "But I'm not."

He stopped in his tracks, although his heart sped up as if he were running. "You're not?"

She shook her head, still refusing to meet his gaze.

His body tensed while his breathing grew strained. Surely he'd misunderstood her. "Well, I mean, of course I'm not happy right now, with what happened today. But I'm happy with you. That's what I'm trying to say."

He watched her lower lip tremble before she pressed it into a firm line. Finally, she looked up.

"I'm not happy, Trip." Her voice barely registered above a whisper.

"You're really not?" That realization practically knocked him on his ass.

"I need more than you can give me." Kelsey's eyes filled with tears again. "For most of my life, I've dreamed about a husband and a family. But now I understand that's not really all I want. What I want is a man who *loves* me. Who *needs* me like he needs oxygen. Who wants the same things I want and isn't afraid of making a commitment." A tear rolled down her cheek as she sniffled. "God, this would be so much easier if I hadn't gone and fallen in love with you. I tried, and I mean, I really tried not to because I knew it couldn't ever work. I knew you would never love me back. Then I got pregnant, and I thought it was a sign. But there are no signs. So no matter how much it hurts, I know what I need to do, because ultimately I know what I need to be truly happy."

"Kelsey." Her bold profession of love left him dumbfounded.

"Last night I asked you, point-blank, if you'd ever consider marriage. You dodged the question, which gave me the answer. I don't doubt that you care about me, but I know you don't love me beyond reason, which is what I'm looking for, what I deserve, and what I hope I'll find one day from the right someone. So unless something's changed . . ." When he blinked without speaking, she said, "Didn't think so."

Before he found his voice, she climbed out from under the covers. As she went into her closet, he asked, "Where are you going?"

She returned holding his grandfather's hat.

"It's time to give this back." Her glistening eyes belied the false smile she wore as she reached up to place his hat on his head. With a slight quake in her voice, she said, "Nothing has turned out as either of us planned, so it's best if we say good-bye and close this chapter of our lives. A clean break so we can still be friends. Good friends."

He pulled her close. "Princess, you're breaking my heart. I don't want to say good-bye, or just be your friend." He kissed the top of her head. "Today has been the worst day. Let's not make any big decisions."

And then, because he needed to convince her and didn't know any other way to express himself, he kissed her. He kissed her like his life depended on it, because at that moment, it felt like it did. When she responded, a bit of relief swept through him. But then she pushed him away.

"If you care about me at all, you'll make this easier for me, not harder, Trip. Please. I lost *everything* today, so please let me at least save my dignity. In the long run, we both know this is the best decision."

He didn't realize he was crying until she raised her hand to wipe away the tear from the corner of his eye.

He'd let himself get close, but it wasn't enough for her. She wanted everything. Yet this kick in the teeth proved it was smarter to withhold himself and his heart. Imagine the pain if he gave her everything and then she rejected him?

Trip couldn't allow himself to be that vulnerable. He didn't want to leave her alone that night, but he couldn't risk staying. Staying might lead to exposing things he couldn't retract.

If she wasn't happy, he couldn't force her to accept his vision of a perfect relationship any more than she could force him to accept hers.

He hugged her again, imprinting his body with the feel and smell of her. "Okay, princess. Whatever you want."

She buried her face in his chest, and through a muffled cry, he heard her say, "Thank you."

Chapter Nineteen

"Gunner, I'm sorry to hear about the baby." Trip's dad's voice sounded almost as depressed as Trip felt. "Deb and I went through the same thing before we had Mason, so I know a bit about how you feel."

His father meant well, but Trip didn't want to discuss the miscarriage. Or Deb's experience. "Thanks."

"How's Kelsey? Are you doing whatever she needs to help her get through it?"

Like any time he thought of Kelsey in the past twenty-four hours, his heart seemed to stop beating for a second or two, and then it wrung dry like an old dishrag.

"I suppose you could say that." Trip couldn't help the burst of sarcasm gilding his words.

"What's that mean?"

Trip heaved a sigh, wishing he could hang up and disappear for a while. "She ended things. She asked me to walk away, so I did."

His father huffed through the phone. "What the hell's wrong with you?"

"Nothing." Trip's brows lowered. "I'm giving her what she wants."

"Is that so?" His dad's sarcasm now rivaled his own.

"Yes. I asked her to reconsider, but she wanted a clean break."

Following a pronounced pause, his dad said, "It's pretty clear to me our history—actually, your whole take on the past—is screwing up your ability to have a normal relationship with a woman."

No shit. "Well, nothing you can do about it either way."

"Maybe not." His dad fell silent for a moment. "So tell me this, does Kelsey have anything to do with your latest request from your trust?"

Trip could lie, but for what purpose? "Partly. When I tanked Wade Kessler's proposed development, Kelsey lost out on a major commission. Maybe I can't give her everything she needs, but at least I can make sure she has the money she'd been counting on to expand her business. Plus, if I buy the land, I can control how it's developed."

"Let's put aside the whole 'I can't give her what she needs' part for a minute. Tell me what you plan to do with that land."

"Turn it into a public park, with athletic fields, a playground, maybe a skateboard park. If there's enough space, maybe I'd leave some of the woods and build a little house for myself way back in the northwest corner of the lot."

"Not much return on that kind of project. As trustee, I have some concerns, but as your dad, I'm proud of you. That's a great resource to give to your community."

"Thanks." Trip formed the beginning of his first smile all day because of his dad's remark. Of course, pride didn't eliminate his frustration at not having control over the fund. "I know you've got your legal duty, but I'm not a kid, Dad. I know what I want. If there weren't a timing issue, I'd wait until I gain control of the fund and then buy the land."

Trip drummed his fingers on the arm of his chair while his dad mulled over the request.

"Well, you do need a house. That apartment you're sharing with your partner isn't ideal."

"So you'll release the funds?" Trip sat forward.

"Let's get back to that other thing first."

"What other thing?"

"That part about not being able to give Kelsey what she needs." When Trip didn't respond, his dad continued. "Last time I saw you, we both said some things that were hard to hear. But still, I know you were holding back. Let's put all our cards on the table once and for all."

Trip stared at the ceiling, debating the topic he'd always been too uncomfortable to broach. After all, he owed his very existence to his dad's affair, which made him feel guilty for being judgmental rather than grateful. But his dad had opened this topic up again, so maybe he should just get on with it.

"Why'd you cheat on Deb?" Trip asked. "I mean, it's not like you were in love with my mom. That I could maybe understand. But to risk so much—maybe breaking up a family—just for a brief fling?"

"Didn't expect that one," his dad replied. After a pause, he asked, "Why does the reason matter?"

"We're a lot alike. We push hard, we take no bullshit . . . we have an eye for beautiful women. So I've always figured the best way to avoid breaking a vow was by never making one in the first place." He shook his head, feeling uncomfortable. "I don't know why I need to know, but reasons matter, at least to me. If Deb was cold and withholding, that would be better than if you were just bored. Or maybe you didn't really love Deb in the first place?"

"I love Deb, so don't doubt that. I met your mom in the middle of a full-blown midlife crisis. I was jealous of the attention Deb showered on Mason, and my head got turned by a witty, fun lady who made me feel like a man instead of a neglectful husband who didn't help enough with the baby." His dad cleared his throat. "Honestly, I can't see how hearing that helps. You're your own man. You're not doomed to make every mistake I've ever made. Son, it's time to grow up and move on, for chrissakes."

"Easier said than done."

"You don't normally shy away from things that are hard."

On that note, Trip pressed further. "Why'd you go back to Deb?"

"Because I loved her. 'Went back' isn't even a fair characterization. I ran back and felt shitty for a long time, praying she'd never find out. I hoped to make it up to her by being a better husband. I wish I could go back in time and do that over, too—be more honest with her right up front."

"But if you loved Deb and cheated, then what good is love? Or maybe you only thought you loved her, but you really didn't? I mean, how does someone really know what love is, anyway?"

"I already told you, I do love Deb. Always did."

"But how did you *know* it was love, not just lust or infatuation or some kind of obsession?"

His dad grew quiet for a while, apparently giving thought to his answer. "Because whenever I thought about the future, I always saw her in it with me. I'd never done that before her, or since. Deb gets me. She lets me be myself. And, say what you will, she forgave my sins and doesn't throw them in my face every time we fight. Hell, I suppose part of me loved her because of the way she loved me." After another quiet moment, he asked, "Do you love Kelsey?"

Trip froze. Would this be how he'd respond every time he heard her name, thought about her, saw her? How would he function this way? The anxiety was worse than dangling from a loose carabiner several hundred feet off the ground.

"There you go again, always with the silence. What's so hard about answering a straight question? There's no right answer, just an honest one."

"Maybe," Trip muttered. "Hell, Dad, I don't know. Why do you think I'm asking you these questions? I've got no experience with all these emotions."

"How do you feel today, now that Kelsey's dumped you?"

"Like shit, thanks." God, his dad was like an obnoxious member of the press corps.

"What's that tell you?"

"Tells me I care about her a lot. She's special, and I wasn't ready for things to end. But that doesn't mean I'm able to promise her a forever."

"For what it's worth, I remember watching you with her that first time I met with Wade. Then you beat the shit out of your brother over her. Before you knew about the baby, you'd stopped seeing other women. And you embraced the pregnancy like a man who was happy about his future. Now you're feeling 'shitty' and asking for the majority of your trust funds just to make things better for her. All things considered, I think you love this girl."

"Well," Trip started, growing increasingly hot and itchy from being so exposed.

"Last piece of advice, then I'll let you go. No one knows what forever looks like. We just do the best we can each day. And when people are in love, any mistakes can be resolved. You look at my marriage as a failure because I made a mistake. But I see it as a success, because we put my mistake behind us and are still together and happy."

Trip scrubbed his face with his palm, unprepared to handle that perspective.

His dad filled the silence. "If you love Kelsey, tell her. Sooner or later, you've got to learn to commit to something bigger than the next ski slope."

"Hey, I made a commitment to Backtrax, and I'm about to sink millions into this town."

"True. There's hope for you yet." His dad chuckled.

"So does that mean you'll release the funds?" Trip asked, happy to redirect the conversation away from him and his outlook on love.

"Yes. But when you build that house, make sure it has more than one bedroom."

Trip chose not to respond to the less-than-subtle nudge toward marriage and family. Before he hung up, he asked, "Can one of your attorneys handle setting up an anonymous nonprofit entity to buy the parcel?"

"Why do you want it to be anonymous?"

"I think Kelsey'd be uncomfortable brokering the deal if she knew I was the buyer. Besides, I'm not doing this to win points with her, I just want to make sure she's got something positive to focus on now. Something to help take her mind off the loss of the baby."

Trip tried not to hear his dad smiling through the phone when he said, "That, my boy, is what love is all about."

Kelsey typed the details of her newest listing into the MLS system. The cute in-town home had an updated kitchen, two-and-a-half baths, three bedrooms, and a fenced yard. Perfect starter home for a young family.

Of course, that thought made her nose tingle, but she'd been growing stronger every day. Three days post-miscarriage, everything she'd lost only crossed her mind about once every hour—a big improvement from being unable to think about anything else.

It took a lot of effort on her part. A complete commitment to repressing any thought of her baby or Trip the instant either popped into her mind. Maybe it wasn't the healthiest approach, but if she gave in to temptation, the raw ache of missing them chafed like a blister inside a new shoe.

Her phone rang, jarring her from her thoughts. "Peak Properties, Kelsey speaking."

"Ms. Callihan, my name is Amy Katz. I'm a real estate attorney representing a nonprofit that's interested in the eight-acre parcel you've listed on Mountain View Road."

Kelsey sat upright. Ms. Katz's words burst like a ray of sunlight streaming through an otherwise gloomy week. "That's wonderful. I'd be happy to meet with someone from the organization to walk the property and discuss the details."

"The principal is unavailable at this time, but is familiar with the land. I've got a power of attorney to oversee the negotiation and closing. We're prepared to make a no-contingency offer of six million, closing within thirty days."

Kelsey's heart sped up. Six million was twenty percent below asking, but a no-contingency offer was worth a lot. No inspections or other due diligence, no financing issues, no community referendums. The family would have their money within thirty days, and she'd have the entire commission to herself. "That figure is substantially below asking, but I'm sure the owners will consider it if you're able to provide confirmation of availability of funds."

"Of course."

"And may I ask, what's the name of this nonprofit entity?"

"White Room Group."

"Is that some kind of skiing association?" Given the deep powder reference, she assumed it might be another backcountry outfit. Should she warn Trip of incoming competition?

"No." Ms. Katz said nothing more, which Kelsey found disconcerting.

"Oh. Well, as you may have heard, the community is fairly invested in what happens with this parcel. Is your client aware there may be some hurdles to whatever its development plans may be, and that buying the land before going through due diligence may be a mistake."

"My client is aware of the risks."

Kelsey's brows pinched together. What kind of organization would spend that much money without tying up every loose end? But it wasn't her job to warn the buyer; it was her job to sell. "Give me your contact information and I'll get back to you with the owners' response."

"Great. But please impress upon them that this is the best offer my client can make."

"I will." After writing down Ms. Katz's information, Kelsey immediately phoned Nick Copeland, who sounded amenable, but needed to confer with his siblings.

Kelsey hung up the phone with a smile. The first one she'd worn in days.

Despite her grief, the world kept turning. Deep down she knew she had to keep moving, too.

This deal would be one healing step forward. A step toward expanding her business and planning for her future. The future of her dreams, not one for which she might've settled because she'd been too afraid of ending up alone.

As she shut down her computer, Avery walked through her door.

"Thought I'd drop in and see if you wanted to grab dinner." Avery collapsed into the chair across from Kelsey's desk. "Emma can meet up with us because her only hotel guests made other plans this evening."

"Um." Kelsey paused, unsure of whether she felt up to socializing.

"Those are gorgeous roses." Avery nodded to the vase of multicolored long-stemmed roses on the corner of Kelsey's desk.

A pang cinched her stomach as she mindlessly brushed the velvety petals with her fingertips.

"Trip sent them." She'd been avoiding him, too afraid that, if she saw him, she'd cave in and run back into the comfort of his arms. It would be so easy. His sexy smile, his safe embrace, his willingness to lock horns with her without getting mad. She missed him, but she didn't want a relationship that lingered in a permanent state of limbo, so she had to cut all ties for a while.

Then, like a child unable to stop picking at a scab, she asked, "How's he doing?"

"Not so great, actually. Grey says he's pretty listless. No glib jokes. Kind of just going through the motions." Avery sat forward. "I'd never have believed him capable of caring so deeply about anything or anyone."

"That's not fair. Look at how loyal he's been to Grey this past year. There's a lot more to him than he lets most people see." Kelsey hugged herself, as if somehow her own arms could take the place of his. "He really did want our baby—once he got over the initial shock."

"Kels, it seems like you two really care about each other, so why have you cut him out of your life?" Avery tipped her head. "It's so unlike you. You're the great romantic. The true believer of 'love conquers all.' If your faith is shaken, well, that scares the pants off me!"

"I still think love conquers all, but only when it's mutual. One person's love isn't strong enough to overcome all obstacles. I'm tired of always being the one who cares more, who loves more, who wants more. I know Trip misses me right now. But he doesn't love me. At least, not enough, anyway. And I've finally realized it's better to be alone than to settle for less than I deserve."

Avery smiled although her eyes were glassy. "If anyone deserves to be loved, it's you. I know you'll finally meet that Prince Charming you've been dreaming of your whole life. I'm just sorry both you and Trip have had to suffer all this loss."

Prince Charming. Kelsey couldn't help but grin at the memory of Fee's introduction to Trip in July. "Me too."

They both sat there absorbed in their own thoughts, but then Avery tapped her hands on the arms of her chair. "So, come on. Join me for dinner. We can go to Mamacitas and have your favorite flan."

Kelsey cracked a smile. "I never have been able to say no to that flan."

"I'll call Emma."

Chapter Twenty

"Trip, can we talk?" Grey tossed his pack in the corner of the office and grabbed a bottle of water from the small refrigerator. "I'm getting more concerned with each day that goes by. You haven't been yourself, which is understandable. But more than two weeks later, it feels like you're getting worse instead of better. You've barely taken advantage of all this snow that keeps falling."

"Sorry. Wasn't aware my mourning period had an expiration date." Trip stiffened, considering turning on his heel and walking out the door. He stopped himself because he knew Grey meant well.

"That's not what I meant." Grey plopped into his chair. "I wish you'd talk to me, or someone. Better yet, maybe you ought to go talk to Kelsey."

"Kelsey asked me to give her space, so that's what I'm doing." Trip sat across from Grey and folded his arms across his chest. "I'm giving her what she wants."

"Yeah? Keep telling yourself that, pal." Grey turned on the computer, pretending to give up on his attempt to get Trip to talk. But Trip knew Grey too well to believe he hadn't just goaded him in order to pry him open.

"Just because you and Avery found a way to patch things up after your big fallout doesn't mean everyone else will follow suit." A streak of resentment burned through Trip, propelling him out of his seat. "If you need proof that I'm getting back to my old self, come out for a drink."

Grey stuck a lollipop into his mouth and shook his head. "That's not what I'm suggesting, and I think you know it."

"Maybe not, but maybe it's exactly what I need." Trip defiantly picked up his cowboy hat and nodded at Grey. "See you in the morning."

Trip strolled through town on his way to Grizzly's, noticing all the Halloween decorations in the store windows, which looked a little funny surrounded by the mounds of snow on the sidewalks. He'd loved Halloween as a young boy, but after his mom died, things had changed, and the door-to-door event had changed to fancy "neighborhood parties" with parents and kids. One of many changes he'd disliked about life with his dad's family.

A cold breeze caused Trip to zip up his jacket and tuck his hands in his pockets as he kept walking through town. Kelsey's office wasn't along the most direct route to the bar, but he found himself walking down that block anyway—across the street, of course. Six thirty, but her office lights were still on. He smiled, assuming she might be diligently working on the Copeland sale. Perhaps his plan had worked, and he'd given her some small comfort.

When he spied her from a distance through the plate glass, his heart nearly dropped to the sidewalk. Mason was sitting across from Kelsey's desk. What the hell was his brother doing with her? Had they made plans to go to dinner?

Jealousy singed his lungs, but he backed away and waited for Mason to emerge. When his brother finally crossed the street alone, Trip called out, "Just couldn't keep away from Kelsey, could you? I can't believe you'd go after her after what just happened."

Mason crossed the street. "Gunner, I can assure you, it's not what you think."

"And I should believe you because you've always been so honest?" Trip tipped his cowboy hat back and cocked his head.

"Actually, I was coming to see you next." Mason maintained a calm expression. "First, let me say I'm sorry about the baby. Dad mentioned that to me last week, but I figured I'd be the last person you'd want to see so soon afterward."

Trip shrugged and cleared his throat, waiting to hear what else Mason planned to say.

"Secondly—and what I'm sure you'll consider to be good news—is that I'm returning to Denver to be near my girls. Dad finally stopped fighting me on it. He's got a replacement coming next week to take over. I needed to meet with Kelsey tonight about whether the landlord would let me assign my lease over to the new guy."

Relief coursed through Trip's body, making him almost lightheaded, but he did his best to hide that fact from Mason. Was it time he stopped suspecting the worst of his brother? They'd certainly both lost a lot this year, and perhaps, on that common ground, they could build a truce.

"Oh. Well, I think that's a good decision. I'm sure you'll be a lot happier near your kids than you are all the way out here. I'm glad Dad buckled."

"I think he finally realized his grand plan for our reconciliation couldn't be forced," Mason said. "Although maybe all the events of these past months have made a small difference. Who knows, perhaps someday things between us can be . . . better."

"Dad would like that." It was the best Trip could offer, since he'd be lying if he pretended to want more just yet.

Mason looked over his shoulder toward Kelsey's office and then to Trip. "Lurking around her office isn't going to solve your problem, you know."

"I'm not lurking."

Mason cocked an eyebrow. "For a guy who projects so much confidence, you sure aren't bold when it counts."

"You've got no idea what you're talking about. How 'bout you stay out of it so we can keep this little truce going longer than two minutes?" Trip crossed his arms.

Mason raised his hands in surrender. "Fine. Just don't go crying in your whiskey six months from now, when some other guy claims the future you had in the palm of your hand."

"I never cry, Mason. You ought to remember that about me from our childhood." Trip couldn't stop himself from tossing immature insults in order to deflect the conversation, even though it made him feel like an ass.

"Fine." Mason shook his head, just like Grey had done earlier. "Guess next time I see you, it'll be in Denver." He stuck out his hand. "Take care."

Trip shook hands, unable to make sense of any of the fucked-up emotions coursing through his body. Mason turned to go. It wasn't until he'd taken four or five steps away that Trip finally replied, "You too."

He stood on the sidewalk, watching his brother walk away. Like some bad scene in a movie, he found himself standing alone, mulling over the choice that took him away from the life he'd led just three months ago to the one three weeks ago and finally to the hell he lived in at the moment. Would anything ever feel normal again?

Before he continued toward Grizzly's, Kelsey came out of her office and locked the door. She hadn't noticed him, so he stepped into the shadows and hid behind the columns of a storefront portico. His heart galloped inside his chest, thundering with the force of a dozen hooves. He held his breath, afraid she might actually hear his heart beating so loudly.

He watched her drop her keys in her purse and cross the street south of where he stood, apparently walking home—in the dark—again. He shook his head when he noticed her snow boots had ridiculous heels, which he realized she could probably run a marathon in at this point.

Part of him wished he could just approach her for another piggy-back ride, like the one he'd offered back in July. But she'd made it clear she wanted time to move on. If he wanted to see her home safely, he'd need to do it from a distance.

Once she got two blocks ahead, he followed behind, careful to keep out of her sight. He hated how careless she was with her safety but, short of stalking her, there wasn't much he could do about it, either.

He stopped at the end of her block, watching her until she disap-peared into her condominium building. Her windows lit up a min-ute later. Through the honeycomb shades, he saw her shadow moving around.

He took three steps toward her house before stopping himself. Rubbing the center of his chest as if it could erase the deep ache inside, he stood on the sidewalk, staring up at her windows like a fool.

Each breath fogged his vision. His muscles strained toward her building, but his feet refused to budge. His mouth grew dry, making it tough to swallow the lump in his throat.

Disgusted by his behavior, he forced himself to turn away and jog to Grizzly's, certain that waltzing through that door would be like com-ing home. Music, the click of cue balls breaking apart, women dressed to impress . . . all the things he'd always enjoyed.

When he yanked the door open, he'd all but convinced himself he'd stayed away too long.

He strode through the partying crowd to the bar. "Red Rocket."

In less than five minutes, two women approached him. Pretty, friendly, available, willing women. One—Gail—he knew intimately. It had never bothered him to be in a room with one or more women he'd slept with before, but for some reason, seeing Gail made him twitchy.

"Haven't seen you out and about in months." Gail raised her glass. "Nice to have you back."

"Good to be back." He guzzled his beer to wash down the lie burn-ing a hole in his throat. He wondered if Gail, like Jessie, had made bets on him and Kelsey. Probably other yahoos in the joint right now were collecting money and joking behind his back.

The atmosphere in the bar and her perfume began to cloy, closing in and making his temperature rise.

"The Bomb Holes are playing over at On The Rocks in a bit." Gail smiled in invitation. "Wanna come?"

He liked Gail. She was friendly, cute, and cut from the same cloth as him in terms of expectations. She'd be the perfect first step toward getting past all this business with Kelsey and the baby. Yet the thought of leaving with her made him sick to his stomach.

The jukebox continued to blare Dierks Bentley's "Say You Do" as Trip glanced around the crowd. Couples and foursomes split off, flirting with one goal in mind. Half of the younger ones had their cell phones out, probably checking Tinder to see if something better had come up. A few rowdy guys were growing loud back in the corner. And Gail's laughter scorched his nerves like dry ice.

He couldn't believe he'd thought coming here would be a good idea. If anything, depression weighed more heavily on him now.

"Trip?" Gail prodded, brushing against his body.

He looked at her and shook his head. "Not tonight, thanks." His stomach churned with discomfort. "Actually, I just stopped in for a beer. Thought maybe I'd find Jon. But I've got stuff to do at home. You ladies have a good night, though."

"Okay, maybe some other time." Gail shrugged, not too upset by his rebuff. "Bye!"

Trip finished his beer and slid the empty bottle across the bar.

"Another?" asked the bartender.

"No, thanks."

Trip spilled onto the street, glancing up and down at the storefronts and people on the sidewalks. He frowned before strolling through town with no particular destination, his head and heart pounding with the certain knowledge of what he wanted. Who he needed.

By the time he finally arrived home, he had formulated a plan to make it happen.

◆ ◆ ◆

Kelsey zipped up Fee's costume and handed her the small plastic pumpkin. The child's long underwear stuck out from beneath the short sleeves, but she still looked adorable. "All set. No doubt you'll be the most beautiful princess trick-or-treating tonight."

"Why aren't you coming with us?" Fee asked, tugging on Kelsey's pink satin skirt. "You're all dressed for Halloween."

"I'm going to hand out candy so your mommy and daddy can take you and Ty around town. But I'll be here when you get back, so you can show me the best treat you get."

"Sara's mommy gives the big giant candy bars."

Kelsey widened her eyes, pretending to match Fee's level of enthusiasm. "Oh, my. Maybe you can hit them up twice."

Fee nodded with a conspiratorial smile just as Maura tromped down the steps holding Ty, who was dressed up like Humpty Dumpty. "Bill's almost home. Are you sure you don't mind doing this tonight?"

"Mind? You know I love all the kids in their costumes." Kelsey smiled.

Maura tipped her head. "You seem . . . better. I'm glad."

Kelsey nodded, forcing herself to steer clear of any regret or doubt. It didn't hurt that yesterday she'd deposited a substantial commission check from the quick, clean sale of the Copeland property. Within another ninety days she'd own a small apartment building. Taking control over one part of her life had helped her cope with her sorrow. "One day at a time, sis."

Maura smiled. "You're the bravest person I know."

"Me too." Fee chimed in and hugged Kelsey's legs.

Before Kelsey could get choked up, she used a trick she'd learned from Trip and deflected. "Where's the candy bowl?"

"In the kitchen," Maura said. "Can you grab it so I can finish getting these two ready?"

"Sure." Kelsey kissed Fee's head and then walked back to the kitchen. Bill strolled through the back door just as she found the candy bowl.

"Hey, Kels, thanks for helping out tonight. I'm really looking forward to being able to participate this year."

"It's honestly my pleasure. We don't get kids at the condo. This will be fun."

"Speaking of fun, congrats on your big sale." Bill opened a mini bag of Skittles and popped a couple in his mouth. "Saw Nick Copeland today at the body shop. He's glad they didn't sell to Wade, especially considering the new owner's plans for the land."

"Oh?" Kelsey's gaze flew to Bill. "The lawyer was all cloak-and-dagger, so I never heard a single word about the mysterious buyer or its plans."

"Apparently the buyer plans to build a community park with a few athletic fields and a playground, maybe more."

Kelsey's mind replayed a conversation she'd had with Trip at the Mineshaft a few weeks ago. *That spot would be a great place for a sports park, with unpaved parking, a football field, baseball diamond, a playground, and maybe even a skateboard park.*

It couldn't be a coincidence, but how? *I have money. Serious money.*

"Hey, Kels." Bill touched her shoulder. "You okay? You look peaked."

She waved him off, despite feeling woozy. "I'm fine, sorry. I just . . . I don't know what happened."

"You looked like you were about to swoon." He chuckled. "Who knew a park would get you so excited?"

"Hardly." She lied. "I'm just tired. It's been a busy week. So, did Nick ever meet the principal?"

It had to be Trip. What other buyer would be so confident that the "Concerned Citizen" wouldn't pick another fight?

"No. Everyone's been guessing, but what makes the most sense is that it's someone who owns a vacation home here and wants to keep a low profile. I say who cares, right?"

Kelsey's thoughts spun. Had Trip spent six million dollars to make up for the commission he knew she'd lost? Was this the latest in a line of gifts, starting with Cowboy, he'd bought to make her happy?

"Bill, is that you?" Maura called from the entry. "Let's hustle!"

"Got to go." Bill kissed Kelsey's forehead. "Thanks again."

She was following behind him to say good-bye to the group when she heard Fee's excited holler, "Prince Charming!"

"Princess Fiona, how lovely to see you again." Trip's deep voice rumbled down the hallway, temporarily stopping Kelsey in her tracks. Her mind went blank, but curiosity drove her to take the final steps toward the door.

She fanned herself to cool down.

When she came face-to-face with Trip, she saw him wearing a ridiculous-looking satin Prince Charming costume. The arms of the white jacket were far too short, as were the horrible royal-blue satin pants. He held a toy unicorn-head-on-a-stick in one hand and a bag in the other.

Her jaw slackened, but she managed not to drop the candy bowl. Through a haze, she asked, "What are you doing here?"

"Looking for you. Glad to see you in your princess outfit." He grinned, dazzling green eyes sparkling at her. Then he bent to Fee and handed her the unicorn. "This is for you."

Kelsey blinked absently, her heart unable to keep a steady beat. "How'd you know where to find me?"

"Avery."

Kelsey's mind couldn't make sense of anything except for the fact that Bill and Maura were now staring at the two of them. "Why are you dressed like that?"

"Trying to live up to the title Fee gave me." He nodded at Maura and Bill.

Kelsey's body grew tingly, her head gauzy. "Why?"

"I thought we'd be alone, but maybe it's better your family's still here." He retrieved a shoebox from the bag and got down on his knees. "These are for you."

Kelsey handed the bowl of candy to Maura while he opened the box. Inside was a pair of crystal-encrusted Jimmy Choo bridal shoes. Suddenly dizzy, eyes watering, she grabbed the doorframe to steady herself. His smile suggested he enjoyed rendering her speechless.

Trip held out his hand for her foot, which she gave him. He replaced her shoe with one of the new ones. "Perfect fit."

"Like Cinderella, Mommy!" Fee interrupted.

"Shh!" Maura tugged Fee against her side.

When he finished replacing the other shoe, he stood and placed his hand in his pocket to retrieve another surprise. "I hope this fits perfectly, too."

Kelsey's body began quaking the instant she saw the tiny black velvet box in his hand. Her knuckles were turning white from the death grip on the door. When she looked into his eyes, she almost cried.

"When you told me you loved me, I should have dropped to my knees right then and there." A thin line of perspiration formed along his brow, but he pressed on. "I'm sorry I didn't, but I'm more sorry I never gave you what you needed, when you were giving me everything I never even knew I wanted. But if you meant what you said, and if I haven't blown it already by being a moron, I'm hoping you'll let me make that up to you today, and every day from now on. I love you, Kelsey Callihan. Will you marry me?"

Fee jumped up and down, clapping. "Yay! Aunt Kelsey's getting married, Mommy!"

"Oh, Fee, since you can't keep quiet, I think we should get on our way and let these two have some privacy." Maura kissed her sister before hustling her family off the porch.

Trip barely looked at them before he popped open the lid to reveal a sizable peach-pink cushion-cut diamond set in a diamond-encrusted band.

"But you said you'd never get married." Kelsey wiped the tears trickling down her cheeks. "You don't believe in it."

"I was afraid." He grinned. "Okay, in all honesty, I'm still a little afraid."

Looking at this giant of a man dressed in a costume in public made it impossible to imagine him being afraid of much, but he sounded sincere.

"Then why?"

"Because I'm more afraid of my life without you in it." When she couldn't speak, he removed the ring from the box and dropped to one knee. "Maybe I should try this again. Kelsey, I love you, and only you. Always you. Marry me, please."

More tears streaked down her cheeks, but she managed to nod while trying to catch her breath.

Trip stood, placed the ring on her finger, and kissed her, only to be interrupted by a sharp whistle and clapping from the crowd that had apparently gathered on the sidewalk and witnessed the proposal.

Trip winked at Kelsey, and then turned around and bowed at the group. The parents released their children, and within seconds, six kids were holding out their bags for candy.

After the group ran off the porch, Trip crushed her against his body. "I missed you so much. I could barely breathe from missing you."

She feared her heart might literally explode from happiness. "I missed you, too."

He kissed her again, then stopped and glanced over his shoulder. "Maybe we should go inside."

"Okay," she said. When he lifted the unicorn off the porch, she asked, "What's with the unicorn?"

"When Fee asked if she could be our flower girl, you told her she could wear her costume and ride a unicorn down the aisle. I thought I'd better be prepared."

"I can't believe you remembered that. I didn't even remember!" She laughed at the refreshed recollection.

Trip grabbed her into his arms again and looked in her eyes. "I remember every moment we've spent together, Kelsey. Every single one."

Kelsey thanked God Trip was so tall and strong, because he was the only thing keeping her from fainting to the ground. "I love you, Trip Lexington, so you never have to be afraid of me, or this," she said, wiggling her ring finger.

The doorbell rang, making Kelsey suddenly wish she hadn't agreed to stand in for Maura.

"Guess this is good practice for next year." Trip shrugged before he bent over to pick up the bowl of candy. He kissed her cheek and opened the door to the sound of another group of loud kids yelling "trick or treat."

Kelsey watched him compliment the little girls, marveling at how she'd risen from the depths of darkness to the absolute peak of happiness in a matter of weeks. A slight pang pressed on her chest at the memory of the child they'd lost. But together she and Trip would eventually create the family she'd always wanted.

As she stood there in her princess costume staring at him in his garb, she realized dreams really do come true as long as you believe.

Epilogue

A month later, Kelsey came home to her two boys, Trip and Cowboy. Trip was leaning over the dining table studying architectural plans for the park, while Cowboy pranced around his feet.

Her heart stretched open wide like it had every other evening since Halloween. She lifted the kitten to cuddle him while peering over Trip's shoulder. "Happy with them?"

"They're just preliminary drawings, but it's coming together." He wound an arm around her waist and kissed her cheek before returning his attention to the drawings.

"Have you come up with a name, yet?" She set the kitten back on the floor and noted the toddler playground installation plans.

"Think I'll just go with Mountain View Park, that way the name and location work together." He smiled like a kid at Christmas. "By the way, just heard there won't be any holdup with the subdivision of the back half acre for home construction."

Their home. One she'd help design. "I'm so excited! I want it to be a homey place with a porch, a picket fence, and a few extra bedrooms."

Trip turned toward her and tugged her against his body, his mind obviously diverted from the park. "Extra bedrooms, huh? How 'bout we practice filling those extra bedrooms, starting right now?"

He kissed her behind the ear, then moved to her mouth. Like always, her knees softened at his touch.

"Sounds perfect to me." Kelsey jumped into his arms, wrapping her legs around his waist. "Giddyap, cowboy."

As he carried her back to the bedroom, she stared at the sparkling ring on her finger and refrained from pinching herself. If this were just a dream, she'd rather stay asleep.

Acknowledgments

Of all the books I've written to date, this one was "a gift" because it flowed effortlessly from start to finish. Even so, I have many people to thank for helping me bring it to all of you, not the least of which include my family and friends for their continued love, encouragement, and support.

Thanks, also, to my agent, Jill Marsal, whom I finally made teary with this one, as well as to my patient editors Chris Werner and Krista Stroever, and the entire Montlake family for believing in me, and working so hard on my behalf.

My Beta Babes (Christie, Siri, Katherine, Suzanne, Tami, and Shelley) are the best, always providing invaluable input on various drafts of this manuscript. Also Heidi Ulrich and the Revisionaries (Monique, Annette, and Rob), for the hours they spent reading and critiquing the story.

And I can't leave out the wonderful members of my CTRWA chapter (especially my MTBs, Jamie Pope, Jamie Schmidt, Jane Haertel, Denise Smoker, Heidi Ulrich, Jen Moncuse, Tracy Costa, Linda Avellar, and Gail Chianese). With this story in particular, Kristan Higgins led a fantastic workshop on layering and, together, we brainstormed parts of this story. Year after year, all of the CTRWA members provide endless hours of support, feedback, and guidance. I love and thank them for it as well.

Finally, and most importantly, thank you, readers (especially those who have been waiting for Trip's story), for making my work worthwhile. With so many available options, I'm honored by your choice to spend your time with me.

An Excerpt from
Unexpectedly Hers

Editor's Note: This is an uncorrected excerpt and may not reflect the finished book.

Straddling her hips, Dallas smeared a handful of chocolate sauce and whipped cream across her breasts.

"Like a sundae." He bent over and licked her, then looked up with a lusty smile as his hand found the red curls at the top of her inner thighs. "This bit of red is the cherry on top."

He licked her again as she writhed with pleasure—her arms still tied to the bedpost—then his head disappeared between her legs.

Bang!

Emma flinched, then shoved the advanced review copy of her debut novel under her pillow before her mother marched in and caught her with smut. That's what her mom would call it, anyway. She imagined everyone's shock if they ever discovered that she was Alexa Aspen, the author of *Steep and Deep*, which many would deem "mommy porn."

Of course, no one would ever learn her secret. When her agent negotiated her publishing contract, Emma had chosen to avoid the brunt of Sterling Canyon's small-town scrutiny by assuming a pen name.

It'd been so easy that, except at the moment she'd signed the contract, she hadn't even flinched. No one would ever believe quiet, conservative Emma Duffy would *read* a book containing smokin' hot sex, much less write one. She could hide in plain sight because people assumed writers only ever wrote about what they knew, and who would ever suspect *her* of knowing much about sex?

Emma smiled to herself while remembering one night in Aspen three years ago, when she'd stepped outside her normal boundaries and . . .

Bang, bang! A quick glance over her shoulder confirmed no one was entering her room. Actually, the noise sounded too distant to be her bedroom door. Grabbing her green cable-knit cardigan, she went to investigate. Hopefully the porch posts weren't cracking apart.

Bang. Bang. Bang.

She trotted down the staircase of her family's seventy-year-old bed and breakfast, The Weenuche, named for a Ute Indian tribe that had once inhabited Southwest Colorado. Emma's presence marked the third generation to run the inn although, technically, her mother ran the business while Emma managed the kitchen and concierge desk. The worn carpet beneath her feet sadly announced to the world that it had been decades since the place had been refurbished.

Who had money to splurge on redecorating when ancient plumbing, sagging roofs, and other emergencies cropped up every month? The unusual spate of monster-sized October snowstorms hadn't helped, either. And while El Niño snowfall should bring more tourists to town, it also inevitably would cause more wear and tear on her battered inn.

Jogging across the small lobby, she shoved open the front door, which creaked against a strong early-November wind. Had the gust not set her back, she might have crashed into the unfamiliar young men in skullcaps and combat boots who were nailing flyers to the posts on the front porch.

"Excuse me!" Emma approached them with caution, tightening her cozy sweater to buffer against the frigid air. "Who are you, and what are you posting on my property?"

The one with the blond goatee and short ponytail smiled. "We're just posting the disclaimer notices so we don't have to get specific waivers for people to be included in the documentary."

Documentary? She scanned the sheet of paper, which read:

REEL DRAMA, INC.
is currently videotaping and
cablecasting scenes at this
location for possible inclusion
in television programs.
If you do not wish to be
photographed or to appear on
television, or to be otherwise
recorded, please leave this
location during our
videotaping.

By remaining in this immediate
vicinity, you are giving REEL
DRAMA, INC. your
consent to videotape, record,
and cablecast your picture,
likeness, voice and statements.

Oh, good Lord. What the heck had her mother gotten them into now?

"I'm sorry, will you please hold on a second? Don't post anything else until I speak with my mother." She turned on her heel and entered the lobby, calling out, "Mom!"

"Don't shout, dear. It isn't very ladylike." Her mother emerged from the back office with a large suitcase in tow. Freshwater pearls complimented her best twinset and wool slacks. She would've looked quite elegant if not for the Velcro orthopedic walking shoes. "I was just coming to find you. I'm leaving now to pick up Vera for our cross-country sojourn. You're in charge, my angel."

The overwhelming scent of her mother's beloved White Diamonds perfume enveloped Emma, making her cough.

"You told me this would be a quiet month," Emma accused, remembering when her mom had first informed her of the plans for Aunt Vera's month-long sixty-fifth birthday trip. She'd been happy to learn of it, because it would leave her more privacy to prepare for the book launch. "You said I'd only be dealing with a skier, his brother, and a small group while you were away."

"Yes, that's right. Apparently the freak October blizzards have made Sterling Canyon an ideal spot for his training."

Training? As usual, Emma had a hard time following her mother's trail of thoughts, which usually made assumptions about which details Emma had been privy to.

Emma raised her arms toward heaven. "So why are there men outside posting notices about filming a documentary?"

"Isn't it wonderful?" Her mother's eyes lit. "People love a comeback story, so this film should be quite popular. The free publicity will bring all kinds of attention to our inn. When it airs, it'll put us on the map so we can compete with that Wade Kessler's new hotel."

"What?" Her pulse beat hard at the base of her neck. The lack of communication astounded her. "Why is this the first I'm hearing of it?"

"I'm sure I mentioned it to you." Her mother patted her arm.

"I think I'd remember if you mentioned a documentary."

"Emma, your head's been in the clouds a lot lately—always off in a daze. Perhaps you just weren't listening."

Emma couldn't deny that possibility. These past several weeks she'd easily lapsed into thoughts about her book, its early reviews, launch preparations, and her next story. Perhaps her mother *had* mentioned it and Emma had just not heard it amid all her nattering.

"Now that I have your attention," her mother began, "all the paperwork and permits are on my desk, and there's a big list of items they need, too. I took care of most things, although you should double-check the list from the nutritionist before you grocery shop this week. Also, I forgot to arrange for a yoga instructor, but you used to teach at YogAmbrosia, perhaps you can do it."

"Me? Then who'll be preparing breakfast, Mom?"

"Oh, yes. That. Then call there and arrange for one of the instructors to come give private lessons here in the morning. Any of those ladies would probably love to work with a real athlete." Her mom smiled and patted Emma's cheek. "It's just so lovely to know I can always count on you, my perfect girl. You always make me so proud."

Normally Emma would bask in the glow of her mother's praise. But the last thing she needed now was to be dodging a camera crew while juggling her duties to the inn and her book launch. And what made her mother think The Weenuche could compete for the same customers as Wade's soon-to-be completed Bear Lodge—a five-star, state of the art boutique hotel?

The entire situation robbed Emma of her good manners. "So you're taking off scot-free while I'm going to end up on camera at all hours, with flour on my clothes and wearing a hairnet?"

"Don't be so dramatic, Emma. Neither of us likes it when you act like your father." Her mother smoothed her own faded red hair.

As always, a chilly two-second pause followed any mention of her father, the man who'd left them both almost twenty years ago to pursue fame and glory in Hollywood. The fact that he'd only ever made the D-list pleased her mother, who'd never wanted to see him rewarded for his philandering and abandonment.

"Think of this as a little adventure." Her mother cleared her throat. "I spoke with the documentary director, Mari, who sounds like a very nice woman. You aren't the subject of this movie, dear, so just smile and make the place inviting." She pinched Emma's cheek. "Maybe put on a little make-up, just in case you end up on film."

"You're really quite something." Emma rolled her eyes.

"I'll choose to take that as a compliment." Her mother waved dismissively and popped up the suitcase handle. "Now help me load this into the car. It's parked out front."

Emma strode out the door, rolling the hefty bag behind her while trying not to be insulted by her mother's assessment.

"Can we continue?" Goatee guy asked as she and her mother breezed past him and his cohort.

"Apparently." Emma sighed and heaved the bag down the few porch steps. "Careful, Mom, there's still some ice."

"I see, Emma." Her mother tsked. "You really must get on this sooner."

"Andy will be here soon to clear it."

"Well, you and Andy will have to make sure to clear all the snow and ice in a timely fashion so we can impress our guests and look good on camera. Remember, people's perceptions are everything—in life and in business." Her mother kissed her goodbye. "I'll send pictures and little gifts from each city. Oh, I can't wait to see Chicago, Washington D.C., and New York. Did I tell you we have tickets to *Hamilton*?"

"Only thirty times." Emma hugged her ridiculous yet lovable mother goodbye.

It'd been just the two of them for a while now. A few years after her father had bolted, her beloved Grammy had died right here in the dining room. Choked on chicken, of all things. Aunt Vera lived in Denver, so they only saw her a few times a year.

Emma and her mom had nursed each other through broken hearts and broken dreams. Although the woman could verge on the absurd, Emma loved her mom and would never, ever want to let her down, so she would bite her tongue now and do what she could to make her mother happy.

"Drive safely, Mom."

"I will." Emma's mother hugged her again. "This reminds me of the first time my mother left me in charge of the inn. Do you remember that ice storm that froze everything and the pipe that burst? Oh, Lord, that was something. Hopefully your month will pass without a major incident."

"Yes, let's do hope." Emma smiled, remembering that storm, and all the candles they'd kept lit because of the blackout, as she helped her mother into the car. She waved goodbye just as a van pulled into the parking lot. Emma assumed that it must be ferrying more of the crew, possibly even the star of the dreaded documentary. Hopefully he wasn't a prima donna.

Another brisk wind blew a cloud of snow in Emma's face, forcing her to seek warmth. She hustled inside, past the guys on the porch, and scampered up to her room to run a brush through her hair, knot it into some kind of lumpy bun, and hide the box of her books under her bed.

She drew a breath, enjoying a rare moment of freedom and privacy. Of independence. Her mother didn't crowd her, per se, but her presence could be suffocating at times.

Emma had grown up well aware of her mother's and Grammy's expectations, having overheard many discussions of the damage caused by loose morals. She'd been privy to more than one such lecture, too.

Not that she'd needed it. She'd seen firsthand how often sex screwed up people's lives.

As a result, she'd locked away that small part of herself that took after her father, even though sometimes the repressed passion simmering beneath her skin burned like fingers caught on a hot oven rack. Her secret night in Aspen had been necessary to avoid self-conflagration.

On her way back downstairs, she heard the murmur of voices and scuffle of bags coming into the lobby. She dashed around the corner to the welcome desk and then froze. Oh. My. God.

Dallas, er—Wyatt. Wyatt Lawson, former slopestyle snowboard International Games and Rockies Winter Games gold medalist, among other titles. She vaguely registered other people, too, but her gaze locked on Wyatt's exotic face. Although born and raised in Vermont, he looked Brazilian with his wild, wavy black hair that hung to his jaw, his bronzed skin, his dreamy hazel eyes set deeply beneath straight, thick brows. Although she couldn't actually see those eyes while staring at his profile, she still remembered them from their one incredible night together.

Her heart leapt to her throat. *Please, God, don't let him recognize me.* Emma had never told a soul about that night, and would be humiliated if her mother or friends ever learned about her brief walk on the wild side. Especially when she'd acted like some kind of cougar, picking up a guy six years her junior.

Of course, Wyatt wouldn't associate Emma with Alexa—the alter ego she'd adopted to break free from being Emma Duffy.

Unlike Emma, Alexa had confidently worn a silky black dress that barely covered her chest and butt. Alexa had rocked high-heeled knee-high boots, had her thick, red hair professionally styled, and worn smoky make-up and loopy earrings. Yes, Alexa had been a bona fide siren that night.

Wyatt had been in the midst of celebrating his victory when she'd spotted him in the bar. Targeted him, truthfully. Carefree, happy, drunk Wyatt—young and proud and on the prowl. He'd been the perfect man for her first and only one-night stand. And they'd had quite a night, until she'd woken mortified at five o'clock, and then ducked out of his hotel room without a trace.

But she couldn't regret it because that night had prompted the kernel of an idea for a story, and naturally Wyatt's image—and certain other things—remained the inspiration for her hero's character. Since then, she'd thought of him as Dallas.

Wyatt now turned those greenish brown eyes her way and smiled at her—the kind of smile he'd give a friend's little sister. She knew her heated cheeks meant her fair skin had turned almost as red as her hair.

"Good morning. I'm Wyatt Lawson." Wyatt stepped aside to make room for a young guy with a cane, wearing a baseball cap and sunglasses. Wyatt patiently followed him to the check-in desk. "This is my brother, Ryder, and that's the film crew, Jim, Buddy, and Mari. Looks like we've all descended at once."

Emma remembered briefly seeing Ryder that night. He'd been an up-and-coming snowboarder, although he hadn't hit the podium. Sadly, two years ago, he'd finally made headlines when a horrible snowboarding accident caused a traumatic brain injury. She'd read that Wyatt had left competition to help his family, and that Ryder had spent a few months in the hospital following his accident.

Looking at Ryder now, she sensed he hadn't fully recovered—physically or otherwise. A pang of empathy for the brothers momentarily set her back. Ryder probably needed special accommodations, and she hoped her mother had addressed them adequately.

It was doubtful Ryder would remember her, but still, she felt thankful that she'd tied back her hair and worn no make-up this morning.

Surely neither he nor Wyatt would connect her to Alexa, assuming Wyatt even remembered that night. *Surely* he'd had many similar encounters before and after their sexcapade.

For the briefest moment, sadness grabbed her, forcing her to acknowledge that a major turning point in her small life had been a mere blip in Wyatt's life story. She shook off the wistful musing before anyone noticed.

"Welcome," Emma said, her gaze roaming the group without making direct contact with Wyatt. "We're so glad to have you. I'll be at your disposal during your stay, so anything you need, just ask."

Wyatt playfully cocked an eyebrow and smiled, this time a little less brotherly. A memory of him wearing that identical look—and nothing else—passed through her mind and shot straight to her girly parts. Goodness, her innocent statement now sounded naughty in her head. How on earth would she survive an entire month living under the same roof with Dallas, er, Wyatt, without giving away her identity?

About the Author

Photo © 2013 Lora Haskins

Jamie Beck is a former attorney with a passion for inventing stories about love and redemption. In addition to writing about romance, she enjoys dancing around the kitchen while cooking, and hitting the slopes in Vermont and Utah. Above all, she is a grateful wife and mother to a very patient, supportive family. Visit her on Facebook at www.facebook.com/JamieBeckBooks.